Vampire Vintage

ASHLYN CHASE

ELLORA'S CAVE
ROMANTICA PUBLISHING

What the critics are saying...

&

5 Hearts "Ashlyn Chase has written a vampire romance with her tongue firmly in her cheek... Although full of fun and laughs, this is a story with a great plot, some hot sex scenes and characters that leap from the pages. The reader will enjoy all the surprises Ms. Chase pulls out to entertain and give the story a lot of pep and sizzle. Go get this story right away, you will not regret it." ~ *Love Romances Reviews*

"Anyone who's ever wished for an immortal soul mate will love this tale of a woman who makes her dream come true. It's an amusing, contemporary read with an inventive plot, sensual love scenes and quirky characters. Women will relate to the realistic heroine who longs to find her true love. Secondary characters add depth, and the girl talk is witty and real. While this is a good read overall, the ending is a bit contrived." ~ *Romanctic Times Reviews*

"*Vampire Vintage* is an imaginative, humorous and erotic page-turner that kept me smiling and guessing until the end. A keeper." ~ *Annette Blair, National Bestselling Author*

"Action, suspense, hot love scenes, humor, wit, dysfunctional families, vampires, extra paranormal characters, and just plain great writing make this story a must read. I really liked this book, Ashlyn Chase had me laughing in all the right spots and holding my breath in others, the chemistry between her characters was perfect." ~ *ParaNormal Romance Reviews*

An Ellora's Cave Romantica Publication

www.ellorascave.com

Vampire Vintage

ISBN 9781419958588
ALL RIGHTS RESERVED.
Vampire Vintage Copyright © 2007 Ashlyn Chase
Edited by Helen Woodall.
Photography and cover art by Les Byerley.

This book printed in the U.S.A. by Jasmine–Jade Enterprises, LLC.

Electronic book Publication March 2007
Trade paperback Publication March 2009

VAMPIRE VINTAGE

Dedication

⁊

To my husband, for "getting" my sense of humor.

Trademarks Acknowledgement

⁊

The author acknowledges the trademarked status and trademark owners of the following wordmarks mentioned in this work of fiction:

The Addams Family: Colyton, Barbara

Armani: GA Modefine SA Corporation

Buffy the Vampire Slayer: Twentieth Century Fox Film Corporation

Ebay: eBay Inc.

Frisbee: Wham-O, Inc.

Harrods: Harrods, Limited

Jell-O: Kraft Food Holdings, Inc.

Kleenex: Kimberly-Clark Corporation

McDonald's: McDonald's Corporation

Matrix: Enter the Matrix, Warner Bros. Entertainment, Inc.

Pierre Cardin: Cardin, Pierre, Individual

Playboy: Playboy Enterprises International Inc

Rolodex: Berol Corporation

Sam Adams Light: Boston Beer Corporation

Victoria's Secret: Victoria's Secret Stores Brand Management, Inc

Windex: S.C. Johnson & Johnson, Inc

Acknowledgements

ᔕᑐ

Thank you to Christy Gissander for critiquing my first draft.

A special thank you to national bestselling author Annette Blair, who read the full manuscript, gave it an enthusiastic thumbs-up and said she couldn't believe I made her fall in love with a vampire.

Chapter One

ஒ

"I'm so embarrassed, I could die! Maura, are you one hunnred percent sure you knew what you were doing?" Ronda grabbed her bra off the branch and slipped it back on. She had a hard time with the clasp and slurred curses under her breath. "Well?"

Maura cringed inwardly and steadied herself so she could step into her panties. "Shh. Like I said before, don't talk so loud. At least not until we get dressed and out of these woods." Yeah, right. She might as well tell seagulls not to circle fishing boats as tell her drunken friends not to talk too loud.

Despite their inebriated agreement with her earlier, her friends had suddenly freaked out when a bolt of lightning split the clear, black night. Maybe they didn't believe in Maura's ability to summon immortals, but they went along with it and she didn't appreciate them accusing her of stupidity.

Barb let out a huff, then whispered loudly. "A lightning bolt came out of the cloudless, starry sky and could've fried us. That was weird and everything, but no immortals were riding it to earth. Couldn't you have screwed up?"

Haley pulled her tummy slimmer halfway up and staggered, barely staying upright. "I can't believe you made us get naked and dance under the moon. What kind of dumb ceremony is that?"

Ronda added, "I think you just wanted to see how far we'd go to find decent men."

Disgusted at their lack of faith, Maura snapped. "I'm not sure of anything except that mortal men are not worth the trouble and heartache anymore. If you think immortals might appreciate an older, wiser woman and want to date one, you have to summon. And I tried to do it—for all of us."

Barb snorted. "Is that what you call summoning? To face in the general direction of Romania and mutter, 'Where the hell are you, damn it?'"

"Look, I tried the nice poetry from my memory of Irish summoning circles, but I was a kid. My grandda made all kind of magic stuff happen."

"Like pulling a quarter from behind your ear? My grandpa did that."

"No, silly. Things you wouldn't believe—like talking in Gaelic to little people I could swear now were leprechauns." Tonight, she had to admit, even to her own ears it sounded like blarney. "Maybe immortals have to hear each of us speaking our own language."

"Irish celebrations, huh? No wunner. They were prob'bly as shtonkered as we are." Ronda's bra clicked into place. "Ah, I finally got it."

"Look, Barb, you have your ways and I have mine. You faced Egypt and spoke to Ra, right?" Maura reached for her camisole and swore when it wouldn't fall off the branch where she'd tossed it.

Barb pointed an accusing finger at her. "Yeah and all I got was some immortal ass's wrath. When I sober up, I'm going to be really embarrassed, not just about the nudity, but for getting suckered into this. Why the Sam Hill did we have to take our clothes off again? We didn't even undress in front of each other in college, roomie."

Ronda answered when Maura didn't. "She said we had to come to the high-and-mighty ones pure to show our commim... com... commiment."

"The word is commitment," Haley said. "As in all of us committed to Bellevue mental hospital if the cops catch us and I'm pretty sure that none of us are pure. Besides, I'm with Barb on dying of embarrassment tomorrow. Commitment's not all we showed by running around buck-naked under the moon."

"No kiddin'." Ronda let out a nervous giggle.

"It's called sky-clad and I'm not exactly proud of my butt without a body shaper, either. Look, I didn't force you to do it, did I? We're all sick of successful men, our equals, going after the little bimbos with the big boobs, leaving us flourishing older women alone, feeling like rejects." Maura couldn't free her camisole from the branch to save her life. She didn't want to pull too hard and tear the delicate fabric, so she stood there in only her bra and panties frowning at the branch.

"'Flourishing.' Good word," Haley said.

"Maura's right, everyone." Ronda mumbled the words from under the blouse she had somehow decided to pull over her head instead of unbuttoning it. "She didn't hold a gun to our heads."

"Hey," Barb cried. "That's my blouse!"

"I'm going to have to climb that friggin' tree."

"Maura, Don't." Barb reached up and touched the branch. "Look, you aren't particularly tall or athletic. Let me do it."

"Is that your way of calling me short and fat?"

"Of course not. I never said that, for shit's sake! I'm just trying to help."

"Maura, your body is perfectly normal for a thirty-eight-year-old woman. You have nothing to be ashamed of."

"Thanks, Haley. But I still wish I could find that friggin' fountain of youth."

"Sorry I got mad at you before," Ronda said to Maura.

Haley smiled. "Yeah, me too. I really love you, man."

"I really love you, man, too." Barb hugged Maura. "Now let me get your top."

"Well…" Maura eyed the branch. "Are you sure? I mean, I know we're the best of friends and everything, but you don't have to risk your pantyhose for me."

Barb shrugged. "What else is new? Friends to the end, right?"

"Right!" the others shouted.

Maura shushed them. "What is it you guys don't understand about 'shut the hell up'?" Then she felt badly and whispered, "Okay—quiet high fives."

All of them attempted a friendly slap of palms, but missed and ended up pawing the air. Haley and Ronda giggled and staggered backward. Ronda tripped over her own feet and landed on her ass.

"Oww. I'm broken."

"Oh, get up. You didn' feel a thing." Haley reached for her and helped her to stand.

Ronda brushed herself off and said, "Yes, I did. I felt cold. Where are my friggin' pants?"

Ronda got down on all fours and began to crawl around, looking for her clothes. She hadn't worn pants, though. She had worn a gorgeous red dress to launch her new ad campaign and landed a huge account.

A pang of jealousy invaded Maura, but she quickly shook it off. Ronda had been celebrating success while she grieved her store's losses. "Hey, Ronda, I've got an idea. While you're down there, why don't you kneel under the branch and I can climb onto your back and…"

"No way! Let Barb get your damn tank top."

"It's not a tank top. For your information, it's a very 'spensive camisole." *Oh great, now I'm slurring too.* Grabbing a fifth of scotch at the liquor store might not have been a good idea, despite Barb's reluctance to cooperate. Plied with plenty of scotch to overcome their better judgment, she and the others kept sipping at it since Barb refused to drink alone.

"No, forget it, Barb. It's really nice of you to offer, but I can just wear my suit. The top should cover my boobs enough."

14

"If not, all the better for your immortal when he shows up." Barb staggered sideways and laughed out loud.

They all shushed her. "Do you want to advertise our location to the rapists? Jeez Louise!"

* * * * *

Adrian picked up the pace as he hurried along the dirty sidewalks of New York. He'd just heard the call he'd waited nearly six hundred years to receive. Unless delusional, his beloved had summoned him. Her voice began as a tinkling laugh, followed by a sigh. Later, the words "Where the hell are you, damn it?" came through as if muttered under her breath.

Hmm…must be a nice, refined girl.

He nodded to a couple of businessmen out for a walk in the pleasant night air. The moon shone full. The heat of the day had lowered to what he'd call balmy weather and Adrian peered up at the sky where he caught a glimpse of a meteor falling to earth. It would burn out before it landed, probably somewhere in the Southwest from the looks of the trajectory. After centuries with nothing useful to do but explore his interests, Adrian had picked up a few books on astronomy, physics and anything else more worthy of note than pop culture.

"Now if I were a mortal human, I'd probably wish on that so-called star." He wondered for the umpteenth time, if he were granted one wish—any wish at all, what would it be? Mortality? Perhaps, but there had to be something more important than being allowed to die. Like living first. Only one dream had eluded him all this time. A special woman. A woman he could enjoy a real connection with. Someone who accepted his fangs as much his big… Well, whatever. He longed for that kind of favorable reception. Not necessarily love.

One thought had him shaking in his black leather boots, though. Another vampire. Female vampires were off his wish list. Not only did they create some of the most unbearably unhappy relationships, but they could stalk an ex-lover for eternity and often did. He wondered what living with his last vamp lover forever might have done to his sanity. He had finally slipped away before she had a chance to follow him. Hiding among the millions of people and scents in the city of New York covered his presence well.

Love had been a disaster for many people he had known throughout the centuries. A mortal woman would need the elusive "true love" with him, especially since he pictured most women dying on the spot as soon as he revealed what he was—an almost six-hundred-year-old vampire. Oh, well. Nobody's perfect.

But to ignore tonight's summons would have been a serious mistake. It didn't happen to any but the most fortunate vampires and might never happen to him again. He increased his speed and jogged down the wide avenues of Manhattan leading to Central Park, certain she had performed the summoning there.

Several anorexic model types, obviously taken in by societal hype, passed him. Women with rail-thin bodies struck him as abnormal in a society of abundance. Why not promote maintaining a healthy weight? He knew the answer. Because too many were becoming wealthy in industries dependent upon altering women's bodies. Idiotic, hungry, corporate vultures.

What would his beloved look like? With no patience for fueling businesses geared toward weight loss products, liposuction, fashions that only stick figures could wear and the misery of not measuring up, he hoped she was at peace with her body, whatever its shape. He never wanted to answer the question, "Does my ass look fat in these pants?"

Yet Hollywood and New York celebrities had no compassion for normal men connected to normal women and continued to propagate a certain image, unattainable for the vast majority. He promised himself he'd remain open-minded, especially since she would have to be open to the truth when he revealed himself. What if she didn't mean to perform a summoning? Or perhaps she'd meant to at the time, but after they met changed her mind. At last the green border of Central Park came into view.

He strolled into the park to see some very tipsy women stumbling out of the woods. Doubtful one of them could have summoned him, he shrank back into the shadows to wait and watch. Hopefully, someone else would walk out behind them.

The tall brunette carried an empty bottle of scotch and had her arm around the short blonde. He knew the bottle had contained scotch since he could smell it on her breath a quarter mile away. Heightened senses aren't always a blessing.

"So, who's designated driver again?" the tall brunette asked.

"You were, Barb."

"Uh-oh. Do we have a plan B?"

The woman with brown hair who trailed the pack, obviously stumbling and weaving more than the rest, called out, "It's my car. I'll drive."

The redhead spoke up, quickly. "Not on your life." And then she laughed.

I know that voice — that laugh! Could it be the retro-beauty sitting with three other women who caught his eye at the bar only an hour ago? She had more than caught his eye. His mouth had watered when he watched her cross her shapely legs and noticed a seam running down the back.

"Better think of a plan C, then," the blonde said.

"I'm not getting into a car with any of you behind the wheel."

The owner of the car said, "Oh c'mon, guys, I'm not that bad. Just because I forgot where I put my dress…"

"Or that you were wearing a dress, or the day of the week, or your own name…" the redhead teased.

17

Because the retro redhead had appealed to him so considerably, Adrian had eavesdropped on their conversation at the bar with his vampiric hearing. Four friends, dismayed that most men only appreciated young, vapid airheads, seemed to be daring each other to try something new — maybe a little crazy. It was the redhead, Maura, that seemed the most enthusiastic and he admired her feisty spirit. He hadn't paid much attention to the rest of them. The one they had called Ronda seemed to be celebrating and the blonde, her name was Haley if he recalled correctly, was pleasant enough. The skeptical brunette had given Maura a hard time, but the redhead stood her ground. He admired that about her too.

"It's Friday and my name is Ronda."

That's it, then. This is the same group of women. The redhead has to be Maura!

All the women chuckled. Suddenly a bat swooped down on them. A couple of the women screamed. The blonde, Haley, pointed at it and yelled, "Hey, Maura! There's your guy!"

Maura jerked her head in the direction of the bat and stood open-mouthed, gaping at it. "Really? You think?"

The brunette laughed hard and almost fell over. The smell of scotch assaulted his nose. When Haley had steadied her, she sat on the grass and reared back, gasping and giggling. "You're too much. You probably believe in Santa Claus and the Easter bunny."

Maura set her hands on her hips and glared at the others. "No, but I do believe in the fang fairy."

The other three erupted in laughter, creating a loud cacophony. Ronda, at the back, fell over. Haley staggered and weaved, then spread her feet apart and placed her hands on her knees to keep from falling.

Adrian sharpened his vision to get a better look at Maura as she made her way down the path under a streetlamp.

Shoulder pads, a nipped-in waist and straight skirt completed the Forties-style navy blue suit. She possessed the proverbial hourglass figure and his mouth watered again. This woman could cause some serious drooling. The dark color showed off her glowing peach skin and beautiful shoulder-length strawberry blonde hair. She had a light sprinkling of freckles across her pert, slightly upturned nose. Even at this distance he could see a sparkle in her aquamarine eyes.

She was what he'd call terminally cute. Ah, terminal. That meant temporary. Still, she sounded like she could be fun for however long…

She turned around and scanned the night sky as if looking for the bat, meanwhile revealing the long seams down the back of her stockings. His cock grew instantly hard. When she returned to face Haley, still doubled over and giggling, Maura bent down to talk to her, which revealed her cleavage. Wow — more than cleavage. The suit without a blouse beneath showed generous perfectly shaped breasts and light rose areolas. What had happened to her top? Did she know she was flaunting her thousand-carat cabochons?

"Haley, get a hold of yourself. I thought you were the least drunk of all of us."

"Me? Hell, no. You're the one who could drink a sailor under the table, then drive us all to Coney Island without playing bumper cars or driving into the ocean."

"I doubt it. I've had more than all of you. I'm just used to it. Hey, does anybody want to meet me at the new blues club on the east side tomorrow night?"

"You've got to be kidding! Two nights in a row?"

"You're Irish," the brunette said. "So you're practically a professional drinker, but not the rest of us."

"Hey, cut the prejudice, Barb. It's not cool. I could say some things about your being Italian, you know."

Ronda, now crawling on her hands and knees yelled out, "Yeah. Don't be anti-semantic."

"Anti-what?" The woman they called Haley laughed like a hyena.

19

Haley spoke as she straightened her posture. "The word you're looking for is anti-Semitic and I think that only applies to people who are Jewish. I don't think any of us are."

Maura pointed at each one in turn. "Let's see, I'm one hundred percent Irish, Haley's English with some Scottish tossed in, Barb's ninety-nine percent Italian and one percent pit bull…"

"Hey!"

"And Ronda's…" Maura peered over the others' shoulders. "Ronda's dead!"

They gasped and spun toward their friend who had stopped crawling and lay facedown in the middle of the path.

"Oh dear God," Barb cried. "What do we do now?"

Haley trembled. "Don't panic. Maura, take her pulse."

"You're the vet. You do it. I'm just a humble shopkeeper."

"I'm not a vet. I'm a groomer."

"Close enough. Check her pulse."

Barb strode as if suddenly sober and kneeled next to the unconscious female. "I've had CPR training, let me do it."

She placed her fingers right over the jugular vein and waited a few seconds. "She's fine. Just passed out, that's all."

"So again, what do we do now? We can't just leave her here."

"I guess we should try to wake her up." Haley walked over and shook the girl's shoulder. "Ronda… Ronda!"

She groaned, but didn't open her eyes.

"Well, we've got to get her to the car. Haley, you take one arm, I'll take the other and Barb can get her feet."

The three of them tried to lift the dead weight, but her head lolled back as they stumbled and staggered until they bumped her head on the pavement.

Maura said, "Damn. We'd better forget about that before we accidentally give her brain damage or pull her arms out of their sockets."

Recognizing his chance to make a positive first impression, Adrian stepped out of the shadows. "May I be of assistance?" While the women stood mute, he lifted Ronda off the pavement and held her as if she weighed no more than a plastic doll. "Now why don't we go call a cab?"

Chapter Two

ॐ

The following evening, Adrian spied Maura at the club, alone at a front-row table for two. Good. None of her friends had accompanied her. She looked beautiful in her Grace Kelly-like outfit with her hair up in a strawberry blonde French twist. But he sensed sadness. Perhaps she thought her vampire hadn't heard her summons or had stood her up. Adrian smelled a few too many chocolate martinis as she sang along with the aging blues band.

Hopefully she used alcohol responsibly, not as a habit or coping mechanism. On the other hand, a good buzz might help her handle the stress of her vampire lover reporting for duty. Sure, she had said she wanted to date an immortal, but a vampire? No more frightening breed existed. What if she had already changed her mind? He certainly hoped not. This was one attraction he felt compelled to explore more fully. He watched her from a discreet distance until she stood, swayed slightly, then planted her feet solidly for balance.

Adrian slipped outside before Maura could settle up her bill and leave, then he waited at the corner. As soon as she appeared, he raised his arm to hail a cab. Several went by without stopping.

He turned toward her and smiled. "It's sometimes difficult to get a taxi on a Friday night."

"In New York?" She chuckled. "Imagine that."

What a wonderful change from women who ignored any attempt at a pleasant exchange. "Do you want to share the cab if I can get one to stop?"

"Oh. Well, I…"

She made eye contact and held his gaze for an inordinately long time. Perhaps she recognized him as the knight who carried her friend to safety. He wasn't using mind control.

"Yes, that would be great. How nice of you to offer."

"It's no trouble at all." The next time he raised his hand, a taxi veered over to the curb and stopped in front of them.

"They must only stop for beautiful women." He held the door for her and waited until she seemed comfortably settled, then jogged around to the other side and slid in.

Maura gave her address to the driver.

Adrian memorized it and reminded himself to act casual as the taxi pulled into the busy traffic. "What a coincidence, I'm heading toward the same neighborhood."

"Oh, do you live in the Village?" she asked.

"No, but I promised to stop by a friend's loft. He's an artist."

She straightened her posture and her expression brightened. "Are you an artist too?"

"No, unfortunately I don't have that talent, but I do appreciate the creative arts—and beauty." Running his eyes over her, he said, "That's a flattering outfit. It complements your blue eyes and lovely red hair."

She looked down at her light yellow formfitting dress that reminded him of lemon sherbet, the kind he'd like to put in a bowl and savor until he licked the spoon. She smoothed it lovingly and smiled. Relieved to see no rings on her left hand, Adrian relaxed.

"Thanks, I love this one. It's from the early Sixties."

"I thought it was reminiscent of that time period. May I ask where you got it?"

"I own a vintage store in SoHo." She beamed with pride. "When it came in on commission, I couldn't resist and bought it from the elderly woman on the spot. I didn't even try it on."

"Yet it fits as if it were made for you. What decades are you fondest of?"

"Well, a lot of my customers are into the late Sixties and early Seventies hippie-retro right now. Personally, I like the sexier styles from longer ago. The satin gowns of the Thirties, beaded flapper dresses of the Twenties are perfect for New Year's Eve or special parties. I even have a few very old items from the Victorian era that should be in a museum somewhere."

"Another coincidence. I'm curator of a wax museum. We actually have a few items of genuine antique clothing on display."

"Really?" Her face lit up with excitement. "What kind of museum? What do you have?"

"It's called the Wax Museum of Demise. We feature artifacts from wars, plagues, bloody rebellions. Anything where many lives were lost, thus changing history and the world."

Maura wrinkled her nose.

Ignoring her apparent snap judgment, he continued. "We try to find something representative of each tragedy, including uniforms from the major wars. On rare occasions I've worn the World War II bomber jackets—very sexy." He smiled broadly and hoped she'd pick up that thread of conversation again. Talking about sexy clothing made him think about stripping hers off.

"You should definitely visit my store, then. You and your partner would love some of our men's items. I have a classic Pierre Cardin black wool coat that still looks new. You look wonderful in black, by the way."

Partner? Does she think I'm gay? "I don't have a partner. I'm not married or gay."

Her hand flew to her throat. "Oh, I'm sorry! I shouldn't have assumed. I thought maybe because you had an artist friend… But then again, I shouldn't make assumptions about that, either."

She let out a nervous giggle and he figured he'd better help her out of the politically incorrect quagmire she had fallen into. "Don't worry. That doesn't offend me in the least. I have many gay friends and even more who are bisexual. I'm not, but a person's sexual orientation doesn't concern me if I'm not directly involved."

"Yes, I feel the same way."

The cab pulled up to her apartment building and she reached for the clasp on her purse.

Adrian quickly put his hand over hers. "No, I insist on paying for the ride."

"Oh, I couldn't let you."

"But I said, I insist. Your company actually made the ride very pleasant."

She smiled and looked at her lap in an almost shy, demure pose. "Thank you. I have to say the same."

When she raised her head, her eyes dilated. A good sign. Adrian knew that meant the sexual attraction was mutual. He even thought he felt her hand jump when he touched it, as if a spark had passed between them. Hopefully it wasn't static electricity.

Adrian reached for his wallet and paid the driver as she exited the cab and stood on the sidewalk. His heart leapt when he saw that she was waiting for him.

Maura swayed on the sidewalk and wondered why she was loitering. No matter how drunk and horny, a woman should never invite a total stranger up to her apartment — even the tall, dark and vagina-worthy ones. However, the moisture between her thighs betrayed her yearning.

And what about her vow, just last night, with all her girlfriends? No more mortal men. *Wouldn't you know it? I swear off men, then a prince of a guy shows up.*

A familiar feeling of trepidation washed over her. Oh no. One of her unwanted advisors was destined to show up. She turned hesitantly toward her left shoulder. Sure enough, there lounged her personal, little drunken, horny devil draped across her shoulder in all his red naked glory, stroking his erection.

"Hello, Susan," he slurred.

My name is Maura, you idiot.

"Yeah, yeah, whatever. So, you want him, don't you?"

I sure do.

"Then why stand here debating with yourself? Invite him up, get naked and fuck the hell out of him!"

How drunk do you think I am?

"I'm here, aren't I?"

Oh, yeah. Good point.

At that moment, she felt a cool tap on her other shoulder. Glancing to her right, Maura spotted the ice-blue angel there with her arms crossed. Her wings fluttered fast enough to take off, but she gripped Maura's shoulder with her bare toes. Uh-oh. She looked ready to declare war any minute.

"Just what do you think you're doing, Devil?"

"Go to hell." The little devil's belly jiggled as he laughed too long and hard at his own joke.

The angel huffed, ignored him and whispered in Maura's ear. "You know what the right thing to do is. Thank the man for the ride, maybe shake his hand, but absolutely no more. Promise."

I… I guess.

The devil laughed again. "See what a killjoy you are, Angel? What sort of pain in the ass guilt did you come to inflict tonight, anyway? Did she eat too much? Laugh too loud?"

"Stop it. You know darn well why I'm here."

"To ruin her fun?"

"No, you idiot. To possibly save her life!"

"Why does everyone call me an idiot?" By now the devil had a chocolate martini in his hand and hiccupped.

The angel rolled her eyes.

Look, you two, knock it off. I can make up my own mind in situations like this. I'm an adult, after all.

"Yeah, Angel. You heard her. Buzz off. She can make up her own mind."

The angel looked terrified. "Not with him around you can't."

"Oh leave her alone. Let her do what she wants. She's a juicy, juicy woman and shouldn't be ashamed of it."

"Oh, for heaven's sake. Dear, do you really want to put yourself in jeopardy?"

The cab driver drove away leaving a tall, sexy, gorgeous man staring at her with dark, smoldering eyes and a subtle, knowing smile. He strolled slowly toward her.

Uh-oh. I'm in trouble.

"No, you're not," they both echoed at once. They peered around her neck at one another, stunned when they found themselves in agreement.

"You know what to do," they both said in unison again.

Maura's heartbeat fluttered in her chest. She really did know what to do. Despite this guy's exceptional qualities, she wouldn't make an exception tonight. Perhaps if she got to know him better…

"I can't take this," the devil spat and disappeared.

"Whew," the angel said and she took off too.

Maura extended her hand. "Thank you for the ride. I hope you'll come to the shop sometime. I'd love to show you my things."

His smile broadened.

Holy crap, did I say "I'd love to show my things?" Maura, you're unbelievable. Drunk or not, a slip like that is embarrassing.

Adrian reached out and took her hand. To her surprise, he raised it to his lips and planted a gentle kiss on her knuckles. "I'd be delighted to see whatever you want to show me. How do I find your shop?"

Her hand trembled, as did all her nerve endings. The electricity running through her body could make her carefully coiffed hair stand on end. "It... It's called Vintage Village. Right in SoHo. You can't miss it."

"I'll stop by, sometime."

"Good. Well, I'll see you, then."

He nodded, "Good night, Maura."

Wait a minute. I never told him my name. How did he know my name?

She waited too long to ask. He had already vanished around the corner and Maura needed her vibrator.

* * * * *

Adrian watched the back of the building from the alley until a light illuminated one of the windows. That must be her bedroom. He crouched, pushed off and soared into the air. Light as a feather he floated down onto the fire escape.

Peering into the second-floor window, he glanced about the room for clues to her taste and personality. Eclectic furniture and bright colors drew his attention, but what he really liked to see was a host of books on two matching bookshelves standing on either side of her dressing table. A sure sign that her mind ranked as highly as her body. Good. His eyes zoomed in on her bedside table to check out the titles.

Young Vampires in Lust, Vampires in Vancouver, Romancing the Vampire. Apparently eclectic taste didn't apply to her reading material. So, Maura had a vampire obsession? This interesting woman's individuality and taste surprised him yet again.

He pulled his vision back to its usual 20/20 and scanned the room as a whole. Maura entered and stood in front of the closet. She kicked off her ivory shoes and they lay discarded beside her. As she reached for the buttons, Adrian's breath hitched. She had just shrugged out of the shoulders, prepared to shimmy out of her lemon sherbet outfit.

Oh, please turn around.

She turned to face the windows and stood with her top buttons opened and a confused look on her face, as if she had forgotten something. Gorgeous, gorgeous breasts! The white lace, low-cut, push-up bra showed off his favorite part of the female anatomy. *Brrrrreasts*! And hers made his mouth water. She lifted one shapely leg and rested it on the edge of the bed. When she had hiked up the hem she reached for the garter's fastener, ready to remove her stockings. As he'd suspected, she wore a white lace garter belt and stockings beneath.

No, wait. Leave the stockings and garters on. Now take off everything else. Don't stop until I tell you too.

Maura removed the dress and turned to hang it carefully next to a long skirt. Facing the closet she reached behind her back, unfastened the bra and let it fall to the floor. *Mmmm… Nicely proportioned from the back too.*

She slipped off her white lace panties next and kicked them onto the discarded bra. Then she bent over to pick them both up.

By the Gods! He beheld her delectable ass. Not one of those little bony asses, but a full, womanly, rounded bottom. Something he could squeeze in the throes of passion. Saliva filled his mouth. Wishing he could use it to lave her clitoris and drive her mad before they coupled, his cock jumped and begged for attention. If he didn't stop himself… What? What could happen? She hadn't invited him in and he'd ruin everything if he lost control, letting her see him on the fire escape while he took care of business. He'd just have to wait for his own pleasure.

She reached for the garter.

Stop. Turn toward the windows.

Maura stood straight and turned around giving him a frontal view of her naked flesh. She still wore the garter belt and stockings, but her full, mouthwatering breasts didn't droop as much as they could at her possible age. They were just right to cup in his hand. That and her lightly trimmed auburn muff, wholly on display for his approval, hardened his erection even more. He remained there and drank in the sight of her nudity, but his greedy voyeurism may have confused her. She shook her head as if trying to clear her mind. Reluctantly, he gave her back her free will.

To his surprise and delight, she walked to her nightstand, removed something from its drawer and sat on top of the bedcovers. "Okay, Mr. Whatever your name is, this is all your fault, so you're going to be my fantasy lover tonight."

Was she talking about him? Adrian moved as close to the window as he dared.

Lying down with her feet flat on the coverlet, she spread her knees wide and aimed the dildo at her pussy. Words escaped him. How could he let her experience this all alone when she clearly wanted a man's contact as much as he wanted hers?

Adrian used his mind control again, as much as he wished he didn't have to and willed her to sleep. The vibrator dropped from her hand and rolled beside her on the bed. In the morning, she'd probably think she had simply passed out from the vodka and fatigue. Meanwhile, he'd provide them both with a certain kind of release and she'd remember it as if it had been a dream.

Okay, so he'd cheat a little bit, but only to give her an experience he knew she'd prefer to an electronic gadget. Getting comfortable, Adrian closed his eyes and tried to ignore his aching erection. He took several deep breaths and cleared his mind. A few moments later, he observed her as if hovering above her bed. In peaceful sleep, no worry lines marred her face at all.

Adrian allowed his astral body to descend slowly until he could affect her. As if actually touching her breasts, he ran his invisible fingers over her, fondling her. She writhed and let out a low, soft moan. When he cupped her fullness an invisible thumb stroked her nipple and she responded just as he had thought she would. Her peaks hardened into erect pebbles and she arched into his hand. Whimpering and continuing to arch in an undulating motion, it was clear she wanted him to suckle her. Happy to oblige, Adrian's virtual tongue licked all around her areola until she writhed with need, then he lowered his mouth and virtually sucked in the sensitive nipple. She cooed her pleasure as he mimicked suckling her breast progressively deeper and harder.

Soon, she moaned louder and arched into his virtual mouth with a slow, steady rhythm. Once he felt she had been thoroughly satisfied on that side, he moved to the other. But what of his own satisfaction?

"Ohhh..." She sighed when he found her other nipple, laved it, then pulled it into his orifice and suckled. As he bestowed the same attention on that breast, his invisible finger found her thigh and traced waves up and down her heated skin. Thankful that in this position, he could levitate, his other hand found his engorged cock and he stroked the length of his hard-on, slowly. *Oh yes.* If she could have a fantasy lover, so could he.

While his hand massaged, rubbed and squeezed every inch of her body, he gave himself the massage he knew she could and would give him very soon.

He neared her pussy lips but only blew gently, not quite ready to touch. She slid her feet out and straightened her knees while spreading her legs wide. Reaching up, her hands searched the air for her lover. He stroked himself faster and harder, knowing he wanted to time his release to coincide with hers.

Her readiness apparent, Adrian placed his virtual mouth even with her clit. Her mons glistened with moisture. He paused in his own pursuit of pleasure and ever-so gently parted her nether lips to study her bud of pleasure. He wanted to know exactly what her clit looked like when swollen with desire. She arched and whimpered as if begging for him to suckle her there.

He shouldn't make her wait any longer. Extending his tongue, he made the motion of lapping at the slit that led to her center of passion. She gasped and moaned in appreciation. Her breathing grew deeper as she raised her pelvis to encourage him.

When Adrian deemed she desperately needed release, he grasped his cock and resumed his frantic hand-job while he licked her clit. She cried out and arched into his mouth. A few more licks and she trembled and moaned out loud, but when she reached for his head, her hands found nothing and merely fell by her sides.

Adrian blew on the swollen bud and suckled. Maura shuddered, inhaled deeply into her lungs and before long screamed in a convulsive orgasm. Adrian's virtual cum shot into space while waves of gratification rumbled over and through him. Maura continued to buck and spasm, coming violently. Suddenly, she pushed against the mattress and sat bolt upright. Even though his astral projection would only appear as a shadow, Adrian broke the connection and dissipated a moment before her eyes flew wide open in shock.

How had she been able to overcome his mind control? No one had been able to do that since… Well, come to think of it, no mortal had been able to do it. Ever!

Chapter Three

ॐ

What just happened? Maura took in deep, panting breaths, not only out of surprise, but… Then it came flooding back to her. A dream. It must have been a dream. The best damn dream she'd ever had in her life! Her legs, weak and rubbery, still fluttered with the aftermath of electricity that had blasted through her body.

She dropped backward and bounced. If she didn't know better… Maura glanced at the pile of books on her bedside table. Her latest pile contained a couple of scenes in which a vampire came to his victim in her sleep and made love to her before biting and feeding. Quickly, she checked her undamaged neck and breathed a sigh of relief. She didn't want just a fang and bang.

She'd have thought about giving up vampire romance novels, but that just wasn't going to happen. Fanged lovers were her favorites.

It must have been all the alcohol. She wasn't used to drinking so much so fast. Being alone at the club and thoroughly bored with the men who hit on her gave her little else to do. It was probably still affecting her.

Maura glanced over at the digital clock radio. A quarter past one. She hadn't been asleep that long, so that must be it. She glanced at her left shoulder and wondered if he'd show up and taunt her. The devil probably thought he had the right to laugh because she hadn't listened to him, but her subconscious certainly had.

Rolling out of bed, she slowly stood, making sure her feet were firmly beneath her. Okay. So far so good. Maura strolled to her computer, removed the quilted cover she had made and named a "computer cozy" for the monitor, then turned it on.

While it warmed up, she unhitched her stockings, rolled them down her legs and took them off. She unhooked the garter belt and placed all of it, plus her bra and panties, in a net laundry bag. From a hook behind her closet door, she removed her long, ivory satin robe. The exquisite robe, tied at the waist, flared all the way to the hem in a typical Thirties Hollywood style. All she needed was a long cigarette holder and for the whole room to shift into black and white.

She plopped herself onto her baby blue, damask, slip-covered chair and opened the file she wanted. Her journal.

Dear Diary,

I know I don't always have all four oars in the water, but so what? I figure that life can be as interesting or as boring as an individual with a brain wants to make it. Maybe I've finally gone over the edge, but I don't think so. I still feel like the same old me...well, okay, me with a hangover, but I knew that was coming.

The thing is, I think I've just had a life-changing experience. It began last night as an innocent night out with the girls. One thing led to another and before I realized it, I was talking about my long-cherished idea of finding an immortal lover. I knew Barb wouldn't go along with it, but the rest kind of got into the idea. I think Barb just didn't want to admit the idea was a great one and she had to remain her logical self at all times...just like when we were roomies in college. But eventually, even she came around. I must be a better salesperson than I thought! I'm glad, although she wouldn't have talked me out of it.

Now getting around to the life-changing part. I know I had way more to drink than I usually do on a Friday night and tonight it's Saturday and I did it again. My poor dehydrated brain is already aching...

Maura stopped typing. Her mouth felt like it was lined with cotton, so she went straight to the kitchen. Water and aspirin would help, eventually. She poured a tall glass of ice water and swallowed a long refreshing gulp. Ah, who knew water could taste so delicious? She refilled the glass to the top and proceeded to her bathroom with it. Tomorrow, she'd pay, no doubt about it, but it might pass a little sooner with some proactive care. She washed down two aspirin, closed the medicine cabinet, caught her reflection in the mirror and gasped.

Ugh! *Disgusting*. Her supposedly waterproof mascara had melted into the puffiness under her eyes. She leaned in close to the mirror. Suddenly those bags looked as if they had been packed to bursting and sent on a wild ride around the country. Maura's skin had always been fair, but pasty white? Jeez, no need to worry about attracting a mortal man like the one she had met earlier. He was obviously just being polite—probably felt sorry for the aging drunken bimbo. *Holy crap*.

"Hey, Susan. Do you think you could possibly beat yourself up any harder?"

Oh no. Maura leaned back far enough from the mirror to reveal the red roly-poly lush perched on her left shoulder. *Not you, again? Why are you here?*

"Because you wished me here."

No, I didn't. If anything, I wished you wouldn't show up.

"Same thing."

Maura's eyes widened. *Son of a...*

"Look, now that I'm here, don't you want to know what I have to say?"

No. I know what you're up to.

The devil let go of his erection and crossed his arms. "Oh yeah? What is it, then?"

You want me to go back to bed and play with myself until I fall asleep again.

"No, that wasn't what I was going to tell you, but now that you mention it, wouldn't it be nice to just lie down with your naked legs spread, rub and massage your aching titties and put that vibrator to use?"

You're incorrigible. And no, to be perfectly honest, no. I don't need anything of the kind right now. I just had the most mind-blowing… Well, what am I telling you for? You must be behind the whole thing.

The devil uncrossed his arms, braced his hands against her satiny shoulder and leaned back, looking pleased. "Nope. Thanks for giving me credit I don't deserve, but it wasn't me."

Oh yeah? Who then?

"I'm not going to tell you. I could, but I won't—even if you beg."

Oh no you don't. You think I'm going to fall for that?

"Fall for what? I'm telling you the truth. I have a whale of a secret and I'm not going to tell you what it is."

Yeah, right. And like I should just believe you because you tell me to.

"Give me a break. I don't lie. Sometimes I tell you what you want to hear, only now I refuse to do even that, because you're not showing me proper respect."

The little devil slid backward against the satin fabric of her robe until all she could see was his round as a red ball ass with all three of his legs sticking straight up in the air. The sight was too much for Maura and she burst out laughing.

Is it any wonder? Look at you! You're more of a clown than anything demonic. In fact, since you keep calling me Susan, I think I'll start calling you Bozo.

The devil blustered, scrambled to his feet and swayed. Steam surged from his head and shoulders. "Don't push me!"

Why not, because you might fall over?

Maura held on to the edge of the sink to keep her balance and chuckled out loud again.

"I mean it. You don't know what you're fooling with here."

Oh shut it. If you're so powerful, why am I not afraid?

"You got me. I actually showed up tonight to help you, but as usual you pretend I can't do anything without your say-so, one way or the other."

Ohhh... You might not tell me this big secret? Like it's something I don't already know. You can't keep secrets from me. You're part of me, you idiot.

The devil smirked and set his hands on his chubby hips. "Oh? You think you're so smart. Think you've got it all figured out, huh?"

Well, of course. You're temptation and the angel is my conscience. Right now I don't need her because I'm doing pretty well without her, aren't I?

The devil reared back and laughed. "Oh, wouldn't it be rich if that were true. Of course, I'd expect a recovering Catholic to come up with something black and white, good and evil, neat and compartmentalized like that."

So, you're saying you're not temptation and the angel's not my conscience?

"If only."

Fine, then you're my subconscious. Either way, you're inside my head, thus a part of me. And you can't hide something like a secret from me forever.

"Wanna bet?"

Prove it.

"Ha! Easy! I'm keeping this secret until you figure it out for yourself. You'll kick yourself to Timbuktu when you find out how easy I could have made things for you!"

Maura gave him the same smug, tight-lipped smile and crossed her arms. *Fine.*

"Fine."

Good night.

"Goodbye." The devil disappeared and she rolled her eyes. Turning away from the mirror, she decided the journal could wait. She'd be better off just drinking the rest of her water and getting some sleep.

* * * * *

Morning rolled around, like it had rolled right over her. The painful sun shone through the window, straight into Maura's oversensitive eyes. She pried herself up to a sitting position and immediately grasped her temples to keep her head from tumbling off her shoulders.

"Ohhh… Two nights in a row. I knew it was going a bad morning." She stayed in that spot until her stomach settled and her head stopped spinning. She drew a few deep breaths and managed to rise and shine like a dirty sidewalk. "Blechhh… My breath!"

She staggered to the bathroom and raised a hand to block the image in her mirror—the one she wasn't ready to face yet. With an open medicine cabinet door, she washed her face and brushed her teeth. At last, prepared to meet the mirror, she closed the medicine cabinet door and let her face swim into view.

Contacts. She needed her contacts. As she withdrew the case from the vanity, she remembered they were still in her eyes. *Damn. Now I'll have to take them out, use some eye drops and wear glasses today. Fabulous.*

She never forgot to take out her contacts at night. How drunk could she have been?

Oh yeah. Bozo showed up. She'd have to find a better name than that for him. Bozo was too sophisticated for that little drunken slut. Maybe she'd call him Fred or Barney. He was, after all, pretty primitive.

Maura sighed, removed her contacts and put them away carefully. Then she used her eye drops. The cooling sensation brought welcome relief. *Okay… Getting there.*

She felt her way to the bedside table and located her glasses. The frames were Fifties vintage, almond-shaped with rhinestones in the tortoiseshell upper corners. Well, that made selecting an outfit easier. June Cleaver she wasn't, but a shirtwaist dress and pearls would complete the Fifties look. Maybe by the end of the day, she'd feel "pure" again. *Ha.* Yeah, right. Friggin' June Cleaver could stuff it.

Once Maura was dressed, she made it to the kitchen and poured herself another tall glass of ice water. *What time is it anyway?* She took a big swig of water and faced the wall clock. "Noon!" She spit water all over the floor and groaned. "Not again."

Now her poor assistant manager would be left opening the store and dealing with the Sunday crowd by herself until Maura could get there. If only she could reach her ass with a good back-kick.

* * * * *

"I'm sorry, Quilla. I'm running late, late, late this morning!" Maura dropped her McDonald's bag on the counter and coffee came whooshing out all over the glass top. "Oh no!"

Quilla, looking particularly earthy-crunchy in her long sack-like dress, grabbed a box of Kleenex and stopped what had spilled from spreading any farther once Maura grabbed and righted the cup. "Looks like you're running on empty too, boss."

"Oh, God. I'm a mess. You wouldn't believe the weekend I had. I'll tell you about it later." Maura finished wiping up the counter. "I really didn't mean to stick you with all the early Sunday customers."

"What early customers? It's been dead and I'm fine here by myself. You could have waited until three this afternoon and had time to get yourself together. In fact, you look like hell. Like you could use a vacation."

Maura wished she could take one, feeling ripe to make one of those "Want to get away?" commercials.

She strode to the back room for some Windex and paper towels. As soon as she returned Quilla left the register to go out on the floor and help a customer. The only customer.

Maura knew her stock by heart. Looking through the glass top to the sparkling jewelry below, she could tell that nothing had moved recently. This was a more serious problem than spilled ugly brown liquid her assistant manager had prevented from seeping into the display cabinet. What was happening with the retro market? The fad hadn't cooled off… Had it?

Quilla returned to the counter with the young woman she was waiting on. The girl had obviously been dying her hair an unflattering shade of flat black, made worse by the regrowth of lighter roots. Black lips and nails completed the — um — style.

"Maura, do you know of anything we might have that could be worn to a Goth party? Something genuine. Not a reproduction?"

Goth. That's a surprising request. "Let me take a look out back."

Maura walked into the small storage area and stopped short, as if suddenly hit in the face by a black, vinyl corset. *Holy crap! Why didn't I think of it before? A Goth section!*

This could be the answer to all her problems. Not only could she increase business with a fresh, new angle, but she could also take that trip to Romania, go on the vampire castles tour, summon her vampire lover and write it all off as a business expense! *Brilliant!*

Her skin tingled with excitement and her fuzzy brain seemed to clear as if by magic. She sprinted out to the God-sent customer waiting by the register.

"When do you need the items and what sort are you looking for?"

The girl raised her eyebrows. "You might be able to get some for me?"

"Maybe. Depends on what you need."

The girl seemed to catch her excitement. "Oh, I don't need it by any certain time, but I have a number of friends who get together on a regular basis for—well, parties, kind of. Anything you can find, the sexier the better. I know my friends would love it too."

Maura translated the information in her business brain as well as her womanly one. She could corner the Goth market with the serious participants and it could add up to major dollar signs. The movement was something she had come across in her pursuit of all things vampire. The mortal, self-proclaimed variety didn't hold any fascination for her, but she knew what went on at these parties. Blood letting, blood drinking and lots of sensual, indiscriminate sex, meaning multiple partners unless claimed by a "beloved", and most cared little about sexual orientation.

She pictured the girls in their black velvet dresses with long side slits and bell sleeves. Underneath they'd have to wear the sexiest black lingerie she could find for them. Front-opening, push-up bras. Black lace g-strings and garters. And, of course the sexy, black, leather lace-up corsets with embellishments of blood red.

Maura moistened between her thighs just picturing such delectable offerings and sensual fantasies. Or was it the money making her so hot? Either way, she was going to Romania and would finally experience the kind of mouthwatering, mind-blowing, out-of-this-world sex that could only be found with a real vampire. Last night's dream, giving her the merest hint of what that might be like, clinched it.

"Here, let me take your contact information." Maura jogged around the counter and reached for her Rolodex. "I'm planning a trip to Romania very soon. I'd been toying with the idea of opening a Goth section, anyway." Neither Quilla nor the young woman needed to know that she had been toying with the idea for all of three minutes.

"That's fantastic!" the woman said.

Quilla's never-plucked eyebrows rose to the point of wrinkling her flawless forehead all the way to her short brown bangs. "Yes, fantastic," she echoed. "When were you going to tell me about it?"

Maura held up one finger, asking Quilla to give her a minute. When the young woman had recited what seemed like a real address and phone number and left the store, Maura turned to Quilla and smiled her most charming smile.

"Do you think you can handle the store for a week, or should I close for vacation?"

Quilla shrugged. "What do you think?"

"I'm sure you can deal with anything that comes up, but I don't want to be unfair. Are you sure you don't want a vacation too?"

"I'm more interested in my paycheck and maybe a little extra since I'll be working all by my lonesome?"

"Uh... How about a bonus after I get back? I may need the money up front for the trip, but I'll get it back with the new purchases fast enough. What do you think? Twenty percent of the profits from the new line?"

Quilla tipped her head up and stared at the ceiling for a few seconds, as if figuring out how much that might add to her paycheck, then smiled and stuck out her hand. "That works for me."

Hopefully it would work out for Maura too.

The women shook on it.

* * * * *

Monday morning Maura twirled through her Rolodex until she came upon the card she wanted and plucked it off its track. "I'm going into the back room to call my accountant and take a look at travel arrangements. I'll see if I can book the trip online. Yell if you need me, Quilla, okay?"

"You got it."

Maura disappeared into the storeroom and yanked the other computer cozy she'd handmade off her monitor. She fired up the machine, then dialed her late father's friend, the accountant, while waiting for the computer to warm up and go through its various calisthenics.

"Berry and Lowry," answered the receptionist.

"This is Maura Keegan for Mr. Berry please."

"One moment."

"Maura, how are you?"

"Great, Stanley. Business could be better, though."

"Really? What's wrong?"

"The store isn't doing well. We need to attract new customers and I'd like to add a new section to the store, shake things up a bit. There's another type of old clothing revival that's especially hot right now. I don't think the trend will be cooling any time soon, either."

"I didn't think the vintage business was cooling. Is it?"

"Not really. It's just that so many designers are getting into retro that they're remaking all new clothing inspired by past styles. Once the public wanted their stuff to be genuine and liked the bargains they could find. Now the snooty names are selling my stuff. Designer labels have always been hot. Then you've got the knockoffs. That's all I can think of to explain it."

"I'm sorry to hear that. So, what do you have in mind?"

"I'm going to begin a new line of gothic clothing and I've had requests for the genuine articles. So far, designers aren't particularly inspired by it."

"And if they are?"

"I don't think the clientele will be interested in their names or price tags."

"Sounds good. So what do you need from me?"

"I'm planning a trip to Romania for the genuine items and future suppliers. It'll be a tax write-off, won't it?"

Maura waited a few seconds for a response. Nothing seemed forthcoming and she hoped they hadn't been disconnected. "Stanley?"

"Uh, sure, Maura. I'm listening — but, Romania?"

"That's what I said." She leaned back and placed her feet on her desk, crossing them at the ankles.

"I guess I didn't expect the items to be so far away, but if that's where they are…"

"That's where the mother lode is, Stan."

"Okay. In that case, you need to keep an account of every minute and every dime you spend that's directly related to your business. Have a diary and fill in how you spent everything. Save receipts. All transportation. Hotels and meals. Any clothing purchases you intend to sell…"

"What about a little sightseeing while I'm there?"

"Any side trips are your own responsibility, but personally, I wouldn't blame you for wanting to do a little touring. Romania sounds like a fascinating and exotic place. Once you get your contacts set up, who knows when or if you'll be back there."

"Yeah, that's what I was thinking."

"Well, have fun, but be careful. Don't venture off by yourself."

"Oh, no, I wouldn't. That's why I asked. There's a tour that would take me to all the most pertinent places and it includes meals, hotels, travel and shopping."

"Sounds perfect. I'll be looking forward to doing your tax return next year. It should make interesting reading."

"Thanks, Stanley."

Maura mentally ticked off the items she could deduct from the vampire castles tour she had been dreaming about. The round-trip airfare, tour bus, hotels, meals, shopping. Damn near everything but the tour guide's tips.

This is a dream come true.

"Or a nightmare," said a familiar angelic voice.

Oh, nuts. Maura glanced toward her right shoulder. There she was, fluttering her wings and hovering. It looked like she was getting ready to land. Maura dodged to the left and brushed her empty shoulder a few times. *Go away. Shoo! I'm going to do this no matter what you say, so don't waste your time.*

"Maura! This isn't like you. Don't tell me he's been hanging around, spreading his negative influence."

No, he hasn't. In fact he went away mad last time and I don't think I'll be seeing him again for a while.

"Really? That would be good news, except that it means you've decided to carry out this foolish plan all by yourself! You surprise and disappoint me, Maura."

So what else is new?

The angel, still floating in the air, flew directly in front of Maura's face with her hands on her hips. "He's gone because you don't need him anymore. You've internalized him. I was hoping that wouldn't happen." Her shoulders drooped. "My poor, poor darling."

What do you mean by that?

"I mean that his bad influence has become a part of your operating consciousness and I-I…" The angel tossed her loose white sleeve across her forehead melodramatically and cried, "I failed!"

Maura shook her head.

I hate to say it, but he was right about one thing. You really do have guilt down to an art form.

The angel's mouth dropped open with a loud gasp, then shut so hard her teeth clicked. "That's it, missy." She flew over to Maura's right ear and hovered. "I'm afraid you're on your own until I can figure out a way to bring you back from the dark side. I just hope you're not too far gone by the time I get back."

Don't hurry. I'm fine, I know exactly what I'm doing.

"That's what you think!" She whispered one last tsk, tsk in Maura's ear and the angel vanished.

Chapter Four

ဢ

Monday evening, Adrian paid another visit to Maura's fire escape. Since the evening was cool, he wore his warm black wool cape in case he decided to stay a while. Tonight she had come home early and he found her already stretched out on her bed, reading. She wore a long nightgown of pale blue lace and shimmering satin that nearly matched her aquamarine eyes. Too bad her eyes weren't visible with her glasses on. If she were a vampire, she'd have no need for glasses since her vision would be as sharp and flawless as his. *Now where the hell did that thought come from? I don't want to turn her.*

After reading one of her vampire romances for a couple of hours, she laid the book against her heart and sighed. Despite suspecting the book was full of nonsense, Adrian found a deep part of himself curious to know what she had just read.

Maura set the book on her nightstand and picked up one of the others.

Don't tell me she's going to do this all night. Adrian wanted to leave her alone this evening, meaning no mind control, just to see what she did with her spare time when not under his influence. If she were going to bore him to death, however, he'd have to rethink that plan. At least he had a thermos of red wine to keep him company out on the lonely fire escape.

She scanned the back cover, smiled and set the new novel aside. Maura pushed herself up and bounded to her feet. As she reached her computer and turned it on, she set her glasses on the desk and then proceeded to the bathroom.

Adrian took a sip of the smooth, rich wine from his thermos and waited for her to return.

When she came back, Adrian spit red wine all over his black pants. *Gaaaah! What's that horrible claylike substance smeared all over her pretty face?* A plastic headband tugged Maura's bangs away from her forehead. Not a great look either, but the disgusting gray coating around her eyes, down her nose and finally stopping at her chin had to go.

Adrian took a long gulp of his wine. Nothing so hideous could improve his woman's face or make her look more beautiful. He'd have to throw that clay crap out, as soon as he was invited in.

Maura settled herself on the chair in front of the computer. Thankfully his view now consisted of her lovely scooped back with loose red hair fluffing between her soft, peach shoulders. He took a few deep breaths to regroup, then let himself relax and watch.

She typed in her password, *Vampire*. Big surprise. When she clicked on her word documents, instead of being presented with the expected blank page, something else popped up. Her posture snapped to attention and she grabbed her glasses.

Adrian zeroed in on the title of the document. Centered and in bold, it read, *The Guide to Mortal/Immortal Relationships. A Code of Honor*. He leaned closer to the window, knowing what he had read, but simply not believing it.

"I thought that book was a myth! And she has it? Hell's bells!"

Apparently Maura couldn't believe it either. He could sense shock waves rippling through her. She scrolled and scanned the document until her hands froze on a new chapter. He focused again to see what she was staring at with such intensity. The heading read "Guide to a Relationship with the Immortal Vampire". She hit the print button, jumped up and ran to the bathroom. When she retuned, her face was scrubbed clean, the headband had been removed and the printed pages awaited her. Maura reached for them with trembling fingers.

Staring at the papers, she must have sensed the supernatural import of this guide. The pages fluttered in her hand. She pulled open a desk drawer and removed a binder then carefully placed the pages inside to protect the precious document. How could this have happened? No one had e-mailed it. She hadn't even opened her e-mail.

He quickly reviewed and dismissed every logical possibility. The computer wasn't already on. She had to turn it on and insert her password. This wasn't sent to her, even as a joke. It wasn't in her e-mail folder. She couldn't have typed it herself, even in a total blackout. The type looked more like handwritten calligraphy and no scanner was present anywhere in the room. Upon studying it closer, he realized some of the flourishes were a tiny bit longer or shorter, the upper line ran with an occasional uneven appearance rather than perfectly straight across the page. It *had* been handwritten. But how and by whom?

Maura held her forehead as if lightheaded and wandered to her bed in a trance. She sank onto the mattress slowly, then opened and thumbed through the guide until she reached the page on vampires. The first sentence read, "Forget all of your juvenile, romantic notions when it comes to the dark ones."

Adrian noticed a shiver run up her spine and she dropped backward onto the bed. She tried holding the guide above her face, but her hands shook, so the words on the page must have looked as if they were written in a fun-house mirror.

Maura gave up and flipped over to rest her elbows on the bed. The papers no longer jiggled around and Adrian could read, but with the document facing toward him, the words appeared upside down and he had to struggle to make them out.

Forget all of your juvenile, romantic notions when it comes to the dark ones. They are almost always a murderous and conscienceless lot. They may seem interested in you as a person, but are more likely interested in what runs through your veins than your brains. Only rarely has there been one with enough emotional strength to overcome his ignoble natural world and create a life apart. It would be almost certain that any vampire you come across would be of the former sort—not the latter. Thus, you must proceed with extreme caution. To succeed in finding love with any vampire could only mean one thing—that you are his beloved.

This was maddening. Adrian could tell she was getting ready to flip the page, reading much faster than he could in this position and he wanted to know everything she discovered. He flipped upside-down and floated in midair until he could read the words right side up. Then his damn cape fell prey to gravity.

Maura peeked up from her reading, did a double-take and caught her breath. Adrian sensed the jolt of sudden fear that gripped her heart and held her immobile. Had she seen him on the fire escape? He darted into the shadows. Meanwhile, she squinted into the night outside her window, shook her head and returned to her reading.

Most likely she thought her eyes had played tricks on her. Because of the freakish appearance of this strange guide and reading its cautionary advice, she might naturally be jumpy.

Whew. That was too close.

Adrian heard papers fluttering to the floor inside the apartment and he peeked around the corner. Maura paced across the room. Her eyes flashed blue fire and her fists were clenched in fury. Her mouth pursed into a thin straight line and she stomped her foot.

"Angel! Angel, you show yourself right this minute!" Her eyes darted all around the room.

What the hell is she yelling? Angel?

"Angel, I know this is your doing. I know it! Now come here and take responsibility for this farce!" Maura planted her hands on her hips and waited. Her face, usually such a pretty pale peach had turned more of a strawberry red.

"Angel! Front and center, now! So I can tell you how wrong you are."

What's going on with this girl? Is she honestly trying to call up a fictional character who plays a vampire on TV?

Maura stormed over to her computer, closed the window on the guide, then opened the internet.

"I'm going and you can't stop me, Angel. Just to spite you, I'm going!"

With a few pounding strokes on the keyboard the monitor revealed scenic vacation pictures. It looked like a travel page.

Okay, so she's going on a trip. Going where?

She entered something into the search bar, but her fingers flew so fast, Adrian couldn't follow along. Up popped a page with photos of places he recognized. Castles. Specifically, Romanian castles!

"I will find the one...my beloved! If you want to pop in and tell me the wrong ones from the right one, that would be cool, but I won't expect your help."

Adrian tried to connect with her mind, but reeled back, clutching his head in pain. The woman was behaving too emotionally to think in a rational manner and let him decipher what was going through her head. Adrian rubbed his temples until the pain subsided.

Note to self, Adrian. Redheaded Irishwomen can go from zero to furious in a matter of seconds. Ouch. He wouldn't try that again real soon.

As she scrolled past the pictures and descriptions, he tried to focus on the monitor again. Destinations and dates flashed by. Promises of chilling tales that had been passed down by oral tradition through the ages.

With stark, raving clarity, he realized she was booking herself on a vampire tour. Adrian guessed that most of it was a bunch of hogwash for tourists, but then two of the castles she scrolled by actually did belong to the undead. *Oh no! She must have read the warnings, but the stubborn girl doesn't believe them.*

If she was planning to do what he thought she was going to do, namely, book herself on a "vampire tour", go to Romania and somehow slip away during the night to summon a real vampire, he had to meet her on that tour and be that vampire. If she summoned any other, she'd probably be invited to dinner, but she'd be the main course!

Adrian continued to watch the itinerary promised by the tour. Nothing bothered him until the next castle on the screen came into view. Holy hell! Suddenly, he felt his head spin and bile rise to his throat. He grasped the iron railing in an effort to steady himself. As soon as he knew his knees weren't going to buckle, he took a long swig from the thermos, draining the last of his red wine. *Bloody hell!*

Adrian couldn't believe his highly dysfunctional family had opened their home to tourists.

* * * * *

Maura picked up the guide from where it had fallen on the Persian rug and walked into the living room with it. She brought along the folder even though the pages had slipped out, figuring she'd put them back in order and store the document away someplace safe. She had only read a small part. Much more existed in the way of an introduction. Curling up on her Victorian love seat she realized that if this wasn't a trick from the angel, it appeared as if it had been given to her by some sort of supernatural power—one that wanted her to have it. Her nerves hadn't settled completely, but she managed to hold the pages steady enough to read them.

The magnificent scrolling letters looked as if they had been written some time ago. As she held the papers they seemed to age. The pages began to turn brown and crinkle at the edges. Maura caught her breath. *Better read fast, before the thing turns to dust!*

Mortal/Immortal Relationships, Behavior and Advice

If you are in possession of this manuscript, think of it not as instruction but more as advice, for you will need it. A mortal romantically involved with an immortal should be aware that certain differences in basic philosophies and values exist along with physiology. This guide is intended to make the reader aware of these differences and to help him or her choose a wise course.

1) Be very specific, when you summon an immortal. Getting your wish may be the worst thing that could happen to you if you ask for the wrong things. Consider your words very carefully. Consider your peril even more carefully, especially with the dangerous fanged immortals.

2) If you are attempting to follow this path as a sexual experiment, don't. Yes, the legendary prowess with which immortals are credited is true. It's beyond comparison and as such you should remember they've had centuries to practice and perfect their techniques. If you go back to mortals after being sexually stimulated by an immortal you may be disappointed for the rest of your life.

3) Reciprocate when an immortal gives you gifts. Do not be concerned at matching a monetary value. A gift you've chosen with the immortal's interests in mind or a gift you've created are both infused with your life force. With an immortal, it truly is the thought that counts.

4) Never ask an immortal to compare you to their past lovers. They've probably had hundreds, maybe thousands. If you ask and they tell the truth, you may not be number one on the list. You could perceive this as a negative answer, even if you're perfectly adequate. Remember that they have little to fear, including the truth.

5) If you are emotionally fragile, jealous or afraid of getting hurt, you might want to reconsider summoning, or if it is too late, end the affair altogether and quickly. Immortals are

not known for being patient or considerate of mortals' feelings, limitations or needs.

6) If it seems as if your immortal is completely in love with and totally devoted to you, it may be true. On the other hand it's possible that it's only temporary relief from sexual frustration. Wait to see what develops between you. If you feel like you are being toyed with, you probably are.

7) Do not expect or demand commitment. Because immortals live forever, they often have a different feeling about it. Monogamy, even with a fellow immortal, is considered impractical since true love is so rare. True love with a mortal is even more unreasonable. Forever is a long, long time to mourn.

8) Do not expect or ask an immortal to grant you immortality. If you have to ask, it's quite possible the immortal is not as attached to you as you thought. It makes you appear needy and clingy. Immortals respect independence and belief in one's self.

9) If an immortal offers you immortality, consider all the ramifications. In the event that your life doesn't turn out as you would like, imagine a "life sentence" without end. In addition, the immortal might not give you a human form.

10) Find a focus for your life to give your life meaning. When your immortal lover leaves you, you have to be able to know your own joy in life so you can remember the time spent with the immortal lover with affection and not bitterness.

A note of caution to immortals if you are reading this.

Your mortal lover comes with an expiration date. The idea of being turned to remain with you is a romantic notion that should be outlawed. The soul-mate exception is so rare, you should probably not even consider it. Bearing in mind that his or her death is inevitable, you should be sure the relationship is worth the heartache.

"Expiration date?" Maura asked out loud. "Who wrote this thing?"

She stuffed the yellowed papers back into the folder, stood and paced around the room. "Devil? Oh, Devil..." She waited several seconds and tried again. "Come here, you little devil." Still, no answer.

Maura jammed her hands on her hips. "Well, that's just terrific. It looks like they're both on strike." Then she remembered the summoning in Central Park Friday night. If the guide was real, she must be about to need it.

Just in case, she ran to her jewelry box and took out the silver stickpin she had made in a jewelry crafting class. She would keep it with her as a gift for her immortal, should she need to reciprocate.

Chapter Five

ჯ

Adrian stood in front of his family's thirteenth-century Romanian castle, arms crossed, shaking his head. How could they have let the place fall into such abominable disrepair?

At one time, the palace had shown as the jewel of Transylvania with the exception of the Bran Castle. Now there was no contest. The other castle, last home of Vlad Tepes, aka Dracula, upstaged Adrian's family home by far. In fact, there were at least ten castles that were in better shape than this one was now.

He'd have to have a chat with whoever was in charge of the estate grounds. Suddenly Adrian was hit by a shock wave of realization. Something must have happened to his father. The family elder would never have let their home go like this. Fruit trees, gnarled by the wind coming off the Carpathian Mountains, looked sickly. Even the tall pines showed large gaps with brown needles or none at all, as if fire had ravaged them.

He trudged up what was once a magnificent stone path leading to the castle doors. Now long grass grew between every broken flagstone. The structure itself appeared sound enough, if you didn't look at the crumbling plaster up close. *Why didn't they try to find me and tell me what happened to my father?* Adrian knew the answer and guilt filled him with sadness like the howling wind filled the dark sky with gloom. He hadn't wanted to be found.

He inhaled a deep breath as he reached the giant wooden doors and steeled himself against whatever he might discover behind them. Adrian gripped the iron ring attached to a heavy chain dangling beside the door. With one hard pull a faint bell sounded inside.

While he waited for someone to answer, he tucked his cold hands in the pockets of his wool coat. A few seconds later the door opened, seemingly by itself.

What the hell? Adrian took a quick look inside, his eyes darting as far left and right as he could see without entering. At last, a lone female, dressed in a long, black gown with a tattered train, descended the wide, wooden staircase.

"Mother!" He barely recognized her. She seemed so thin and pale. Adrian charged into the palace and up the stairs to embrace her. As he held the frail woman, the doors clanked shut on their own.

"What happened here? Where's Father?"

"Adrian. How good of you to come home for a visit."

Feeling like a much younger, more vulnerable vampire, he regressed into his boyhood speech and manner, stamping his foot. "Why didn't you send for me when Papa died? I was always the last one to be called, even for dinner. I was the one you left behind at the rest stop and didn't notice was missing until you were almost home."

"That's because you were so forgettable. I mean that in the nicest way possible, Adrian. Your brothers were always creating havoc everywhere we went, but you were the good boy, doing what you were told, being quiet and blending in." The older woman suddenly reeled back in shock. "Papa's dead? Why didn't I know about it?"

"You didn't know either, Mama? I thought you were tied to one another forever and could sense each other's very breath."

"We are. I thought he was still upstairs in his study. Wait a moment." Adrian's mother cupped a hand behind her ear while Adrian waited in confused silence.

"He's still there, still breathing. In fact, he's breathing rather heavily. Oh, damn. I'll bet the maid's in there again."

The woman turned on her heel and marched up the stairs with her hands on her hips, as if prepared for battle.

Adrian shook his muddled head, vigorously. *If Mama was all right and Papa was all right, what had happened here?* Perhaps his father was ill? He quietly followed after his mother, at last catching up with her as she heaved open the thick door to his father's study.

The older man stood at the edge of his desk, pants around his ankles, pumping his stiffy in and out of the maid.

"Damn it," his mother shouted as she stormed into the room. "We have company. Stop fucking the maid."

Adrian turned away. Obviously, his father was as healthy as ever.

"I'll have plenty of pep left over for you, my dear. Now just give me a minute, I'm almost there."

Adrian peeked around the doorframe to see his mother turn her back and wait while his father gave a few more thrusts into the young blonde and then jerked with his release.

"Ahhh… Thank you Violeta." He withdrew, pulled up his trousers and fastened them. While he buttoned his white shirt, the maid rolled off the desk and scurried past the two witnesses of their afternoon tryst. Adrian watched her short skirt bounce up and down displaying a full, round ass, sans panties, as she jogged down the hall. He could see their juices running down her leg. She smelled delicious. Like flowers and sex.

His mother folded her arms. "Our son has come to visit."

"Really?"

His papa's broad, white smile lit up his face. A handsome devil, he wore his perpetual black hair loose.

"Which one?"

"Adrian. He came all the way from America and this is how he finds you." His mother tsk-tsked the old man.

"Don't be silly. He's a grown man. What is he, now? Almost six hundred years old? Besides you know you love it when you catch me fucking the maid — or the gardener. And I know you love fucking the chef, then me catching you and spanking you for it. Don't pretend you're not turned on right now."

"Of course I am, but this is different. I've never been caught catching you before. I don't know how to react. Most people find extramarital sex something shameful and being caught in the act is supposed to be embarrassing."

"Nonsense. I enjoy all the extra sex I can get. If you think the maid is hot, son, you should see the gardener. Feel free to indulge."

Adrian stepped into the room and extended his hand to his father. "That won't be necessary. I'm just glad to see you're in good health, Father. I'm glad to hear your English improving."

"Yes, we practice regularly since we see so many more English-speaking visitors here than we used to. Even the staff is learning a little English."

"By the way, you have a gardener?"

"Of course. You don't think I could keep the place looking like this by myself do you?"

Adrian raised his eyebrows. "Like it's abandoned, you mean?"

"The atmosphere is good for business," his mother said. "We'll explain later."

"I know about the tours, Mother. What I don't know is, why?"

"Your father quit his job."

"I thought you liked working, Papa?"

"I thought so too. Now I find I like loafing even more."

His mother rolled her eyes. "Yes, it seems as if we cannot live in the style to which we've become accustomed, with willing servants and the like, unless there's some form of income."

"Don't be embarrassed about the maid, Mother. Like he said, I'm almost six hundred years old. I think I can handle the fact that my parents need a little variety in their sex life to keep it fresh."

Pink tinted his mother's white cheeks. "It's just that I don't think this has ever happened before. Our children always knew we had satisfying sex lives, but only with each other. Yes, I admit it. I like to catch him going at it with someone else, but afterward, we get so hot for each other the sex just explodes. How can I explain that to one of my sons?"

"I think you just did and it's all right. I understand. Whatever little sex games get you off. I like to think my parents are enjoying themselves."

"Good, well, I hope you don't mind when your father makes me scream, later. The other wing is closed, so you'll need to stay on this side."

"I won't be staying. I have a hotel room in Brasov."

"You didn't have to do that, Adrian. We'd be delighted to have you stay with us."

"I'm not alone on this trip."

His father raised dark eyebrows and elbowed his mother. "That's wonderful, Adrian. We'll even understand if you make her scream."

Adrian chuckled. "I'd love to, believe me. We're not at that stage in our relationship yet. We'll be on a tour, stopping at various locations around the country. I just wanted to give you some advanced notice that I may be bringing someone special around." He glanced at the torn tapestries on the wall and the well-worn rug. "Now I'm glad I did. Can you fix up this dump? I'd like to impress her."

His father clapped him on the back and guided him out of the room. "We'll see what we can do. I'm glad you found another vampire to bring home. It's about time you got over Vampirella."

"I was never attached to her, Father, and if you remember it ended in disaster. I haven't spent any amount of time with one person since, but I think I may have found the woman who could make me want what you and Mother have always had."

"Who wouldn't want what we have?" His father asked the rhetorical question with pride. "A fine home, wonderful children and a satisfying business where we get paid just to be ourselves."

Adrian's mother squeezed his arm. "That's wonderful, Adrian! Tell us more about her."

"I think I'd just rather bring her home and let you meet her. How's Tuesday?"

His parents looked at each other. "Vladimir, I think we have a group coming on Tuesday, right?" his mother asked.

Adrian stared at his mother. "I know you have a tour that evening since we'll be on it, but Mama, are you going senile or is this another sex game? Papa's name is Petrov."

"Not anymore, son," his father said. "I changed it. On Tuesday, you may call me Vlad."

* * * * *

Maura had never been this excited in her entire life. She had landed in Bucharest, Romania, and her dream was about to come true. Why else would "The Code" have appeared? She was going to need its advice, it had said. She wished she could have brought it with her, but sadly, the folder in which she had tried to keep it hadn't provided enough protection. She wondered if anything could have kept the guide from vanishing overnight. Yet she remembered its words well enough to write down the gist of it on regular notebook paper and keep it in the back of her trip journal.

61

She fingered the small steno book in her coat pocket while she waited at the baggage claim. In it she would keep her notes and transcribe them in greater detail, each evening. Time had a way of erasing memories and Maura didn't want any of hers to be lost.

Perhaps that's why she was inspired by vintage fashions. Clothes could evoke such sentimentality. She remembered every emotion she felt at her prom whenever she gazed at the dry cleaning bag that held her turquoise sequined gown in the back of her closet. Her Catholic high school uniform hung in front of it and evoked a different set of emotions. But she was proud to try it on now and then to see that it still fit...well, almost. All right, so it was a little snug at the waist and gaping at the bust, but she used it as proof that she wasn't letting herself go—much.

Glancing around the airport she didn't see anything in the way of gothic fashion at all. Certainly the suits worn by business-men and -women and most of the casual attire of traveling families didn't qualify.

At last she spotted a young woman in what could only be called "vampire vintage" and grinned her foolish head off. The whole ensemble was exactly what she needed for the store. The woman's black dress showed off a pair of black lace-up boots under a handkerchief hem and she wore it with a black and red corset on the outside. The long sleeves of the dress ended in a bell-shape and floated away from her body, sensuously, as if made of gauze.

Maura wove her way past the other travelers at the baggage claim to speak to her. "Excuse me. Do you speak English?"

"I think I can manage it," said the cheeky brunette with a British accent.

"Oh, yeah. I guess you can." Maura chuckled and suddenly felt uncomfortable about pursuing her question. Would the woman think she was nuts? She didn't usually let what people thought get in her way, so she certainly wouldn't now. "Do you mind my asking where you bought your outfit? I absolutely love it."

The girl grinned. "Isn't it wicked? There's a gothic store in London on a side street near Harrods. I'm going on a vampire tour and thought I'd dress the part."

"Really? So am I. Does yours start tomorrow from Brasov?"

"Yes. We're to meet our guide tomorrow afternoon at a local pub, the Brasov Beer Stein. I believe that's what the name of the place translates to in English. I understand the tours are mostly in the evening."

"Oh? I just thought it started late so those of us with jetlag could sleep late and wake up refreshed."

The woman laughed. "More likely it's for the atmosphere, so we'll all tremble at the setting sun and threat of waking vampires." She extended her hand. "I'm Jordan Fredericks."

"Maura Keegan."

The women shook hands and Maura liked having made a new friend. An adventure shared is always fun, but there might be a time when she'd like to be alone—with her vampire. She hoped chumming around with a friend wouldn't get in the way.

"How are you getting to Brasov?" Jordan asked.

"I guess there's a train and a bus. I found out the train is faster and since we're going to be on buses most of the week, I figured I'd take the train."

"I reckon you can't wait to get there?"

"You said it."

* * * * *

As it turned out, the pub was on the ground floor of the hotel where Maura was staying. She shared a pint of ale with Jordan, figuring the bartender would probably be stumped by a request for a chocolate martini. She didn't want to be one of those Americans who expected to get everything the same way as at home. The ale was much stronger than a Sam Adams Light and if she had known... Well, it was too late now. Besides, she'd probably sleep like a baby.

When she staggered upstairs and opened the door to her room, she had to admit the European first-class accommodations seemed rather basic to the New Yorker. One narrow room with twin beds and a sink was adequate for her for one night, however and by the time she met her vampire, she'd want a room with a good-size bed. Maybe he'd invite her to stay at his castle!

Her head was swimming with questions. How would she know where to leave her summons? How long would it take him to seduce her? How would he do it? A thought she hadn't considered intruded and her eyes popped wide open. *Oh God, what if the vampire who appears after my summons isn't a male?*

Clutching her chest, she answered her own question quickly. *It's okay, the guide said to be specific.* She took a few deep breaths. She'd better try to word her specific summons tonight to be sure she got the words right. After coming all this way, it had to be right.

She opened her suitcase and rummaged in the side pocket for her journal. She wanted to review it even before selecting her outfit for the next day and hanging it up.

"Don't worry, Susan. I'll help you."

Oh, for the love of...

Maura turned slowly toward her left shoulder and there he was, in all his drunken, red glory. He reclined on her shoulder with his hands folded behind his head, smiling like a... Well, like a horny devil who knew something she didn't.

Wipe that smug look off your face and for the last time, my name isn't Susan, Fred.

"My name isn't Fred, either, but you don't see me getting all pissy about it, do you? Try to relax, Susan. I'm here to help."

Maura rolled her eyes and collapsed on the single bed. "Oww."

"At least the mattress is nice and firm." He chuckled.

Look, I haven't even got my coat off yet. Do you think I could get comfortable first?

"Well, if you don't need my help, by all means, take your time. I just wanted to help you with the real reason you're here before the white fluttery one shows up and ruins everything."

Fine. Help me, then.

"To answer your first question, how will you know where to leave the summons? You'll just know."

That's your idea of help? I'll "just know"?

"Do you want me to make something up? Would you feel better if I said, third castle to the left, first corridor, in the drawing room, under the candlestick? Is that what you want? Maybe I should get Colonel Mustard on the tour."

Oh, all right. I'll try to listen without questioning you from now on. Now what else can you tell me?

"Stop!" A familiar female voice called out.

"Aw, nuts." The devil spoke out of the corner of his mouth directly into Maura's ear. "Sometimes I wish she could be like a bird and fly smack into the glass window."

The angel landed gently on Maura's right shoulder. "I heard that. Thank you for not giggling, my dear. That would only encourage him."

"I need no encouragement."

"True, unfortunately. Maura certainly needs me, though. I'm glad I saw what was going on down here before it was too late."

"Killjoy!"

"Idiot!"

Stop it, both of you. I'm too tired to listen to you bicker, so leave me alone. If you don't like it, you can kiss my stubborn Irish ass.

Her unwelcome angelic visitor gasped. "Well! I never…" the angel protested.

"I don't doubt that." The devil snickered and whispered in Maura's ear. "Nice one, Susan. Don't worry. I'll be back, but I'll make sure she's occupied for a while, first."

Maura threw her arms in the air and shouted out loud. "Out! Both of you!"

They vanished and not a moment too soon. A knock sounded at her door.

"Uh… Yes?"

The door opened and to her surprise, the handsome man from the cab ride in New York, the same one who rescued her friend, stood there. "May I come in?"

"Um. I guess."

He stepped into her room and closed the door behind him. She could be mistaken, but this guy certainly resembled him.

"Are you all right?" He glanced about the room. "I thought I heard you order somebody out and thought you might need some assistance."

"Oh. Ah, no. Only mice. I thought I saw a couple of the little rodents in my room. I don't mind sharing, but not with varmints."

The tall, dark and chivalrous man looked familiar. Was it the guy she shared a cab with? Hard to say since she was plastered at the time and he looked slightly different now that she was just pleasantly buzzed. If it was him, then he looked even handsomer in focus. That didn't happen often.

As Maura took in the dangerously sexy, six-foot hunk, sultry dark eyes, masculine jawline, muscles in all the right places beneath the black shirt he wore with rolled-up sleeves, he simply smiled. His long black hair, tied neatly behind his head was so smooth it reflected the light with a bluish sheen. Healthy-looking, tan skin covered sinewy forearms.

His unperturbed, laid-back style endeared him to her immediately. Had he insisted on finding a flashlight and searching her room for a mouse she "should" be afraid of, or worse, had run from the prospect of a small, furry creature, he'd have lost his appeal. As it was, his mesmerizing gaze captivated her. If only he were a vampire. Maura sighed.

Adrian's mind went blank. He couldn't think of one intelligent thing to say. Here he was face-to-face with the only woman to capture his imagination in centuries. He had been invited into her hotel room and he was tongue-tied. *Say something, damn it. Do you want her to think you're a freak on your first day together?*

It had been too long since Adrian had done this, specifically trying to pick up a mortal woman without using his mind control on her.

So what should I do now? Say, "Hello my name is Adrian and I'll be your vampire today?"

Maura offered her hand. "Are you from New York? You look so familiar — like someone I've seen before."

Ah, thank you, dear lady.

"Yes, how coincidental." Adrian took her hand and raised it to his lips.

A chaste peck on the knuckles made her blush. A woman in her thirties with some worldly wisdom that can still blush! Adrian held her hand a little longer than usual, delighted when she smiled and didn't snatch it away.

"I'm surprised to see someone from home here in Romania, of all places!"

"You never know where I'll turn up." Adrian held her gaze, not particularly happy with his scintillating dialogue. He thought briefly about turning to the ol' vampire's mesmerizing trick, but he wished to share something mutual with her. He'd just have to muddle through.

His cock was hyper-aware of her too, sending its signals to get his attention, as if raising a red flag. Still, it would be best to see where the conversation would lead on its own, now that the ice was broken. He'd like to keep talking and get to know her the "normal" way...whatever that was.

Adrian cleared his throat. "My name is Adrian and I'm here on a tour. It starts tomorrow afternoon, so I'll only be in Brasov until then." He tried to sound as if he didn't know her plans.

"Oh, so am I! I'll be on an English-speaking vampire tour. I heard about it years ago and wanted to try it ever since."

"Another coincidence. It sounds as if we'll be on the same tour."

Maura tipped her head and rested her hand on her hip. "You know, that's an unusual accent you have. It's not exactly American."

Adrian smiled. How could he explain that he had been following bloody rebellions, wars and famines since he left Transylvania for good in the 1400s? He wasn't even sure what year it was, then. He just knew that his once friend, now sworn enemy, Vlad Tepes, aka Vlad the Impaler, son of Vlad Dracul, went too far by punishing disobedient subjects and "unchaste" women by impaling them on sharpened stakes.

It was different when they were fighting the Turks. They were the enemy and soldiers know they might die in war, but his own subjects? Unforgivable. And unchaste women were his favorite type.

To play God, deciding who should live or die, just to feed his need for blood made him ill after that. He had worked to avoid the desire altogether, but when he had to have a nip or go crazy, better to be from a victim ready to meet their maker.

"I've lived in different places. I grew up right here in Romania."

"Really? Yet, you're taking a guided tour in English. Don't you remember your native language? Your homeland?"

Adrian smiled. "I left a long time ago. I still speak Romanian, but I've never seen some of the castles we'll be visiting. I'd like the fresh perspective a more complete tour would give. It will be an education I should have had before I left."

"I know what you mean. I've never visited the top of the Empire State Building or the inside of the Statue of Liberty. I keep meaning to do that."

"And how long have you lived in New York?"

"Most of my life. I was born in Ireland but came to the United States as a kid. I went to Catholic middle and high schools in the city, then college."

Adrian pictured Maura in her cute Catholic schoolgirl uniform and his fangs ached. He'd be all right if he could get to his special vintage within the next hour. "May I buy you a drink in the pub downstairs?"

Her body language practically shouted indecision not only in her hesitation, but in the way she looked to her left for a few seconds, then to her right, as if weighing both sides of the argument.

"I would, but I'm a little jet-lagged."

"Of course, dear lady. I understand." He made a slight bow and reached for the door handle.

"But, I'd love to have a drink with you some other time. We have the whole week, after all."

Since his fangs hadn't descended, Adrian gave her his best grin. "Yes, we do. I'll look forward to it."

Chapter Six

❧

As hard as it was to turn him away, Maura knew it was the right thing to do—damn it. She pulled her trip journal from the front zippered pocket of her suitcase. The attached pen dangled from its long ribbon as she settled onto the uncomfortable bed.

First evening in Romania.

Met a Brit earlier today wearing a perfect example of what I'm affectionately calling "vampire vintage". Sadly, she bought everything in London. If I don't find enough of what I need here, perhaps I could extend my trip and make a quick stop in the UK. Any excuse for a holiday, right?

I'll probably find everything I need right here in Romania, though. I have a week to explore the shops and marketplaces and haven't yet begun, but if I meet my vampire lover, I could get distracted, big time!

Met a man tonight I'd definitely be interested in if it weren't for my new mission. Chiseled features, dark hair and eyes and under his all black clothes I detect there's a toned, muscled physique. Talk about sexy as hell! There's something about those eyes. The way he looked at me…it was as if he knew me—intimately. He's so hot I almost wish I hadn't given up on mortals just yet.

I wonder…if I fooled around before summoning, would that count as cheating? Who knows? Who could I ask? The good news is I might be able to see him in New York if things don't work out with my vamp. Well, that's all the news that's fit to print.

Maura tucked her journal away in the pocket of the suitcase. Opening the case, she mentally ran through wardrobe possibilities for the next day. She had packed lots of knits that coordinated and would travel well. Black and white was the theme for the week, with accessories to add a splash of color.

Glancing around the room, she didn't see a closet. There were some hooks on the wall, but no hangers. That would never do for her clothing. She draped her robe over one of the hooks, but her clothes would have to be spread over the other twin bed in the shape of a flat Maura, like a life-sized paper doll.

She extracted her slinky black pants from the bottom of the pile, shook them out and was pleased to see nary a wrinkle. Laying them out on the bottom half of the bed, she thought her white knit top with a silky purple paisley scarf would work. *I know my butt looks good in those pants, so if I happen to meet my vampire right off the bat, I'll be ready. Ha! Vampire…right off the bat. Vampire bat. Maura, your mind's weird.*

Her walking shoes were almost sneaker-like, so she opted for her sexy, black, open-toed kitten heels. Later in the week she'd resort to jeans and sneakers if her feet protested wearing a one-and-a-half-inch heel.

Satisfied with her choices, she crossed to the suitcase again. Pajamas, nightgown or nothing? Not knowing if she'd wind up sharing a room with another female later in the tour, nothing seemed the most efficient choice. That way, her nightwear would stay fresh.

She washed up in the sink, brushed her teeth and flicked off the light. *Bedtime. Ah, clean, starched sheets…cool and fresh against my naked body.* If her flesh could sigh, it would have. Her heavy eyelids were desperate to close and had been for the past hour. She wriggled around to get comfortable and was asleep in seconds.

She didn't know how long she'd slept before a soft touch partially awakened her. Maura's eyelids fluttered open. With moonlight streaming through her window, when her eyes adjusted to the darkness. She glanced around the room but saw nothing.

Sleep beckoned, but that touch haunted her. Astral touches were something she had heard of, yet this was her first experience with one. Maybe it was a dream, like that wild wet dream she had in her bedroom a few nights ago. She was about to go with that explanation and try to return to sleep when she felt another one.

This time it was more than a touch. It felt as if a hand were gliding over her cheek and neck. The stroke was gentle, but Maura trembled. A few soft kisses landed on her shoulder, slowly licking up her neck. Gentle hands stroked her hair, as if telling her she was safe. Heat and desire replaced anxiety as the mysterious hand kneaded her breast through the covers and she realized this had to be her vampire lover. He anchored her head in place with the pressure of his lips on hers. His hand moved down to cup and squeeze her ass, causing her to undulate with need.

She moaned and leaned into his touch. Warm, liquid desire pooled between her legs. It was similar to the beginning of her earth-shattering dream, but this time she was definitely awake. As soon as the pressure on her lips eased, she whispered, "Yes. I've come to you."

Books spoke of this ability vampires had. Now welcoming him, she tossed off the covers and exposed her nakedness. Another hand joined the first and both of them together massaged her sensitive mounds. Maura felt her womb clench and knew she was riding a storm inside, becoming desperate for release. The anticipation of coupling with this vampire immortal filled her with sexual excitement.

But what if it wasn't her vamp? What if it were something else? A spirit? A succubus? Maura shivered, yet she was anything but cold. As if to put her mind at ease, a scrape against the side of her neck answered her question. Warm pressure replaced the scrape as if a kiss had been planted over her jugular vein. It was followed by a deep drugging kiss to her mouth.

Soon after, he nuzzled the slope of her neck, then trailed a string of kisses to her cleavage. Suction applied to her nipple followed and Maura arched into the pleasurable sensation. One invisible hand continued to squeeze and massage her other breast while the second traveled slowly but deliberately southward. Her breathing became ragged. She only wished she could enjoy the smell and taste of her secret lover, but everything felt too lovely to question.

She moaned aloud and writhed in impossible pleasure when the hand cupped her mons and rubbed with a firm rotation. Fingers parted her folds and stroked the inside of her labia. The bastard stopped just short of her clit and she wanted to scream. Then one finger penetrated her. At least, she hoped that was only a finger. It felt pretty slender. Ah, yes—another finger joined it. Whew. She hoped her vamp was well endowed, since their size was legendary. A deep, primitive growl emitted from her throat. Maura loved a well-filled fucking and prayed she'd get one soon.

Having her center filled and stretched was heavenly, but he still hadn't touched her... "Yaoww, Batman!" Maura jerked and bucked under the clit massage. "Oh God." He had the perfect spot, pace and pressure as if he had been making love to her all her adult life. "Yes, I'm yours! Take me. I beg you."

Suddenly, she was flipped onto her side and the mattress dipped behind her, as if a solid body had joined her in bed. A hard ridge rubbed against her ass. She reached around, determined to touch it, but a hand clamped her arm hard to her side and held her immobile. Bound on her side by the unknown force, her clit massage continued. She couldn't see anything but her own quivering body. No hand appeared where she felt its hard grip. No fingers touched her clit—not even her own. The sweet torment continued and there was absolutely nothing she could do to stop it. She was forced to submit to the inexplicable pleasure.

Heat reached her skin as the electrical energy coursed through her body and reached its peak. She moaned out loud, her volume building beyond control. Her legs vibrated, wildly. She knew she was going to scream so she turned her head into the pillow and shoved it against her mouth. Seconds later, she shattered. While she yelled, screamed and came undone, deep, rich spasms rolled over and all through her, rocking her to the core.

* * * * *

When she awoke the following day, she tried to remember exactly what had taken place after her incredible, amazing, mind-boggling orgasm. No matter how she tried, she recalled nothing subsequent to that moment. Had she passed out? Did he screw her?

Holy crap, I hope I didn't miss our first time together! That would just suck.

Maura dressed quickly, glad that she had laid out her clothes the night before. Breakfast was being served for only a few more minutes and after last night, she was starving. She hurried down the stairs and found the dining room nearly empty.

Only one other patron sat there and he raised his glass as if in a toast or invitation. It was the gorgeous guy who came to her door and offered assistance, so of course she'd join him. Maura did her "sexy walk", the one where she turned her heels and swished her hips before sitting down at his table.

"Good morning," he said. "You look lovely this morning. I trust you slept well."

"Yes, thank you. And how did you sleep?"

He shrugged. "As well as I ever do. I'm afraid I'm a bit of a night owl, but fortunately I seem to need less sleep than most."

A waitress rolled a cart over to their table.

"Oh good. I'm starving." But when Maura turned her head to check out the delectable offerings, she saw some crusty rolls, butter, jams and honey. A pot of hot water, tea bags and a carafe of orange juice accompanied the offerings. "Oh, well. A continental breakfast is better than nothing."

Adrian spoke to the waitress in an exotic-sounding language that mesmerized Maura, despite knowing he could have told her to spit in the water glass. The waitress nodded and returned a moment later with a pot of coffee and an uncorked bottle of wine.

"I know how Americans love their morning coffee. I wouldn't want you to go without."

The waitress poured Maura's coffee into a teacup, then she refilled Adrian's wineglass. Maura smiled and cocked her head. "You're very kind. How many languages do you speak?"

"Several. Most Europeans do."

"Yet you live in New York? You're an American now, aren't you?"

"Yes, I'm American and I originally come from this area, but I think and speak in a conglomeration of languages since I've lived in many places."

"Really? Tell me about them."

"There's not much to tell. When I was a young man, I moved around Europe and even the Middle East for a while. I settled in France eventually where I bought a vineyard. I moved to Great Britain and then Ireland before coming to New York."

"So, you're fluent in Romanian, French, English and American?"

Adrian chuckled. "Mostly French and American, I think. I still own the winery in France, but I have my museum as well, so I go back and forth between them."

Ah, so that's why he's drinking at nine o'clock in the morning. It's probably like juice to him. "Is that wine from your vineyard?"

"Yes, it is. It's a very special vintage and I carry some with me wherever I go. This particular bottle is from a harvest that could have been better, but alas, I send the best to a very exclusive clientele."

"I see. So it must be very tasty."

Adrian's mouth curled at the corner and his eyes dropped. "It is indeed. My customers pay dearly for it."

"Oh, well then, I won't ask to buy any, as much as I wish I could." She gave a little laugh to indicate she wasn't made of money, but appreciated the uniqueness of his product. Secretly, she wondered if he was loaded. *Another business? Exclusive customers?* It all sounded pretty good. She almost hoped things didn't work out with her vampire lover, but then she remembered last night and her intoxicating virtual bondage experience. She instinctively knew there would be more where that came from. *Don't get distracted. Keep your eye on the goal, Maura.*

Adrian downed the rest of his glass. "So, dear lady, what do you have planned until the tour begins?"

"I had hoped to do a little shopping. I own a clothing store and we're expanding, I wanted to see what's available from the local seamstresses."

"That's an excellent idea and fortunate timing. A local folk fair is going on today. You'll find people from all the surrounding villages set up to sell their goods. There are some very beautiful handmade embroidered items you might like."

Maura wasn't really looking for the typical Slavic embroidered peasant blouses, but she could always take a look and hope for the best. Maybe she could find some red on black, or black on red, or black on black embroidery. She could always look. Shopping would fulfill her time requirement for her tax write-off at any rate.

"That sounds good. Where is it?"

Adrian looked pleased. "If you'll give me a moment, I'll take you there."

* * * * *

In the hotel's kitchen, Adrian began searching for the remainder of his wine. The staff had dispersed until lunch, so there was no one to ask about its hiding place. It wasn't in sight on the counter and it better not be in the refrigerator. He hated it cold. Red wine wasn't meant to be chilled and the proprietor knew enough to realize that. Just in case, he checked the industrial-size steel fridge and was oddly relieved when it wasn't in there, even though he needed it.

If he were to take Maura to the fair, he would have to protect himself from a longer than usual exposure to the midday sun. That meant he had to drink more wine. He turned to the cabinets and began rifling through them. If it wasn't there, he'd have to go to the wine cellar and open another bottle. What a waste that would be. He didn't plan to come back here after today and an open bottle of wine would only be good for about three days.

Ah! *Found it.* He brought the bottle to his lips, tilted his head back and glugged the lifesaving liquid down his throat. It warmed him immediately. He could feel a rush of heat rise from his stomach up to his face and down to his toes. The unusual amount at once could make him tipsy, but there was nothing to be done about that now.

Adrian returned to the lobby and spotted Maura waiting by the front door. She'd stand out in a crowd simply by radiating natural internal beauty, rarely found in the city. Women there were often made of hard edges and sharp barbs. Not this one.

In profile, with the light behind her, Adrian could see that Maura's shape in clothing was almost as alluring as when she was nude. Well, not really, but she sure knew how to flatter her figure. The smooth pants cupped her ass without panty lines and she must be wearing the kind of bra made to go under T-shirts. The fluid line of her torso flowed uninterrupted over and around her soft, full breasts. Adrian imagined how good it would feel to spoon her while in his actual body—or eat her with a spoon.

Come on, Adrian. Be smooth. Be charming. Be like you were as a cocky, young vampire when no woman could resist you. But this one could and he was already falling for her. Either that, or the wine was going to his brain. Yeah, the wine must be causing this dull, slow fogginess. Regardless, he wasn't going to use his mind control on her. He wanted to take her willingly when they coupled. Ideally, they'd have more than a one-night stand.

He came up beside her so silently, she jumped and put a hand to her chest.

"Oh! You startled me. I didn't hear you."

Adrian smiled and placed his hand on the small of her back. "Sorry. You startled me too — with your beauty."

Maura rolled her eyes.

Okay, so much for the lines. She's probably heard them all. Adrian shook his head and escorted her outside. The blinding light hit him in the eyes and he quickly pulled a pair of black sunglasses from his pocket and jammed them on his face. Ah, better.

She turned to look at him and smiled. "Sexy shades! Where did you get them?"

"In New York. Some little boutique in the Village."

"Really? I live in Greenwich Village."

"No kidding." Apparently she didn't remember much from the cab ride and maybe that was best. She had wrinkled her nose at his museum's theme and had thought he might be gay. Sometimes a guy lucks out and gets a second chance to make a first impression. Or in his case, possibly a third. At least this time she was sober and remembered him.

"Are you in the mood for a walk? It's not too far from here."

"Oh yes, a walk sounds great. The world rushes by too fast to appreciate the details as it is. Once you're in any kind of vehicle, you miss the nuances."

"You're so right, dear lady."

She dropped her head and looked at the sidewalk. "Um, can I ask you to do me a favor?"

"Of course. You can ask me anything."

She leveled her gaze at him and offered a weak smile. "Would you mind not calling me 'dear lady'? It makes me feel kind of old. I'm not a young girl anymore, but I'm not ready to be an old lady, either."

Adrian took a step back. "I'm sorry. I didn't mean to infer—"

"I know, I know." She waved her hand as if to erase his thought. "It's silly, but I guess I'm getting a little sensitive about my age these days and you look a little younger than me."

If she only knew. Adrian crooked his elbow and offered his arm. When she slipped her hand around it, he figured his gaffe wasn't fatal. They walked together across the uneven bricks and the breeze plus the shade of each tree they passed offered welcome, cool relief.

"You shouldn't be sensitive about getting older. I consider a woman who has lived long enough to gain experience and wisdom more magnificent with every year."

She grinned but her eyes quickly met her moving feet. "That's a nice philosophy. Most men don't really believe that."

"I do. One thing I don't do is lie just to puff up someone's ego. I learned a long time ago that the person you flatter falsely can get so full of themselves, they think you don't deserve their time or attention anymore."

"Gotcha. I did that when I was younger with a couple of high school boyfriends. Dumb jocks. Oh, sorry. Are you into sports? I didn't mean anything by it."

Adrian chuckled. "Not to worry. I enjoy watching them, but I don't play games." He turned to her and hoped she'd read his other meaning.

She nodded. Looking ahead, she pointed to a pristine church looming at the top of the square. Elaborate and imposing, the building looked as if it were the patriarch protector of the town. "Isn't that a beautiful church? You don't find ornate architecture like that in America."

Adrian took in a deep, proud breath, remembering when that church was new. "It was built in the fifteenth century as are many of the beautiful buildings you will see. Some of the castles on this tour are even older."

"The long history is one of the reasons I came to Romania. Did you know that despite all his faults, Vlad Dracul built much of this ancient city? This kind of historical landmark I could never see at home. It takes my breath away."

"Yes, many things you will see are breathtaking." *She thinks I'm ancient. Now who feels old?*

She cocked her head and turned toward him. "It sounds as if you've already been on the tour."

Oh no. Don't give away too much too soon, Adrian, or she'll get suspicious. Whatever you do, don't mention Vlad. "I like history and read up on some of the places we'll be visiting, but no, I've never taken this tour before."

It must have been the wine, but if he didn't kiss her soon, he was going to pull her into an alley and...well, scare her to death.

"Maura, may I call you Maura?"

"Please do. 'Miss Keegan' makes me feel older than 'dear lady'."

"Stop here a minute, Maura."

She stopped walking and looked up at him. A soft questioning, yet trustful look filled her eyes. Under the shade of a wide, gnarled beech tree, he took her by the shoulders and positioned her against its trunk.

"I see a perfect photo opportunity here."

"Oh." She giggled. "You want me to pose, or get out of the way?"

Adrian smiled. She was so adorably unaffected. So young at heart. How could she not know it? "Stay right where you are. I want to take a picture of you."

She smiled shyly, but nodded. "Okay."

Now what? You don't have a camera, you idiot.

"I want to remember you exactly like this." For all time. Still holding her shoulders, Adrian leaned in and angled his mouth over hers. Not knowing what she would do he was taking a chance, but at this point it was too late to matter. She really was his dear one, his *cherie*.

She tipped her face up and her lips parted, slightly. With her persona so open to him and her eyes drifting shut, she looked so vulnerable. If she fell prey to one of his kind with lesser morals, he'd never forgive himself and his heart would be broken for the rest of time.

She waited, eyes closed for another moment while he simply stared at her. When her eyes fluttered open, she looked down and stammered. "I—I'm sorry, I thought you wanted to…"

Adrian put a finger under her chin, tipped her face up to his again and said, "You were right." He descended and captured her lips in a tender kiss. When she didn't pull away he wrapped an arm around her and pulled her closer. The hand resting on her shoulder slid around to her back as he opened his mouth and deepened the kiss.

Maura let out a little sigh and let her arms glide around his waist, holding him close. She met his tongue with hers and swirled around it. Heat invaded Adrian's body as sunlight never could. A soft, warm glow filled his heart. He wanted to hold her like this forever. Even though, no matter how long he tried to keep her, there would come a day…

"Just what do you think you're doing, young lady?"

Ashlyn Chase

Maura felt cool air fanning her face. Oh, no. She opened one eye just enough to see the angel flapping her wings like a hummingbird.

I'm kissing. Go away.

"You barely know this man."

Well, I'm getting to know him better as we speak...or, I mean, think.

"Think? Do you really believe you're thinking about this? I'd say you're acting without thinking. Behaving rashly. Being—"

Shut up and go away!

"Don't worry, Susan. I'll help you out."

Damn. She closed her right eye and opened her left. There sat the little red devil.

Not you too. I don't want your help. I don't want either of you here. I just want to be left alone to enjoy this wonderful man's skilled mouth. Damn, does he know how to kiss!

"He's knockin' your socks off, isn't he, Sue?"

It's Maura!

"Okay, Maura. He's got you hot, bothered and ready to jump his bones, then."

Adrian broke their passionate lip lock.

Maura sighed. "And how."

Adrian pulled back. "Did you say something?"

"Oh. I, um. I was just saying, 'Man. Wow!' You're a great kisser."

His full lips spread into a wide smile and she was relieved to get away with the stupid out loud slip of the tongue. She'd rather be slipping her tongue back into his mouth.

Adrian left one arm behind her waist and guided her around the tree to resume their walk.

"Weren't you going to take a picture?"

82

"Ah, that's right. I was, but I just remembered that I left my camera back at the hotel."

Maura had an impulse a moment before and she wasn't going to talk herself out of it—or let herself be talked out of it, either.

"Adrian?" she whispered and stopped walking.

He turned to face her. "Yes?"

"I'd like to take your picture too." Maura leaned in and tipped her face up, hoping he'd get the message.

He did. His face swooped down over hers and their lips connected more solidly than before. He opened to her and she pressed her tongue into and around his mouth. He tasted of wine. It was neither dry nor sweet. Almost like a spiced wine. It was hard to pinpoint the unique flavor. There was a slight metallic taste mixed with full-bodied fruitiness. It wasn't bitter, though. Nope, nothing bitter about it. Holy moly, this man could kiss! His lips felt soft, silky and magical. They fit perfectly over hers, as if they'd been created in the same form.

Not only could he kiss, but he knew how to hold a woman when he kissed her. He took possession of her body, pulled it against his and made her feel enveloped. Wrapped in a single cocoon that held both of them.

He explored her mouth with all the thoroughness of their first kiss and more. His tongue was gentle and probing one minute, demanding the next. Then he'd pull it back and create a vacuum she couldn't wait for him to fill again.

Oh, god. Why did I do this? I could lose the will to find my vampire this way and I only have a week. I have to stop this.

Maura, reluctant as hell, pulled away. She stared at his chest and watched it heave with deep breaths.

"You know, Maura. According to old Romanian law, we're married now."

She gasped and jumped backward, breaking his hold on her. "You can't be serious."

He laughed. It was the first time she had heard him laugh out loud and it was a deep, rich sound that reverberated inwardly landing somewhere in her solar plexus.

The angel wasn't there, reprimanding her and the devil wasn't there, laughing his ass off, so she figured she was safe. Adrian was probably making a joke.

"Jeez, Adrian, you had me going there for a minute."

He quieted but still smiled broadly. "Don't worry. I won't hold you to it." Glancing around he said, "I don't think there were any witnesses, anyway."

Maura shook her head. "Maybe we should just get to that fair."

Chapter Seven

ᔕ

The fair proved to be an interesting and eclectic mix. Booths with appealing foods surrounded Maura with mouthwatering aromas, designed to whet the appetite. Local crafts, abundantly available, caught her eye too. Clothing? Not so much. She bought a few items from one vendor for a great price. The woman acted incredibly excited, as if she had made her rent for the rest of the year. Maybe she should have bargained.

Her favorite was a long, black velvet, fishtail skirt with braided detail. She also found a long, black, glossy pencil-skirt. It looked neither comfortable nor practical unless the buyer wanted bondage without straps. She figured a gothic woman might enjoy slits to her preferred thigh height. She saw some lovely black lace skirts and bought one with open panels in strategic places. A few off-the-shoulder black blouses looked sexy and not so reminiscent of peasant-style, so she bought three to complete the outfits with the skirts.

Adrian kept quiet unless she asked his male opinion. Only then did he offer it. So far, she was doing well if his taste was anything like Goth men. Chances are, the items she picked would delight anyone, male or female.

The nearby shops also presented some wonderful buying opportunities. Maura was able to find some of the sexier items she was looking for and some surprises that absolutely delighted her — namely the corsets.

She didn't know whether to sell them or keep some of the unexpected treasures for herself, so in several cases she bought two similar items. Adrian's reaction to the corsets pleased her immensely. When a man uses the words "delectable and tempting" the confection would probably water the mouths of more than just the gothic community. Certainly the average male in New York and beyond would thank her. These selections in her display window might even attract more men to the store.

The first item she bought was a black satin corset that buttoned up the front. Adrian simply raised his eyebrows and nodded. The next was a black leather corset that boasted the ability to fit a waist from eighteen to twenty-six inches. Since most Goths seemed rail-thin to her, she knew this would be a smart purchase. Stretchy panels on the sides made the instant alteration possible.

The next one had no opening in front. Adrian took it from her and turned it around to see the other side. It laced up the back and he looked as if he might possibly drool. Maura bought two.

All of those fit fairly straight across the breasts and didn't have garters attached. They could be worn outside clothing as well as inside. She wanted some with the garters and more support for breasts like hers. Pulling out each black or red piece of that description, the most well-boned and sensuous landed in her purchase pile.

Then she spotted one made of white silk with full cups. Embroidered in white with seed pearls, it was probably meant to be for a wedding trousseau. *God, it's gorgeous.* She lingered in front of it longer than she should have and the shopkeeper started talking to her as if she and Adrian were engaged, saying how beautiful it would look on her wedding night, winking at him. That's when Maura decided it was time to go back to the fair.

Adrian stopped her at the door and turned her to face him. The electric touch of his warm fingers on her arm penetrated, but not nearly as much as the strength of his dark stare.

"I want you to try one on."

"What? Me?" She glanced nervously over her shoulder at the smiling shopkeeper. "Which one?"

"I saw one that would look stunning on you."

"Not the white one…"

He laughed and shook his head, but his eyes burned and nearly ate the clothes off her body. She reacted instinctively with a sudden ripe throb in her breasts that traveled down below.

Adrian let go of her arms, walked to the back of the store and Maura followed him as if there were an invisible thread between them. And not just because he was her translator, helping her to bargain.

"But I'm shopping for my store."

From one of the corset racks she had previously searched, he pulled something that had escaped her notice. How could she have missed it? It was gorgeous burgundy satin with black lace trimming the thighs, full cups and center. Partially open in front, laced up with black cord, it also had detachable garters.

He leveled a smoldering look her way as he handed it to her. "I want to see you in this."

Maura's eyes widened and she slapped a hand over her mouth. "You want to see me in it?" *Oh, dear God. This is getting out of hand. A kiss is one thing…*

He nodded. "Of course, if you're self-conscious you don't have to show me here."

"I don't have to show you at all."

"No, but if I buy it for you, I'd expect a peek."

Suspicious, she cocked her head. "A quick peek, huh? Is that like your idea of snapping a photo?"

"Maura, my sweet." He set the corset on the shelf above the rack and took both of her hands in his, then he spoke in a low voice only the two of them could hear. "I can feel your heat. You know there are flickering embers between us. It's only a matter of time before they ignite our passions. I'm not a man to deny myself pleasure and I don't think you're that kind of woman, either."

Maura almost swallowed her tongue. He was coming right out and telling her they were going to sleep together, though she'd bet sleeping wasn't what he had in mind. He wanted to fuck. No matter how prettily he put it, that's what it boiled down to. So much for thinking he was a gentleman.

"Adrian, as much as you're right about the potential fire, there's something else. Someone else I'm supposed to meet on this trip."

"Oh? What's his name?"

"I, uh…" Exasperated, Maura threw her hands in the air. "It's none of your business."

"If I have a rival, I think I should know who he is. Don't you? Otherwise, how can I prove to you I'm better than he?"

In a moment of pure oppositional defiance, Maura blurted out, "What makes you think it's a he?"

Adrian raised his eyebrows and looked positively stunned. "Oh."

* * * * *

Instead of returning to the fair, they decided to go to their hotel and get ready for the tour. It would be only a couple of hours before the group met. On the way back, Adrian kept glancing over at her, wondering what her reluctance was about. He knew she had no silly hang-ups about having premarital sex and she wasn't gay.

His vampiric hearing picked up the quickening of her heartbeat each time they touched. The temperature around them rose whenever he walked close to her and those kisses! Any more response on her part and they'd be tearing at each other's clothes right on the sidewalk. Had he frightened her by expecting too much, too soon? He could have sworn he smelled her musky, wet scent. Had he been premature when he pictured them sharing wild, uninhibited, erotic sex?

Suddenly the truth hit him like it had been shouted in his ear. Of course! She was looking for her vampire. He broke into a grin and let out a deep breath. He felt a little stupid for not realizing it right away, but somehow thought she would give up the search as soon as he swept her off her feet. It was ironic that she was saving herself for him, but in a way, sweet.

When they entered the hotel lobby, Maura spoke for the first time since leaving the shop.

"Adrian, I'm sorry. I didn't mean to be rude." She looked squarely at her feet while talking to him, but he could see the high color in her cheeks.

He placed one finger under her chin and tipped her face up enough to look at him. *Oh, those aquamarine eyes.* She would only get deeper under his skin and he knew it.

"Maura, I'm sorry too. I'm usually a gentleman. I don't know why I was so forward with you."

She smiled and touched his cheek. "Don't worry. It's a compliment, really."

"You're an exquisite woman. If things don't work out with your…" What? Was he going to play along with the bisexual ruse? Or should he just come out and tell her what he knew. He told her he didn't like to play games.

While he was momentarily paralyzed, Maura finished his thought for him.

"Yes. Definitely." With that, she squeezed his arm and ran up the stairs, presumably to her room.

Okay, now what? Adrian plodded up the stairs too. He didn't know exactly what he was going to do with himself for two hours other than taking a cold shower, then napping if he could, or twiddling his thumbs if not.

As he reached the top step, he saw Maura's door close and heard a soft thud as if she had let herself fall against it. Amplifying his sharp hearing as he strode toward her door, he heard her say with unmistakable clarity, "God, I need a cock!"

Adrian didn't hesitate. He stopped and knocked on her door. He heard her let out a startled gasp before she opened the door a crack and peeked out.

"I just happen to have one right here in my pocket."

Her eyes widened. "You heard me?"

Before he had a chance to answer, she grabbed his black lapel, growled, "Get in here." And yanked him inside. Kicking the door closed, she launched her lips at his open mouth and pawed him like an octopus in a tank of caffeine.

Adrian could hardly believe what was happening. His Maura wanted a cheap screw, a quick wham bam, thank you, ma'am. What about her mission? Had she forgotten it, or was he being used as a fill-in? Maybe she needed a good hard fuck to get the tourist out of her system?

While kissing him frantically, Maura pulled him over to the bed and collapsed on it, bringing him with her. Adrian heard her heart beating wildly and smelled the feminine musk between her thighs.

His mouth slammed into hers in response. *I don't care if she's using me or not. I'm going to give her the ride of her life and it won't get me out of her system.*

Adrian peeled off his black jacket while she worked on the buttons of his shirt. She grabbed at the bottom hem and nearly ripped the fabric as she yanked it out of his pants. As soon as he was shirtless, he began unbuttoning her white blouse while she unbuckled his belt, popped open the button on his slacks and jerked down the zipper.

"Easy, sweetheart. No need to rush."

"That's what you think," Maura ground out between clenched teeth.

With that warning in mind, Adrian used his lightning speed to get naked and get her undressed too. Falling together onto the freshly made bed, Maura clasped his enormous erection.

"Holy cow!" She leaned back to confront the log in her hand. Okay, so it was more of a branch, but it definitely qualified as porn-sized.

Adrian glanced down at his swollen manhood, of which he'd always been proud. "Does my size frighten you?"

She held his throbbing member with one hand and stroked it with the other. "No. We'll make it fit. You might have to be careful on the initial thrust."

"It's not a rocket."

"If you say so."

Adrian kissed her ear. "I'll simply need to stretch you a bit, first."

Maura still gawked at it and answered absently. "Yeah. I always stretch before I exercise."

"What?"

"Sexercise... Ride the rocket. Do the horizontal bop? Never mind."

Maura scooted down until she was eye to eye with the one-eyed monster. She hesitated only a moment and then licked around the head.

A shudder of pleasure rippled through Adrian's body. "Oh, yes. I like that. Nothing would please me more than if you lick me since sucking the whole girth may intimidate you."

She looked up with a wicked expression dancing her in eyes.

As he'd hoped, she took the encouragement as if it were a challenge and wrapped her lips around the tip, sucking it in progressively farther each time. Adrian trembled inside and moaned in appreciation. He rarely met a woman who didn't shrink in fear from his size, even under mind control. It was refreshing not to have to spend several minutes persuading her that it would be all right.

Superb tugging sensations continued to build not only in his body, but also his heart. She licked, sucked, explored and made love to his cock, exquisitely. She cupped his balls and manipulated them expertly in her hand, then licked and sucked those too.

Shit, she's good. I knew that someone who's all woman, like Maura, would rise to the occasion.

Adrian stroked her hair and enjoyed watching her take more and more of him into her mouth, until he had to close his eyes while she applied stronger, more deeply satisfying suction.

"Oh, Maura. What you do to me. It feels so good, no wonder fornication is illegal."

She looked up with a twinkle in her eye. "As least it's not fattening."

"Huh?"

"Isn't that a saying? Everything people like is either illegal or fattening?"

Adrian smiled. "So you like it, do you?"

Maura nodded and Adrian swooped under her arms and pulled her up to hover over his face. He delivered a long, slow, deep kiss, then flipped her onto her back, prepared to return the favor with his cunnilingus skill. She raised her arms over her head and rested them on the pillow, then opened her legs for him in complete surrender. He couldn't believe how turned on, yet protective, he felt with her in that trusting position.

He leaned over and cupped her breast placing a soft kiss on each peak. "I usually spend a lot of time in foreplay. I could fondle and suckle these beautiful breasts for hours, but since we don't have much time…"

She sighed. "Don't worry. I've been primed and ready for days."

He couldn't help chuckling, knowing exactly how he had been astrally driving her crazy with lust, but leaving their ultimate joining until they could do it face-to-face. Then, later, face to ass, straddling him, even swinging from a trapeze if she wanted it that way. He couldn't wait to fuck Maura every which way possible and he expected that before long, he would. Adrian took a moment to lean over and attach his mouth to her puckered nipple. She moaned and arched into his suction.

"I love that. Suck me harder."

He had no trouble complying. He gently squeezed her fullness and sucked her in deep.

She moaned beneath him and arched her back to get even more of his mouth around her breast. He pulled back, scraped his teeth across her nipple and leaned across her, so he could suckle the other one. He could have hovered above her and freed up that other hand, but not until he had told her everything. She might be open-minded, but a shock like that could kill the mood. There was only one reaction he wanted from her and he didn't think he'd get it if he sprung his secret on her right in the middle of a lusty screw.

As he continued to massage and savor, tease and titillate, he couldn't help wondering about that inevitable revelation. The woman might think she wants a vampire and yet, on another level, she might not believe they exist. Maybe she's simply protecting her heart by asking for the impossible. He should actually witness her summoning before telling her that her dream had come true.

Adrian might be a little tongue-tied when speaking to a woman who mattered, but he was quite adept at using his tongue for other purposes, so he cut short his attention to her breast and moved down, wedging himself between her legs.

She opened wide and welcomed him into her most personal space. Smiling into her hooded eyes, Adrian stroked the slick ridges of her labia. "If we had more time, I could turn you inside out and I'd bet you'd scream for more."

Maura licked her lips. "I'm not sure I can wait much longer. I really need that big cock rockin' my world."

Adrian grinned. "Patience is a virtue."

"I'm not feeling very virtuous at the moment."

He didn't want to miss his chance, so without his usual slow torment, his long tongue reached for her clit and his fingers slid into her pussy.

Maura bucked and let out a yelp.

Pleased with her sensitivity, he proceeded to flick her clit with his tongue and finger-fuck her hot core. She moaned out loud and undulated, grinding her sensitive pussy into his mouth and hand with abandon. He spread his fingers apart and inserted another one. Soon, she was thrashing and nearly yelling. Adrian tried to hush her, but she seemed unable to control herself. At least, she got the hint and grabbed the pillow out from under her head. Holding it over her face, she screamed into it as she bucked, vibrated wildly and came for what seemed like an eon. Her orgasmic waves washed over Adrian and enormous pleasure filled him, knowing he'd satisfied her. He just hoped her lust wasn't quite slaked. He had more to do.

Adrian sensed her deep relief as she descended back to earth. When she lay panting, he crawled over her and poised his cock near her opening.

"Are you ready?"

"I need to catch my breath. But other than that, I couldn't be more ready. I want you to fuck me so bad."

"I just need to add one more finger and stretch you enough to take my cock."

She chuckled and bent her knees while spreading her feet farther apart. Her open heart and willingness was refreshing. Adrian leaned over and kissed her. Three fingers penetrated her core and worked their way in and out of her until he knew she was stretched enough to accommodate him.

"Please," she begged. "I want you, now."

He positioned himself between her legs with their genitals touching. His cock ached to plunge inside her, but the last thing he wanted to do was cause any pain. "I'll go slow. Just relax and breathe, okay, Maura?"

"Listen, if a whole baby can come out, then you can go in. Let's give it the good old college try."

Adrian smiled, pushing only the head of his cock inside and she cooed softly. Entering her wet center felt so damn good. Despite wanting all of it in there, he pulled back, then rocked forward on his knees and entered her a little more. She let out a little moan and seemed quite content to take more of his shaft. With his next thrust, she rocked toward him, skewering herself on most of him and took in a deep breath.

"Are you all right?"

"Hold on." She let out the breath she was holding on a sigh. "Perfect. Go ahead and fuck me silly."

Adrian snuggled her neck, delighted to know his Maura could take his size and enjoy it. He filled her as far as he wanted to and she let out a little mewl but seemed fine...better than fine. He sensed her desire spiraling as was his own. Energies radiated all through his body and kept him firmly in the moment. He increased his speed and depth, propelling himself in and out of her hot, wet tunnel. His pleasure built quickly and he perspired as he held back his orgasm. It had been too long and he needed this as much as she did. Maura was groaning with desire as if she were coming close.

Adrian wanted to give her some seriously thorough fucking, but the building hunger in his cock craved release. He held back what promised to be a monumental orgasm for her enjoyment as long as he possibly could, waiting until he sensed her approaching the edge. "Oh...*cherie*!"

"Hey!"

Adrian slowed the pace. "What's wrong?"

"I've been called by the wrong name before, but never during sex. I don't know who this Cherie is, but my name's Maura."

Adrian tried, but couldn't suppress his chuckle. She frowned as if she thought he was laughing at her.

"*Cherie* is French for dear one."

"Oh."

She seemed abashed, so he gave her a kiss on her cute, freckled nose. "What do you say, go again?"

Maura nodded but broke into a sweet smile at the same time.

They kissed heartily and then Adrian picked up where he left off. In seconds, the inevitable moment was upon them again.

Maura was worthy of the greatest pleasure he could give her. She plopped the pillow over her face again, only to have loud moans leak around the sides. She wrapped one of her smooth legs around Adrian's waist and he grabbed the other one, anchoring her foot to the bed. By controlling her body only that much, he was able to slip his hand between them and increase the pressure on her clit with his fingers. She shivered and trembled, just as he thought he was going to explode. At last, he let loose a roaring orgasm. Maura let herself go in an uninhibited display of bucking and screaming into her pillow. Not only did he feel the earth-shattering sensations rip through his whole body, but he could smell the mingling of their juices as she suddenly gushed an inordinate amount. If this were anyone else, he'd take advantage of the situation, feed and erase the mortal woman's memory of it. But, no. He wanted her to accept him and want him as much as he wanted her.

"Incredible. You're simply incredible," he whispered.

Apparently all she could do was pant her appreciation. "Yeah." Puff, puff. "You too." Puff, puff.

They lingered coupled for several minutes, relaxing and letting their breathing subside to normal before he rolled off to the side. Adrian's whole body was sated. Smiling to himself, he realized their sexual unions would be rich and recurrent and they'd only get better…and then she sat bolt upright.

The pillow dropped onto her lap leaving her hair in a static mess. She looked as if she'd been hit by lightning. Her eyes wild, she practically shouted. "What did we just do?"

Adrian propped himself on his elbow and looked at her curiously. "I think we just had sex…at least that's what they call it in my neighborhood."

"I know we had sex." She put a comforting hand on his arm, "Oh, it was fantastic too, but what the hell did we do that for? Unprotected sex! How stupid am I?"

"Ah, you're worried about health issues. Relax. I have no diseases and I can't get you pregnant."

"Oh." Her shoulders relaxed and she whooshed out a deep breath. "That's good to know. I feel a little better."

"How about you? Any diseases I should know about?"

"Just brain damage."

"Is it contagious?"

"Maybe. If you hang around with me you may find yourself doing some pretty foolish things."

Adrian smiled and said, "I'll risk it."

She didn't look completely reassured. In fact she looked as nervous as his first victim. This wasn't good. Not good at all. He wanted her to fall in love with him for him. After that, he could tell her he was a vampire and she'd either freak out, overlook it, or, hopefully, count it as a bonus.

Maura turned and looked at his naked reclining body, drinking in the sight of him. *Holy shit. I'd ask myself what I was thinking, but I know what I was thinking*. Adrian was magnificent and not only because of his impressive cock. As much as she'd sensed a hard, toned body beneath his clothes, looking at his well-muscled arms, thighs and abs made her mouth water and her brain empty — nothing but wind and tumbleweeds in there.

"I'm sorry. I'm afraid I..." She pulled the sheet up to cover her nakedness, knowing that if he saw her body, he'd be sorely disappointed.

Adrian tugged the sheet down to uncover her breasts. "Afraid? You?"

"I got swept away."

She looked to her right. Where was her angel? She should have been there to prevent this from happening. At the very least, Maura expected her to fly in and admonish her for utter stupidity. Maybe the horny little devil would show up to congratulate her. But nothing happened. They were keeping quiet.

Maura couldn't understand. They were constant pains in her ass only to desert her when she actually needed them. Maybe she insulted and shooed them away one too many times and now was on her own. But if they represented her conscience, did that mean she didn't have one anymore? Picturing herself at orgies and looting Victoria's Secret, she shuddered at the implications.

Adrian sat up and took her in his arms, stroking her back as if to soothe a repentant child. "I never realized you'd regret it. You don't seem like the kind of girl who's saving herself for marriage."

Maura snorted. "Hardly."

"Then what's wrong?"

She sighed. "Look, I told you I was supposed to meet someone on this trip and now I..." *I went and messed things up by falling for a damn tourist.*

"Ah, yes. The anonymous someone." He leaned back and tipped her chin up, but she couldn't look him in the eye.

"What aren't you telling me?" he asked.

"I... It's complicated."

"Let me help you out, then. You came to Romania to meet a man. Someone you don't know, yet. But you knew he'd be special and you knew you'd find him here."

She gazed up into his wise face, shocked. *How could he know that?*

Adrian took her hand and kissed it. "And now your search is over. You've met me."

Oh, crap. It was just a line. Maura rolled her eyes and couldn't believe she wished he'd meant it. If only Adrian was her vamp instead of a smooth-talking, charming, sexy-as-hell mortal.

"You don't understand." She let out a deep sigh. "Let me put one thing in perspective for you, for us both. This was a casual fling. Don't get me wrong, it was great. Utterly out of this world and amazing. But it was just sex. A one-timer. I'm sorry if you thought it meant more."

Adrian frowned and stood up. He dressed quickly and headed toward the door. Before he left, though, he stopped with his hand on the doorknob. He turned toward her and looked like he was about to say something. After a long hesitation, he simply shook his head and left.

Chapter Eight

෨

The tour guide counted heads. "Eleven, twelve, thirteen." Then he nodded and looked pleased. "My name is Enric and I am to be your vampire tour guide over the next six days. My English is pretty good, but if I say something not perfect, you can correct me. I always like to learn new tings."

Adrian leaned toward Maura and whispered, "I'd be correcting him frequently, if I cared enough. Thankfully, I don't."

Maura elbowed him, wanting to hear every word, perfect English or not.

Enric tapped his clipboard. "Ve have many beautiful castles and palaces in Romania. You vill only be seeing those that have been rumored to house vampires. Don't vorry, I'll protect you." He gave a laugh that no one echoed, so he cleared his throat and moved on. "Ve know if the current occupants are friendly and I'll not take you anywhere too dangerous. You all have your garlic and crosses, right?"

The crowd chuckled. Adrian folded his arms and seemed slightly annoyed. Maura thought that maybe it was because she brushed him off after they'd had sex. That wasn't very gracious, come to think of it. Yanking him into her room, tearing off his clothes and practically jumping him…then tossing him out like an old shoe? As she reflected back on it, she had to admit that, yeah, it wasn't really his fault. She'd have to be nicer to make it up to him. Oddly, her Catholic upbringing popped into her head and she found herself thinking, "What would the Golden Rule say? Do it unto others as you would want them to do it unto you?"

Okay, now that was disturbing. She pulled herself back to the present and tried to listen to what the tour guide was saying.

"I know you are all anxious to visit the Bran Castle. It is rumored to be the base of Vlad Tepes, son of Vlad Dracul, and it's one of the most beautiful castles in all of Romania. It has protected the city of Brasov since the thirteenth century. We begin our tours so late in the afternoon for a reason. Ve vouldn't vant to arrive too early and possibly miss meeting the dark one himself." Amid the stunned silence, his laugh sounded a bit maniacal.

The crowd groaned and murmured their regrets. Some for being so stupid as to believe his ruse and some for the fact that Vlad wouldn't be making an appearance.

"Don't vorry. There is much to see and you vill find all of it interesting. I promise. Now your bags have been taken to the bus and soon you vill all be on it, vinding your vay through our picturesque Carpathian Mountains. Please to have your cameras ready."

Remembering her last episode with picture taking, Maura smiled up at Adrian. She was surprised to see him smiling down at her too. *Crap, we've already started sharing secret jokes and making memories. Why did I have to meet a mortal who's so damn sexy on this, of all trips?*

Adrian placed a possessive arm around her waist, furthering her ambivalence. With him close like that, she could smell the wine on his breath. Fabulous. Just what she needed. An American wino following her around like a lovesick puppy the whole time she was on her vampire mission in Romania.

Well, he'd better not hang around once her vamp found her. He was a nice gentleman and she'd hate to see him go toe-to-toe with a real, live vampire.

Maura shook off his arm and walked ahead of him to catch up with Jordan. Today she was wearing another Goth outfit, sensual, but also practical. A black jumpsuit made of some stretchy material. It almost looked like faux leather, but it was thin and light. Maura would have to ask her more about it. The suit laced up the front with a thin black cord through large chrome grommets, so as to give peeks at Jordan's pale skin beneath.

"Hang out with me, will you, Jordan? I may need rescuing from a friendly tourist. Too friendly, if you know what I mean."

"Of course, luv. You don't like the gorgeous bloke in black?"

"It's not that. I like him a lot. I just don't think it's a good time for me to get involved with him. But I don't want to hurt his feelings."

"I understand." Jordan looped her arm through Maura's and hung on to her. "I'll be your new best friend."

"Thanks. Love your outfit, by the way. Is this another one from that shop in London?"

"Yes. I did most of my shopping for this trip there. You're wearing a cute outfit too."

Cute? Maura wouldn't have called a monochromatic pair of white knit pants and matching sweater cute, but whatever. She didn't need to argue with her only ally. Together they'd look like a photonegative. So would she and Adrian, for that matter. He was wearing all black once again. He even wore a black jacket with his black shirt and pants and his dark hair was held back in black leather cord. Damn the man. He looked like sex on a stick. Not only that, but when she looked up, she noticed him waiting for her by the folding door of a smaller than normal bus. Unfortunately she and Jordan wouldn't fit through the opening together, so she had to let go of Jordan's arm and let her board first.

When Maura came up to him, he offered his hand, to help her onto the first step. She thought the bus driver should be doing that, but the man sat in his driver's seat, facing forward, waiting for everyone to board. It wasn't what Maura would call "the short bus" although she felt like she belonged on one. She had to learn to discipline her lust without resorting to a chastity belt.

She and Jordan found a seat together. When Adrian boarded last, he seated himself right behind them. Maura couldn't help being acutely aware of his presence. The hair on the back of her neck prickled. She could almost feel his breath and it smelled like wine...of course. Did the man drink constantly?

Enric counted heads again and nodded to the bus driver.

The picturesque city passed by Maura's window and she would occasionally point out something to Jordan that interested her. Adrian would lean forward to speak softly about it in her ear. She had to admit it was nice to have two tour guides and one who spoke not only the local language, but also whispered in perfect English with a French-Slavic-British or something accent in a low, silky, sexy voice. Every time he spoke, she wanted to jump his bones. Damn the man.

By the time they reached the highway, more of a paved two-lane road, Enric stood and rubbed his hands together enthusiastically.

"Now I am going for to give you some history of Romania."

A couple of young male passengers in the back groaned, but Maura couldn't wait. History was something that had captured her interest in high school and as far as it pertained to American fashion, she was pretty confident about her knowledge. Eastern European history was something she knew nothing about and learning anything new would be a treat.

Enric launched into his spiel. "Dacia was an ancient kingdom and later a Roman province between the Carpathian Mountains and the Danube...This area is now known as Romania."

Adrian leaned forward. "Pay attention, there'll be a test at the end."

Maura smiled, but kept her attention riveted on Enric.

"The jawbone of a caveman, who lived here in Romania, vas found recently. It is the oldest fossil from an early human to be found in Europe and vas carbon dated to thirty-five thousand years before Christ."

The crowd oohed, aahed and murmured.

"So now don't you all feel young?" Enric looked very pleased with himself when the occupants of the bus chuckled.

Adrian guessed that he was easily the oldest person in the bus, but the information didn't make him feel particularly young. At least he wasn't hearing the same old crap about Dracula, so he perked up his ears and gave his attention to the eager young tour guide.

"The Transylvanian Dacians are first mentioned in contacts with the Greeks around the year 650 B.C."

Okay, now it's getting a little boring. If he starts explaining the geological layers, I may have to take a nap. Before that happened, however, he thought he'd try to do something to spice it up a bit, at least for Maura and her friend.

Enric chattered on. "So, as you can see, Romania is a very old part of the vorld."

Adrian leaned forward and whispered, "On the first day, God made Romania. All of the unimportant places came later."

Maura turned slightly and he could see she wasn't smiling. Maybe he wasn't that funny. *Try harder, Adrian.*

"There vas a lot of invasions and vars during the early A.D. period," Enric said. "People came from as far as northern England for the second Dacian war. Only the neighbors were invited to the first one." He smiled and waited for his audience to chuckle politely.

Leaning forward again, Adrian whispered, "And when the English are invited, they bring their bloody bangers and mash and there goes the neighborhood."

Jordan chuckled at that one, but Maura turned around and gave him an unmistakable look of irritation. "Shush. I'm trying to learn something."

Adrian slumped back in his seat and pouted.

"Between 700 and 800 A.D. invading Slavs took over a large area including Bulgaria, Romania, Macedonia, Turkey and parts of Greece. That's how ve all got these pretty accents."

People chuckled at that and Enric beamed.

"In the fourteenth century many monasteries were being built in different parts of the vorld. In Tibet the Buddhists built theirs, Spain built Catholic monasteries and in Romania, the historic Sihastra Monastery vas built. It vent through a rocky period vith the Communists but they didn't do much bad to it. Almost ninety percent of Romanians are Eastern Orthodox and one percent is Eastern Rite Catholics. That means that only nine percent ve don't know vhat they are."

Uh-oh. They were coming up on the breathtaking view of the Bran Castle. Adrian almost visibly cringed because he knew what was coming. Dracula.

Enric beamed and said, "Of course some people think that the other nine percent are vampires!" This news was met with cheers and applause. Enric grinned and rubbed his hands together.

Adrian steeled himself for whatever the kid had to say. Chances are this tour was designed to promote the myths of Transylvania that gave the region its fascination and fame. He didn't know why he hadn't thought of that before. Biting his tongue would be difficult. If the kid did a good balanced presentation, he wouldn't have to refute some of the more ridiculous "facts".

"Drac is a Romanian vord that can be interpreted as either devil or dragon. Vlad Dracul, born around the year 1390, joined the Order of the Dragon shortly after his son, also named Vlad, vas born. Dracula means son of Dracul. The younger Vlad, who grew up to be known as Vlad Tepes, the Impaler, vas born somewhere around 1430 or 1431."

So far, so good. Adrian relaxed into his seat, hoping the kid was going to give a factual transcript of what was known without the nonsense.

"Now it is important to know a little bit about the father and family to understand Dracula. His father, Vlad Dracul, vas the illegitimate son of Prince Mircea, the ruler of Wallachia, the area of present-day Romania south of the Carpathian Mountains. His mother may have been Princess Mara of Hungary. As such, he had to achieve his status with more difficulty. Vlad Dracul, the father of Dracula, grew up in other countries, possibly Germany, Luxembourg and Hungary. He did spend some of those years in the court of the king."

Adrian knew all of this, but the busload of tourists was so silent you could hear a pin drop.

"Ve know that Vlad the elder appeared in Transylvania as an official in charge of securing the Transylvanian border with that of Wallachia. He had already married and given birth to a son named Mircea after his father, the prince. So, if you've been paying attention, you know that Vlad the Impaler had an older brother named Mircea. Vlad was the second son of Vlad and grandson of Prince Mircea. It gets confusing vith all the names that repeat, yes?"

The tourists nodded. One American woman from the back called out, "Keep going. We're still with you." The rest of the bus laughed and Enric chuckled too.

"Okay, good. Now if that isn't bad enough, he eventually had three more children. The second of them vas another Vlad, while the youngest vas another Mircea."

The same American woman spoke again. "I guess people didn't get very creative with new names back then."

Tourists laughed while Adrian remembered the other sons—Vlad the Monk in particular. How two sons with the same name could be so different...

"So, shortly after Vlad the Impaler was born, Vlad Dracul vas selected by the king to rule Wallachia. The king had also founded the Order of the Dragon, so he knew he could trust Vlad Dracul to carry out the goals of the Order. Yes?"

The crowd nodded their understanding.

"One of the main goals of the order vas to fight Islam. But, Vlad Dracul vas still having trouble gaining the throne, even vith the title of 'Prince of Wallachia'. So he took a second spouse, Eupraxia, sister of the ruler of Moldavia, vhich created a powerful alliance and secured him the throne."

The kid was doing a good job with the facts and hopefully the folklore would be minimized. Vamps didn't need any more publicity.

One of the Brits asked, "How old was Vlad the Impaler when all of that got settled?"

"About five years old. And those first years are very important to form personalities, so I'm told. Maybe you can picture the richly dressed Vlad Dracul, svaggering about the house, raving, 'I am the prince and son of a prince. Those who don't respect me vill come to fear me! I swear it!'" Enric's voice had taken on such a different, commanding tone that he seemed more like an actor on a stage than a tour guide on a bus.

The bus's occupants murmured and nodded as if they were witnessing daily life for the five-year-old Vlad Tepes and suddenly his actions as Vlad the Impaler made perfect sense. Adrian had no patience with psychoanalysis and couldn't excuse his friend's behavior even if he did have an uncertain or confusing childhood. Adrian's childhood was pretty bizarre too, but he'd managed to deal with it.

"I don't vant to get too far ahead of myself," Enric was saying. "I only vant you to look out the vindow to your right and see the incredibly beautiful, grand and inspiring Bran Castle as it comes into view. This is rumored to be the headquarters for Vlad Tepes. It was originally built in 1212 as a fortress for the knights of the Teutonic."

Gasps and awed murmurs from the tourists verified what Adrian had always thought. Bran Castle was the most striking and scenic castle in all of Romania and perhaps all of Europe. Many debated its validity as the famous Dracula Castle, but Adrian saw it was his last known address. With its white façade and brick-colored roof, it looked more like a fairy palace than one belonging to the darkest figure in history.

Dracula had exquisite taste. Why would he live in a dark, rotting palace covered with bare twisting vines? Adrian reflected upon what his parents had done to their family home and shuddered. How could they adopt and authenticate a stereotype like that?

"Vlad Dracul, the father, has a less terrible reputation than his son, known as Dracula. Perhaps if the father vas a dragon, then the son vas a devil. Many think so."

Adrian had to keep his opinion to himself. Even though he did not believe in the devil, things he had witnessed and heard about his friend, Vlad Tepes—Dracula—gave him pause. It was hard to know if the whole thing could be blamed on madness alone. He believed evil was involved. Evil existed, even if he didn't think it could be embodied in one entity. But most vampires weren't supernaturally evil as in "from hell". Hell was where the heartless were.

Suddenly bringing Maura home to meet his insane family seemed like a helluva bad idea. Would his parents mention being friends of Dracula? *How stupid of me? Of course they will! What would Maura think of him once she heard about all the horrible things he had done in the long ago gruesome past?*

Enric rubbed his hands together. "Now for how the vampire legacy all got started!"

Crap.

* * * * *

Maura trailed behind the group as they toured the castle. The grand extravagant entry had led to room after room of lavishly decorated opulence. Guards were posted at key points to protect the valuable antiques and artwork that would tempt an unscrupulous person to steal some priceless souvenirs.

Everyone else had sighed in disappointment when told they couldn't see the dungeons in Dracula's lair, but after hearing the horrible history of Vlad Tepes and his reign of terror, she would be just as happy to skip this castle altogether. She knew her vampire lover could not possibly be here. Could he? Maura shuddered.

She tried to pick up any "vibes" from this place. Other than grim dismay, nothing much was coming through. On one hand, she wouldn't mind if this were the right castle simply to be its occupant, but on the other hand, she didn't want to cut her tour short, or find her throat ripped open!

Even with the stories of the life, possible death and mass killings of the actual Dracula, her tour was filled with fascinating legends, overwhelming beauty and her curiosity was permanently piqued. Maybe if she lingered in one place for a while, she'd feel something else?

Adrian had stopped walking with the rest of the group and seemed to be waiting for her to catch up. Now suppose she did feel the call here? How the hell was she supposed to slip her carefully worded note where only a vampire could find it with this infuriating man watching her every minute?

"Are you coming, Maura?" Adrian's brow furrowed and he seemed impatient. Perhaps he wanted her to protect him? Maura inwardly chuckled at that idea. Here she was, a five-foot-five, middle-aged woman, while he had to be six-feet easy and in his rugged prime.

"You don't have to wait for me, Adrian. I'll be fine. I just wanted to spend a little more time looking at these—um, gold urns." She pointed to a large dark cherry sideboard that gleamed. It looked as if it were in the same perfect condition as the day it was hand-hewn.

He frowned and continued to wait.

Damn him. Why had he appointed himself as her bodyguard? Did one quick fuck mean that much to him? Perhaps he thought there was more where that came from, even though she had specifically told him it was a one-shot deal.

Remembering their tryst, she relented a little. It was a very satisfying half-hour and the prospect of more sounded pretty damn good, despite her reservations. Hadn't the guide mentioned that vamps were apt to have had hundreds of partners? Why should hers mind if she had a little fling before they found each other?

Maura sighed and walked over to Adrian. He smiled and appeared to relax a little. As they strolled down the long corridor to rejoin the group he glanced over at her a couple of times.

"What?"

"Maura..." Adrian hesitated, then stopped just before the room where the group was gathered. He faced her squarely and took both of her hands in his. "You may not take the vampire lore seriously, but those legends didn't come out of nowhere. They're dangerous creatures."

"And?"

"And you shouldn't be so blasé about it. Being alone in a vampire's castle is a terrible risk to take with your life. They say he escaped through the catacombs, but he could have returned that way too. You just don't know."

"What are you saying? That you think I have a death wish?"

"Do you?"

Irritated, Maura just let out a huff and walked into the room to hear the end of the most recent story. Apparently this castle had been occupied after Dracula by a prince that was overrun and unseated a couple of times, each time gaining back his throne and avenging himself in the quick, brutal deaths of his enemies—unlike the slow, painful torture of Dracula.

Well, that's an improvement, anyway. Maura imagined that if he hadn't been overthrown, he might have been a nice guy.

One of the tourists asked, "Does he still live here?"

Enric shook his head. "No, he was assassinated centuries ago."

Well, that answered that. No wonder she wasn't getting any call-me vibes.

Maura watched the tourists wander back out into the hallway prepared to regroup and continue on. She spotted an interesting portrait on the wall. As soon as the others were out of her way, she took a few steps closer to study it. A man with the likeness of Gary Oldman, only with darker hair and lighter skin looked back at her. His expression was regal, but intense. If the eyes followed her around the room, she'd probably get the willies. No, she was getting the willies anyway.

"That's Vlad Dracul—the elder. He was a great man."

Maura turned to see Adrian leaning against the open doorway.

"How do you know?"

Adrian strolled up to her slowly, hands clasped behind his back. "What would you say if I told you I knew him?"

Maura snorted, then laughed. *What's he trying to pull?* "You don't really expect me to believe that, do you?"

"It doesn't matter if you believe it. The truth is the truth and another person's doubt doesn't make it less of a fact."

Maura stared at him, mute. He turned from the portrait and looked directly at her face with the same intense black eyes that the painting bore. They seemed to glitter.

Her heart lodged in her throat and she felt a prickle travel up her arms and neck. She tried to wrap her mind around his words, then it hit her. *Holy crap*! Was he identifying himself as a vampire from centuries ago? Did he know what...who she was looking for? Or was he just playing some sort of mind game?

She took a step back and crossed her arms. "Adrian, if you have something to say, just say it."

As he opened his mouth to speak, Enric poked his head in and said, "Are you coming? I don't want to lose you."

Maura waited for an answer, but Adrian walked away. Damn. *Thanks a lot, Enric.*

When they rejoined the group and Enric spoke about the tapestries on the wall, she couldn't concentrate on what he was saying. All she could think about was what Adrian had been about to tell her. Should she force him to tell her? If so, should she pull him aside, or wait? Adrian took care of that problem by whispering to her.

"Later, over cocktails, I'll explain."

Maura glanced quickly at his serious face. "I may need more than one."

Chapter Nine

୫୨

Maura struggled up the hotel's stairs with her suitcase and bag of purchases. As she turned the corner of the narrow, winding hotel staircase, the heavy bag's flimsy handle ripped, spilling the contents on the stairs.

"Oh, crap." Maura scrambled to pick up the pretty things that lay all over the stairs, apologizing to the people below her. She mumbled, "I guess I should have left this on the bus."

Behind her, Jordan plopped her own suitcase on a step and began to gather up the newly purchased clothes. As she picked things up, she oohed and aahed them—especially Maura's gift from Adrian.

"Blimey! Where did you find this brilliant bit, Maura?" She grasped the burgundy satin corset by its black lacy straps and held it up to her bodice, as if mentally trying it on. The peanut gallery below her tittered and someone gave a wolf whistle.

Maura felt her cheeks heat and a nervous giggle followed. She whispered that it was a gift from Adrian, then heard more whistles and catcalls from even more onlookers as they filed in the front door below.

"It's for my shop." She raised her voice and said it again to be sure everybody knew.

Adrian was at the bottom of the stairs, looking up with a sly smile on his face. *I believe that one was for you, Maura, dear.*

She would have been uber-embarrassed and annoyed, except for the fact that Adrian's lips didn't move the whole time she was hearing his voice. Jordan didn't turn around or act like anyone had said anything. She simply continued to gather the clothes.

113

He'd better be a ventriloquist. Maura stared at Adrian and mentally verbalized the word, *What*?

I simply said that the item Jordan was admiring belonged to you, ma cherie.

Jordan still didn't react as if anyone had spoken, but Maura heard him loud and clear. As if struck, she staggered backward and landed on one of the steps with a thump.

Jordan jerked her head up and asked with concern, "Are you all right?"

Maura, hyperventilating, placed her hand just below her neck. "I…I'm fine." After a few slow, deliberate breaths, she recovered and stood. Taking the items from Jordan, she said, "Must be klutzy today. Sorry about that."

Jordan shook her head. "Shit, I don't blame you. Today was unsettling. I feel a little off-center myself."

"Yeah. I think I'll just take a bath and go to bed."

"I hope they have at least two tubs," Jordan said. "I'd like a relaxing bath too."

Adrian had hoisted his suitcase and come up behind Jordan. "You didn't forget about our nightcap, did you, Maura?"

This time his mouth moved and Maura was relieved. Perhaps she had just imagined the fact that he was speaking without moving his lips before. As Jordan pointed out, it had been a freakish day.

"No, I didn't forget."

Jordan lifted her eyebrows and grinned, then gave Maura a deliberate, ticklish jab at her waist, causing her to jump. Obviously, she wouldn't be an accomplice in Maura's effort to steer clear of the handsome tourist.

"Let me help," Adrian offered.

Jordan stepped around Maura and continued up the stairs while Adrian reached for her suitcase. Once he had hers in one hand, his own in the other, he gestured for her to continue up the stairs.

Maura didn't know whether to be embarrassed, infuriated or grateful. Since he was buying her a much-needed drink later and she was very curious about whatever he was going to explain, she settled on grateful.

"Thank you, Adrian. I'll have to buy a bigger suitcase before we board the bus for the next place."

He simply smiled and carried her bag up the stairs and down the hall, stopping where she stopped. Maura fiddled with her key and opened the door, but when she walked in, he didn't follow her.

Momentarily confused, she didn't know what to do, so she laid the pile of clothes in her arms on the double bed. *Shit, is he waiting for me to invite him in?*

"Yes," he answered.

Maura's jaw dropped and she staggered backward again, sitting down hard on the bed this time. "What the hell? Are you able to read minds?"

Adrian smiled and his eyes darkened. "Only one."

Maura didn't know what to think. In fact, she didn't want to think at all. She had been accused of keeping her mind blissfully blank whenever she tuned out her friends — which she desperately wished she could do now.

"Can I come in?"

"I...I don't know. Can you?"

Adrian, still smiling, looked at his feet briefly before answering. "Not unless you invite me in."

Maura, still not certain she was interpreting things correctly, really needed that drink.

"Um, why don't we go have that cocktail? Just shove the suitcase in and I'll relock the door and come with —"

"You really don't want to let me in, do you?"

"Not until I hear what you have to say."

"It might be better said privately."

Maura shivered, both with excitement and fright. Should she let him in and find out he's her vampire lover? Should she insist on going to have that drink? What if he wanted a snack first?

A flash of inspiration provided her with a way they could talk privately, yet prevent her from winning the imbecile of the year award if Adrian turned out to be a vampire, but not *her* vampire.

If we can communicate through telepathy, why don't we go have that drink and you can tell me like this? No one will overhear us, right?

He hesitated, but eventually nodded and stepped away from the door. Maura retrieved her suitcase, brought it inside her room, grabbed the stickpin out of the case's front pocket and joined him in the hallway. Her stomach was doing loop-de-loops.

Adrian took her hand and kissed her knuckles. "You're safe, I promise you."

Letting out a long breath, she felt better for about five seconds.

* * * * *

The bar buzzed with activity, forcing Maura to grab the only available table. A tiny round table for two. Meanwhile, Adrian walked up to the bar to order their drinks.

He didn't even ask what I wanted. That was presumptuous.

Nervously, she glanced over at Adrian to see if he had read her thought. He turned toward her and winked.

Well, at least if he had, he wasn't upset about it.

Maura removed her multicolored bangle bracelets to have something to fiddle with and concentrate on. Anything to prevent her from thinking real thoughts. *Shiny, pretty colors. Hear the tinkling sound they make when they fall together. Pretty,*

116

pretty bracelets. Yuck, I smell cigar smoke. I guess they're more lenient about secondhand smoke in Romania.

They are.

The comment sounded like Adrian's normal speaking voice, but she heard it in her head, as if he were standing next to her. Yet there he stood at the bar, clear across the room.

Then he said something else in his telepathic voice. *Chocolate martini, right?*

Right! How did you know?

I'll explain later. I just didn't want to be presumptuous. He turned and flashed her a sly grin before the bartender approached him.

You're going to have to explain to me how this works. Can you turn it off and on? Why can't I hear your random thoughts?

Because I've had years of practice and can control them easily. You'll learn how.

Soon, I hope. I don't want you eavesdropping. Some pretty crazy shit rolls through my brain sometimes.

I know what you mean.

Maura's eyes popped open. A moment later, she went back to fiddling with her bracelets. *Shiny, pretty bracelets. Blissfully blank mind. Shiny, pretty bracelets. Blissfully blank mind…*

It's okay, Maura. You don't need a mantra. I can shut off the telepathic sense from here.

Oh, good! Please do.

A few minutes later, Adrian returned with a martini for Maura and a glass of red wine for himself then settled into the chair opposite her.

"So how did you know I like chocolate martinis?"

"I have a highly developed sense of smell and we shared a cab in New York."

"You smelled my breath and knew I had a couple of chocolate martinis?"

"More than a couple and some pretzels too."

Maura slapped her forehead.

Adrian took her hands in his and stared into her eyes. "Don't worry about it."

Returning his stare she answered him in her head. *Don't worry?*

"I'm not counting how many drinks you have, nor will I ever."

You'd have a heck of a nerve if you did. You seem to like that wine a lot.

Adrian just smiled and their conversation went on, but to bystanders, they must have looked mesmerized by each other with their silent knowing smiles and long gazes.

Maura adjusted uncomfortably in her seat. *So, what did you want to tell me?*

"I think you know."

Please, just say it.

"I'm a vampire."

Maura hadn't thought he'd just pop right out with it like that, even though she asked him to. When he did, a shiver shot up her spine and goose bumps peppered her arms. Her mouth went dry and she could only stare, mute.

Isn't that what you wanted? Didn't you come on this tour hoping to meet a vampire—a very special vampire? He brought her hands to his mouth and placed a tender kiss on each. *Your vampire lover?*

Well, yeah, but... Maura fidgeted and then let go of one of his hands so she could tip her head back and swallow half her chocolate martini.

"I thought you'd be pleased."

I thought you'd be taller.

118

He chuckled and shook his head. *I should have fixed you up with my brother Boris.*

That's okay. I was just kidding.

I know. I enjoy banter. I haven't had this much fun in centuries.

Really? What a dull eternity.

At least it's not dull anymore. Let's get out of here.

"Maybe I'll just switch to that wine you like and you can get a whole bottle and a couple of glasses…" she said out loud.

Adrian looked like he'd swallowed his fangs. "I…I can't let you drink from the same bottle, love. I'll be happy to get you a bottle of something else and the two of us can each have our own nightcap."

"Are you afraid I'll drink too much of yours?"

"No. Just let me get you something else, whatever you like."

She cocked her head and examined his face. *So what's wrong with the type you're drinking?*

"It's a very special vintage, Maura. It comes from my own vineyard in France. When I know I'll be frequenting a certain pub, I give the bartender a bottle to keep for my use only."

Oh.

"It's how I really make my living. The museum is just a hobby. I keep an owner's reserve for my own use and sell the rest to certain exclusive customers."

Vampires?

"Yes."

The light dawned slowly in Maura's brain, but when it did, she gasped. *It's blood!*

"No. It's wine, but there's a special ingredient that I managed to isolate and propagate that you wouldn't care for."

Do you have to be so cryptic? Just tell me what it is.

Adrian looked at the table and sighed. *All right, but if I tell you, please don't ask any more about it even if it sounds improbable.*

Fine. Out with it.

"It's a precious drop of blood from Joan d'Arc."

Who's Joan Dark?

Her name in English is Joan of Arc.

Joan of Arc?

"Yes. So you see, it's very rare."

Are you sure you weren't duped? Did the same guy try to sell you magic beans? The Brooklyn Bridge? A few acres of swamp?

"It's authentic. It's also the reason I'm able to walk in the sunlight and I don't have to drink from humans."

Maura tossed back her martini and drained the glass.

Adrian stroked the hand he still held. "Would you like another martini? Or did you want to get a couple of bottles of house wine and skip dinner?"

"I'd like a bottle of anything cold with a high alcohol content, please."

He stood and kissed her hand. "I'll be back with a nice fortified bottle of white wine. I think you'll like it."

Adrian?

Yes, love?

This is the strangest conversation I've ever had. She glanced at her left shoulder, then her right. *Well, almost the strangest.*

"Then you'd better brace yourself, because I want you to meet my family."

Your family? Why?

"Because. Who can say when we'll be back? I should make time for a short visit and I want them to meet you. I have the feeling we'll be together for quite a while."

Both reassured and unsettled, Maura gulped and nodded.

* * * * *

Adrian and Maura spread a blanket on the grass outside. He felt certain his choice of location was private since they situated themselves at the highest point overlooking the hillside village below. Cloaked in darkness with the stars above, they could easily have a midnight tryst, provided she was willing.

He couldn't help wondering about her earlier reaction to his news. Maybe she thought she wanted a vampire lover, but deep down, once it became a reality, she had second thoughts. Truth be told, any sane person should.

"What did you mean about bracing myself to meet your family, Adrian?"

"They're... I don't know quite how to describe them. Unique?"

"Unique? In a good way or a bad way?"

"Both." He reached for her hand and she extended hers to his grasp. Relief washed away his nervousness as she meshed their fingers together, curling hers around his.

"Maura, I left home when I was a very young man. I think I realized that my family was pretty dysfunctional, even by vampiric standards."

She sat up straighter and cleared her throat. "Dysfunctional—how?"

"Oh boy." Adrian dropped his forehead into his hand and wondered what to tell her. Trying to think of a way he could explain them that she would understand, he hit on a pop-culture reference that he hoped would work.

"Actually, they're quite loveable in their way but may take some getting used to. I tried to come back home a couple of times, but even though I love them... Do you remember the TV show, *The Adams Family*?"

"Uh-oh." She tensed and looked off in the distance. "Go ahead, tell me what to expect, so I don't run away screaming and embarrass us both."

Adrian stroked her cheek and chuckled. "Don't worry. We won't stay long at all. I just want them to meet you more than I want you to get familiar with them."

Maura bit her lower lip and her forehead furrowed. "Why?"

"It has to do with a certain prediction they made for me. I want to show them they're wrong." Adrian noticed her eyes widen and could almost smell her fear.

"Wrong? About you? Why? Did they think you were gay too?"

He chuckled. "No." Somehow he had to turn this around. He wanted this to be a romantic rendezvous, not a game of twenty questions with each answer leaving her more confused than the last.

"What did they predict?"

He shrugged. "Doom and gloom, basically. They insisted that I belonged with my own kind, embracing what I was, instead of fighting it. They said if I lived among mortals, I'd be miserable. I want to show them how unmiserable I am and it's all because of you."

Adrian turned to face her and brought his lips to hers. Just before their mouths would have touched, she interrupted with another question.

"So why can't you send them a postcard? 'Having a wonderful time with my new mortal girlfriend. Wish you were here.'"

"We'd better leave out the 'wish you were here' part, or they might show up."

She jerked away and gasped. "Are you serious? Would they?"

"No, relax, Maura. I was kidding."

She wrapped her arms around her knees and seemed to be hugging herself into an upright fetal position.

122

Adrian sighed, realizing she wasn't ready for lovemaking—not right now, anyway. They had a long way to go before she was relaxed enough to take his cock, even though it was hard and throbbing again. Damn, that happened every time he was around her and they had only fucked once. Maybe he could use a little mind control? *No. I want her as an equal. That means equally involved and willing.*

That was another thing. How would she react when she found out that he could manipulate her with his mind, or astral project into her bed? They had a lot of ground to cover and had barely scratched the surface.

Maura stood up and began to pace. "I don't get it. Why did they think you'd be miserable among mortals? Are they prejudiced or something?"

What now? Should he begin lying to her just to get her in the mood? She'd find out eventually and then the trust he'd been working to build would be shot to hell.

"I'm afraid so, love. They do believe in their superiority and if you're willing to be honest, there's some justification. Superior strength, more highly developed senses—"

"More bloodlust." She folded her arms and glared at him.

This wasn't going well at all, certainly not the way he had planned it. Adrian sighed and shrugged. "Please understand. I'm trying to be completely honest with you. You said you wanted to be prepared. Perhaps if you understand the way they think—"

"Then what? That will make their prejudice okay?"

Adrian stood and snarled, "No! It's not right, but it's real and it goes both ways. How would your family feel about you dating a vampire? I'd love to live in an ideal world of rainbows and butterflies, but we don't. Realize that."

Adrian stepped backward, surprised by his own impatience and lack of control. "Look, Maura. I'm sorry. It's just that I've lived a long time. Hundreds of years. And I've seen what our people can do to each other." When he began to advance, she raised her arms as if to push him away, her face set in a "stop right where you are" expression.

"No, you look. I was told that I'd know my vampire when I found him." She tipped her chin up in defiance. "I simply don't know if I've found him yet."

He deliberately controlled his emotions and tried to sound casual, like he had before. "You were told? By whom?"

Maura went silent. When she looked down and to the left, Adrian knew she was lying. "I'm not the only one who needs to be honest, *cherie*. Now who told you that?"

"I… You wouldn't believe me."

Adrian stuffed his hands in his pockets. "Try me."

A blush colored her face. "Why? Why should I tell you? What difference does it make?"

She had a point, but he was still curious. "Because it's nonsense. Humans can live right next door to their soul mate without knowing it for years. And vampires are no better. For all their acute senses, they have just as much trouble knowing their beloved as soon as they meet.

"Vampires are only able to communicate mind to mind with their beloved, but they have to join their bodies first before they can do that. Even so, we all have to go through the process of getting to know one other before we 'just know' a relationship with that person would work. Haven't you ever been attracted to someone and dated and wound up realizing they weren't who you thought they were? Perhaps you couldn't stand the man once he was no longer putting on his best face?"

Maura frowned and kicked at the grass. "I suppose."

"Wouldn't it be the same with me? With any vampire? Wouldn't it be much worse if the vampire lied to you, said his family just loved human mortals, only to have you discover the truth the hard way?"

"Like how? Being passed around on the hors d'oeuvre tray?"

"Exactly." He held her gaze, hoping the seriousness of his voice penetrated her foolish, idealistic head.

She sucked in a deep breath and her eyes seemed to be pleading with him. "I wanted it to be you. I really did. But…"

He stepped closer and pulled her into his arms. "Then stop second-guessing."

"But I haven't even done the summoning, yet."

"And you won't if I can help it. Do you realize how dangerous that is? Do you know what sort of thing you could call upon and ask to come to you?"

Maura's face fell. "I went to all the trouble of writing exactly what I wanted, being careful of my wording, thinking of a good place to leave the note and then I was just waiting for the sign."

"May I see what you wrote?"

She bit her lower lip and looked at her feet. "No. It's embarrassing."

"All right, but did it ever occur to you that you may have summoned me already? Perhaps back in New York, simply by thinking about doing it, planning to do it and wishing for your vampire lover in your mind?"

She jerked her head up and gawked at him. "Can that happen? I mean, really? Like I said, some pretty strange thoughts cross my mind, sometimes."

"Not if it's just one random thought, but if it crosses your mind over and over again and perhaps you say something out loud…" Adrian took her hand, cautiously. "Do you believe it's possible to worry about something so much that it eventually happens? I think they call it a self-fulfilling prophecy."

"Oh." Her gaze wandered away from him, to her left again and then as if a light bulb flicked on in her brain she exclaimed, "Oh!"

"I guess you know what I mean, hmmm?"

"Yes, or at least, I think I do. My girlfriends and I were talking about doing the summoning and we did it as a group in Central Park one night. It was even my idea."

Adrian nodded, knowing exactly why he went to the park that night. "And I'll bet you were thinking about it even before that."

"Well, yeah. It was one of those random thoughts at first, but it grew and got stronger until I was sort of obsessed."

He slipped one hand behind her head and the other around her back and pulled her closer. He could feel her heartbeat and breathing quicken. "Here I am."

Chapter Ten

❧

A loud drunken hiccup assaulted her left ear. "Hello, Susan."

Maura closed her eyes and gritted her teeth. *Not now, you moron. He's just about to kiss me.*

A familiar flutter of air on her right cheek and a high-pitched squeal preceded her other unwanted visitor. "Yes and then he's going to make love to you. You mustn't let him."

Bite me, Angel.

"That's exactly why you can't allow it, because now that he's identified you as his, he's going to bite you! I'd bet money on it."

Adrian lowered his mouth over hers and she sighed. His kisses were fabulous.

"Did you hear me? He's going to bite you! Right after the act."

What do you mean? It's not an act. I know he loves me. He just hasn't said it yet.

"You tell her, Susan."

For Chrissakes, my name is Maura!

"Maura, Susan…whatever. And, by the way, my name isn't 'Moron' either."

Well, if you think this is convenient timing, you're both morons. Now get the hell out of my head. He can read my thoughts, you know.

"He can't hear us," they both said in unison.

Well, he can hear me. All I have to do is call him telepathically and he'll kick your asses.

"And how's he gonna do that, Susan?"

Damn. He had her there. *So, how does one get rid of one's conscience? Oh, I know! Just refuse to listen to it.*

"You should always listen to your conscience, dear. You can make big mistakes if you don't."

Adrian pulled her even closer and she could feel his passion growing by the way his muscles moved against her. That wasn't the only thing that was growing. His huge erection pressed right against her stomach.

"And I told you, Susan. We're not your conscience."

Then who the hell are you?

"We're not a who. We're a what."

All right. If you're not my conscience, then what is?

She heard the devil let out a bored sigh. "Your conscience isn't a what, Susan, it's a who. It's the sum of all the past people who've instilled your values. Maybe you're the moron here."

Get out. Get out, get out, get out!

The pressure on her shoulders eased. All was quiet, except for the muffled groan Adrian made that sounded like he had tasted something so good, he was almost in paradise. Like the way she sounded the first time she took a sip of a chocolate martini.

He kissed her harder and groaned against her lips.

Oh yeah. He means business.

Maura pushed on his shoulders just hard enough to break the kiss, but was still prisoner in his firm grip.

"What's wrong?"

She panted for a few seconds and said in a breathy voice, "Nothing. But if I don't jump your bones soon, I'll burst."

Adrian swept her up in his arms as if she were made of balsa wood. "I'm going to take you somewhere more private where we can make love with as much zeal as we want."

"Zeal? We're going to have zealous sex?"

Adrian's eyes glittered like black obsidian and he said, "Indeed. Hold on."

Stars sped by until they were blurs of light. Maura's head and stomach were still moving after the rest of her body had stopped and she couldn't focus on her surroundings.

"Dear Lord, where did you learn to run like that?"

Adrian shrugged. "Probably at the end of the Crusades." He spoke casually, as if it were the same as learning to paint while vacationing in Paris.

Maura finally managed to pull herself together, adjust her vision to the moonlight and view the sweet-smelling, grassy meadow surrounding them.

"This is a pretty spot. Where are we?"

"France."

Her eyes popped. "Really?"

"No. Just kidding. I'm not a jet."

Maura pushed at him, playfully. "Don't tease."

Adrian pushed her shoulders. "Why not?"

Surprised, she pushed at his chest, harder. "'Because I said so."

Adrian pushed her right over backward. "But I enjoy it."

Before she hit the grass, he swooped in beneath her to break her fall. Catching her around her waist and neck, he flipped and rolled, gently lowering her to the grass until she rested on her back.

Her stomach lurched again, but she quickly recovered. "Nice reflexes. Was that your little way of saying don't push me, or I might push back?"

He nuzzled her neck and said, "Glad you got the message." His hot breath on her cool skin made her tingle.

Without further need of words, she slipped her arms around his neck and he lowered his mouth to hers. Tingles passed through her lips and became butterflies fluttering down her torso until they reached her belly. At that point an automatic clenching in her womb began. It was as if she was calling to him to complete their connection, body into body.

He tasted like his wine, but it seemed sweeter somehow. Perhaps it was the way she was feeling about him? Her heart was melting like warm chocolate. Much of her ambivalence had fled and she was ready to give in to the pleasures of a perhaps "meant-to-be" relationship with an immortal.

"Adrian, I have something for you."

He waggled his thick brows. "You certainly do."

"She let out a tiny snort. "Well, that too, but first..." She reached into her pocket and extracted the stickpin. "I want you to have this. I made it in a jewelry class."

He took the sterling silver pin and examined the bauble at the end of it.

"I know it's not much—"

"Not another word, *mon coeur*. I love it. What an interesting stone. What is it?"

"It's not a stone. It's a shell. A piece of abalone from Mexico."

He tucked it in his pocket, leaned in, whispered, "Thank you," then fused his lips to hers.

After a long, tender and deeply satisfying kiss, he nibbled her upper and lower lip, gradually pulling away. Her eyelids fluttered open and she stared into glowing eyes—dark brown with a gold sheen. She hadn't noticed the golden glow flooding his irises before. Perhaps it had always been there, but she suspected not. She would have noticed.

Adrian leaned back on one elbow with his head propped on his hand. The glow seemed more evident up close. Farther away, his dark eyes sparkled. As she stared at his face, one side of his mouth turned up.

Damn, he was devastating. It was bad enough before, when the wetness between her thighs was a purely physical reaction to a physical attraction, but now she could tell by the tug on her heartstrings that her emotions were getting involved too.

The *Mortal/Immortal Relationships Guide* popped into her head. It had sounded skeptical about a monogamous relationship with an immortal, but the thought of sharing him with anyone else drove her nuts. She reached up and stroked the stubble on his cheek.

"Adrian?"

"Yes, love?"

Maura shivered. She was going to break one of the guidebook's rules. It wasn't exactly a rule, though, was it? The book had said it was advice. She had ignored advice before. Plenty of times. In fact, if she didn't, her friends would have driven her crazy since they were all full of advice and rarely concurred. If she were ever to listen to her inner voice, she'd have to ignore a lot of advice.

"Can I ask you a question?"

He brought her hand to his cheek, turned his head and kissed her fingers. "Anything."

"Are we for real?"

He leaned back and frowned. His eyes bore into hers as if searching for the meaning of her words.

"I don't mean anything by it, really," Maura stammered. "I don't have any claim on you. I just want to know if I'm the only one feeling, well, you know…"

The lines in his brow faded and his frown relaxed into a lazy, sensuous half-smile. "Don't worry, Maura. I'm feeling what you are."

He leaned in and kissed her again, soft and slow. It was reassuring to know he was experiencing something, but she couldn't help wondering what the emotion was. Maybe if she knew, it would help her figure out what was going on in her own head and what to do about it.

She wasn't usually so disoriented. Maybe some of it was due to her unknown geographic location but even more due to her emotional insecurity with this much trust and fear. Her heart was bouncing all over the map. Maybe she was in unknown territory, but this was becoming more complicated than she realized.

"Adrian, when we slept together before, I didn't feel this way. I thought you were a tourist. A damn sexy, infuriating tourist with incredible, uh…skills, but I thought it was a one-time thing and back then that was all I wanted."

He cocked his head, as if wondering what this babbling crazy woman was talking about. "And now?"

"Now…" She let out a deep sigh. "Now I want more."

Adrian grinned. "And you shall have more. Much more." He grabbed her arms and held them above her head as he unbuttoned her blouse.

She didn't mean it that way. Well, she did, but that wasn't the gist of it. He licked his way down her neck, causing her viscera to quiver. *Oh, God! Maybe I should wait and talk about this later.* Her whole body trembled and she wanted her hands free to tear off his clothes. Her awakened desire demanded she wrap her legs around him and then sheath his cock in her damp center.

Maura struggled against his grip. "Let go of my hands. I want to help."

Not letting go, he merely paused. "You have a lot of wants tonight." He resumed what he was doing, pulling her lacy stretch bra over her nipple with his teeth. Then he proceeded to suck.

"Oooooo…" Writhing and moaning in pleasure beneath him, her mind went blank, empty of all desires except one. The urge to mate. Her cunt ached with it.

"Adrian, please…"

He didn't ask what she wanted, he just suckled harder and deeper. She arched and moaned so loud she nearly drowned out soft growls from the back of his throat. When he had completely satisfied that breast, he scraped his teeth against the other lacy cup and dragged that down until her other nipple was exposed too. He licked and kissed it. "You want me to suck this beauty too?"

"Oh yes," she said in a raspy voice that didn't even sound like hers.

Adrian let go of her wrists slowly and as he laved and suckled her, she pulled his hair free of its tie. All she could do was run her fingers through the silky strands, caress his neck and shoulders and hold him against her breast. Her whole body tingled and whatever reservations she may have had once evaporated. She wanted this man—vampire—more than any successful business, more than family, more than… God, more than anything.

Her womb clenched whenever he applied more pressure or suckled her deeper and she bucked instinctively, reaching out for him with her pelvis. Adrian's hot mouth finally left her breast, wet and instantly cool. Then and he trailed kisses down her midsection. When he reached her waistband, he popped the button and dragged the zipper down with his teeth.

"Dear Lord, Adrian. I need your body. I need to be skin to skin with you. Please take your clothes off and let me suck your cock."

"Not yet."

"Yes, yet!"

He leaned on his elbow and looked up at her curiously, as if trying to understand her. "This is our joining, Maura. It shouldn't be rushed."

"But, I thought we already joined."

"Not like this. I'll remove all of your clothes if you like, but I don't want to cheat you out of all the pleasure we can have by becoming overanxious. Therefore, I'll leave mine on until I've satisfied you, thoroughly."

"Oh!" It sounded more like a squeak than a word.

How could she turn that down? Her juices were running, her mouth watered and if she didn't drool soon, she'd be astonished.

Adrian helped her to a sitting position, pushed her blouse off her shoulders, removed her bra and stared at her bare breasts. *It's as if he wants to devour them. At least I hope he does.* He seemed to find them attractive.

"I do and I will, many times before we part."

Unnerved, Maura snapped, "Part?" Then she digested the rest of the sentence. "Wait, are you reading my mind without permission, again?"

He dipped his head and licked her cleavage. "Only that once. You practically shouted it."

Adrian attached his mouth to her nipple and sucked her in deeply. Bracing herself against the ground, Maura threw her head back and let out a cry of sheer joy. Being topless and exposed to the world as Adrian suckled was heaven, but she still wanted to be naked. To sit on the yielding earth, completely bare-assed and open, letting the breeze caress and cool her overheated skin.

Adrian let her breast pop out of his mouth and the tenderness of the night flowed over her damp nipple. If it were possible, she swore her nipple puckered even more.

He moved quickly, took hold of her slacks and as she lifted her butt, he pulled. Thankfully, her panties came with them and she was able to kick them off. Adrian gathered her clothes, folded them and placed them on some rocks about ten feet away.

Maura felt blessedly free. Ordinarily, with all of her perceived flaws exposed to the scrutiny of a man, even by moonlight, she'd be self-conscious. But, amazingly, with him she wasn't. Adrian's lustful eyes roamed over every inch of her, making her feel overpoweringly sexy, perhaps for the first time in her life.

He kneeled beside her and then straddled her even though she was still sitting up. He began by touching the top of her head, then ran his fingers slowly over her scalp. The gentle pressure of his fingers trickling through her hair caused her to tremble in a way altogether different from the cool air passing over her impassioned body. She sensed herself falling, yet she knew she wouldn't hit the ground with a thump.

Allowing herself to be lowered with trust, she closed her eyes until she felt the tickle of grass under her back as her body met her fresh-smelling bed. When she opened her eyes again, Adrian was leaning over her. Their eyes met and bore into each other while he ran his persistent hand over her collarbone and caressed his way to her plump breast.

Her soft flesh being massaged and kneaded made her close her eyes and moan in pleasure. He had already piqued her desire enough and she ached for completion.

Maura clutched his hand and brought it to the seat of her yearning hunger. He smiled in understanding and cupped her mons. Leaning over her, he kissed her nose and proceeded to crawl backward on his hands and knees until he reached her bellybutton.

Maura quivered in anticipation. *Please don't stop there, darling. I'm begging you.*

Adrian only paused long enough to place a soft, sensuous kiss on the slighted rounded part of her tummy. She had always been self-conscious about not being perfectly flat there, but no longer. She felt like a woman. A whole, curvy, perfect-in-this-moment woman.

She waited for whatever Adrian would do, placing her pleasure in his hands. He put pressure against her thigh, pushing her lower legs open. The touch of his leather pants skimmed over her as he moved to the inside of her parted legs. Then he pushed on her other thigh until she was spread wide and sensed him kneeling at her apex. Cool air greeted her dripping wet pussy.

His loose hair tumbled onto her leg and Adrian kissed her thighs, then trailed tickling kisses slowly up to her groin and over her mound. His warm tongue teased as he kissed his way down the other side and liquefied her.

When he parted her folds, he paused. "Beautiful. So beautiful."

Even those few words spoken with such a sensual cadence carried meaning beyond compare. She thought she might weep. He stroked her labia and inhaled, then kissed her swollen bud and she nearly came undone. No one had ever made her feel like every part of her was desirable.

Crawling up between her legs, he looked into her eyes with his black, intense gaze. He lowered himself enough to lay the rigid column of his erection against her belly. "You're mine. You know that, don't you?"

"Yes, Adrian. Always and only yours," she whispered.

"Good." He crushed her lips in a scorching kiss, then dropped his pants and placed the rubbery tip of his penis at her portal. "I want to be sure you'll never forget."

He only pumped her entrance once, smiled wickedly, and then returned to his former position. His face even with her mons.

Maura cried out in desperate frustration.

As his tongue went to work on her clit, Maura buried her fingers in his hair and howled in ecstasy. Gurgling sounds she had never made before emerged from the back of her throat. She thought she had experienced every sensation sex had to offer, but how mistaken she was.

Adrian took her clit into his mouth and suckled. She jolted, spasmed and exploded, screaming. Swept away in passion's fierce current, her legs vibrated wildly as the most intense orgasm she had ever experienced racked her body. The damn guide was right. She could never go back to mortal men, now. Not after this.

Maura cried openly. Adrian crawled up beside her and enfolded her in his arms. He just held tight, letting her sob until she snuffled and quieted.

"I don't know why I'm crying. I feel so stupid."

"No. You mustn't worry. I understand it is often like that with mortals and vampires the first time they make love."

"But this isn't our first time."

"Yes it is, my sweet. As you said before, that was just sex. I knew it would be different this time."

She sniffed again and asked, "How? How did you know? Does this happen to you a lot?"

"No. I only suspected it might. It has never happened to me before."

Maura gawked at him. "You've never gone down on a mortal before?"

"Not one that I loved."

A lump formed in her throat. Trembling, she could feel the tears returning. She didn't want to cry again. She was happy, damn it. Happier than she had ever been in her life.

Adrian kissed her ear, then let go of her long enough to undress.

She spread her legs wide and appreciated the view she had of his erect, hard cock as he moved into the V between her thighs.

Looking into her eyes with glowing intensity, he said, "I love you. I want to see your face as I'm making love to your body." He reached for his clothes and folded them. "Bend your knees. Let me slide this under your bottom."

She did as he asked and he remained on his knees in front of her raised pelvis. He placed his engorged penis at her opening and they both watched as he sank his cock inside her. Both of them moaned in unison.

Then they began fucking. She reared back her head and drank in the sensation of his cock penetrating her center over and over again. By his entering her at this angle it made every stroke more effective. On withdrawing an even more powerful suction built between them eliciting grateful howling moans, almost as if the wind were pulling the sound from her lungs. She held her knees apart and watched with joy while he thrust in and out of her.

"Does that feel good, darling?"

"Oh, so good."

"Do you love me?"

Maura hadn't realized it, but she did. The feelings she had been having had calmed and developed into that warm, gooey feeling of new love.

"I do."

Adrian smiled. "Hang on, then." He used his finger to stimulate her clit sending her skyrocketing into another screaming orgasm. As she jolted and bucked, his body began to jerk. Feeling as if she had temporarily left her body all she could feel was the power of her own release.

Several loud grunts later, she knew he had come, but he didn't let up on her. She had just returned to earth and then realized she was already climbing to another peak. Her third orgasm came rip-roaring over her before she knew it. Still he persisted. She was about to beg him to stop when a fourth hit with such ferocity and force she wasn't sure she had the strength to beg, so she whimpered.

His fingers traced her ear as he kissed and licked a path down her neck. His tongue lingered at the base, over her jugular vein and wandered over it in circles. His hot breaths came faster and deeper. Eventually, he jerked away.

Even though he broke contact, Maura knew what he wanted and she wanted to offer it. Taking about five seconds to think it over, she cocked her head to the side and swept her hair out of the way. Exposing her flesh, without words she gave him permission to bite.

He inhaled a sharp breath and groaned. "Maura..." While she waited for him to finish his thought, she heard him panting. At last, he blew out a deep breath through pursed lips and regained his composure. "Don't be a silly girl."

"Excuse me?" She turned sharply and glared at him. "Did you call me a silly girl?"

"No, I said don't be one. Never offer a hungry vampire your neck. If I didn't have the Blood of the Warrior in me, I'd have drained you."

"The blood of the warrior?"

"That's what I named my private reserve. My wine. Without it, you'd be toasted."

"I think you mean, 'I'd be toast.' You're the one who's toasted."

"I meant to say you would be no more."

"But, I thought we would...you know. Have sex, then you'd bite me and have a little snack but leave me enough to wake up refreshed."

"You read too many books. If I take blood from you, you'll feel tired and drained. But you are willing to let me taste you?"

They faced each other squarely and Maura couldn't pull free of his gaze. He hadn't mesmerized her in the vampiric sense, she was fairly sure of that. But, in that moment she was defenseless against his allure. A magical bond had been created between them and it was only gaining strength. Eventually, at the price of being thought foolish, she nodded.

He closed his eyes and dropped his head as if in prayer, but she knew better than that. After a few moments of silent meditation, he looked up again, cupped her face and leaned in to kiss her. When her tongue slipped past his lips, she felt something sharp against it. *His fangs.*

He pulled away and opened his mouth until she could see them. "It's all right. I'm not going to hurt you. I want there to be no misunderstanding as to what I am."

"I understand. I'm not afraid. Well, maybe a little afraid, but I know what you are and I still trust you."

Adrian took her in his arms and pulled her tight against his chest. "Perhaps you shouldn't."

* * * * *

The bumpy bus ride took them through some harrowing mountain roads, often without a guardrail. Whenever the bus swayed too close to the cliff, or passed a car, narrowly missing a collision, Maura grasped Adrian's arm so tightly he was glad he had found a "wing-man" for her friend Jordan.

A single Canadian man named Roland, built like a lumberjack, seemed like the perfect companion for her. They laughed and chatted in the seat behind him and the very nauseous Maura.

Adrian leaned close to whisper in Maura's ear. "I don't understand why you wanted to stay on the tour. You completed your task, didn't you?"

She looked up at him with a mixture of discomfort and annoyance. "One of them, yes. But I don't understand why you didn't complete yours last night."

"You were exhausted, both physically and emotionally. You couldn't have stood it. Tonight, if your health improves, I promise to leave you the stamina."

"No way. I love having my energy drained."

She managed to chuckle and Adrian kissed her hair. Even when she was miserable, she was still good company. A younger mortal woman would probably be complaining and whining. A female vampire would be biting and drinking the driver.

"We're almost to the village where we'll be staying for the night, *cherie*."

"Thank God."

"God has nothing to do with it. We're arriving quickly and safely because of skillful driving."

Maura rolled her eyes and groaned. "Is that what it's called?"

Adrian wrapped a protective arm around her and she rested her head on his shoulder. They rode that way in silence until the bus turned off the paved road onto a dirt one. Maura jerked her head up, hoping to see that they had arrived at the hotel.

"Are we there yet?"

Adrian simply raised one eyebrow and focused on her anxious face, hoping his meaning was clear.

"Sorry." Maura gazed out the window at the landscape. Adrian knew the uneven road would lead them around some hairpin turns as it ascended and hoped Maura would make it. She really didn't have any choice.

"How are you feeling?"

She wrinkled her nose and said, "Gross."

The bus rolled over some rocks embedded in the dirt, lurching left and right. Maura slid one arm around Adrian's back and the other around his waist as if she were holding on to a mast in a stormy sea. He smiled and stroked her hair as she clung to him. He had never experienced a woman's neediness without irritation, but, admittedly, something about his stubborn, independent Maura holding on to him as if he were the steadying force of gravity itself, brought out a loving protectiveness he had never known.

"Adrian?"

"Yes, love?"

"I'm gonna hurl."

Chapter Eleven

🔊

Adrian yelled something in Romanian and the bus screeched to a jarring halt. Maura bolted toward the door when the driver opened it. As if that weren't mortification enough, Adrian followed her out of the bus.

There was nothing she could do about him. She couldn't outrun a vampire and if she opened her mouth to speak, more than words would tumble out. She dove under the bus, but Adrian met her there and held her hair back as she liberated the contents of her stomach into a wheel rut.

"Oh, for God's sake! Why did you have to come with me?" Maura shot him an angry look, then crawled to the side of the road and sat down hard. "I feel disgusting."

He sat beside her, pulled out his handkerchief and extended it in offering.

Maura shook her head. A familiar heated blush rose to her cheeks. It was the curse of the redhead as far as she was concerned.

"Please don't be embarrassed, Maura. I've seen much, much worse."

"Yeah, at least I didn't run into a stake and then puke my guts out while bleeding to death on top of a pole. That wouldn't be nearly as attractive."

"Don't be cross with me, *cherie*. I would rather die than let anything happen to you."

She looked up at him in silent wonder. Right about now nearly every man she had ever dated would be turning away, retching and trying to think of how to let her down easy when dumping her.

Adrian felt her forehead. "You're warm. Perhaps you are getting ill? My family's castle is nearby…just above the village. Let me take you there and forget the rest of this silly tour. If you want to buy clothes for your store, I'll take you shopping. If you want to see castles, I can show you castles. But right now and perhaps for a few days, you need to rest. Think about it."

Maura sighed and then clamped her mouth shut, worried about her breath. *Oh, this is just lovely. I won't be able to talk to anyone until I can brush my teeth.*

Adrian stood up and said, "Wait here."

He bounded up the steps of the bus and returned moments later with a half-filled bottle of water. "Jordan was drinking it, but said she'd be happy to give you the rest."

Maura dropped her head into her hands and groaned. "Why me? Why this trip? I waited so long for this. If I'm coming down with something, I'll be hugely pissed."

"I can guarantee that none of the castles on this tour are more fascinating than the one you've already seen." Adrian extended his hand and said, "Come on, Maura, they're waiting. It isn't much farther."

Eventually, she reached for his hand and allowed him to hoist her up. One swig of water, a swish and a spit later, and they climbed back on board the bus.

Once settled in their seats, the bus started up again. Jordan tapped her shoulder.

"Are you all right?"

"I guess. I'm feeling a little better now. If this damn bus driver can find the damn hotel without throwing us all over the damn bus, I'll be feeling much better."

"That's a lot of damning," Adrian said.

"Are you sure you're all right?" Jordan asked.

"I could use a breath mint."

"I happen to have some chewable tablets that settle the stomach. Want a couple?"

Maura nodded. Turning around, she raised the water bottle. "Thanks for this. I don't suppose you want it back."

Jordan giggled. "No. Please, keep it."

To Maura's great relief, the minty-fresh stomach tablets doubled as breath mints. When she faced forward again, the village and the dilapidated-looking hotel rolled into sight. Hmmm… Castle or rustic charm? Castle or rustic charm? Okay, so it's a no-brainer.

"Uh, Adrian? Is that invitation still open?"

He grinned and folded her hand into the crook of his arm. "Yes. It is."

* * * * *

Maura and Adrian left their bags by the side of the road and said goodbye to Jordan, Roland and Enric.

Enric looked crestfallen. "Are you sure you want to leave the tour? Tonight's castle is completely different from the one you saw yesterday and genuine vampires inhabit it! They greet the guests and put on quite an exhibition."

Shit. He could hardly wait for Maura to see his family putting on a show. Maybe he could talk her into being somewhere else when the tour arrived.

Maura quickly reassured the young tour guide. "Oh, we'll be there, Enric. Don't you worry. I'm just not sure we'll be continuing on after that. I need to see how I feel, but I'll be sure to tell you when I see you later tonight."

Fabulous.

When the last person disappeared into the hotel, Adrian picked up all of their bags with ease. Since she had bought another suitcase that morning, they had four. Two for Maura's clothing, one for his and another one lined in foam and full of wine.

"Jeez, I forgot about how strong you vamps are."

"This is nothing. Can you stay here a moment while I run these up to the castle?"

Maura glanced around at the eerily quiet town. "I... You do mean run, don't you?"

"I'll back in a flash. I just want to take a moment to tell my parents you're coming." And be sure his father's penis was in his pants.

She gave him a quick kiss and he disappeared in a blur.

When he arrived, the place looked worse than it had before. He hadn't seen it in daylight and now he noticed even more damage to his ancestral home. The beautiful oak doors looked as if they had been beaten with chains and probably were. Adrian shook his head and dropped the suitcases on the stoop.

He pulled the large iron ring and heard the same faraway tinkling deep inside the castle and soon after, the door slowly opened on its own. No one seemed to be around. Then he remembered it was still daytime. How could he forget something as basic as that? He guessed he really had been out of the loop for a long time. He entered and the doors closed with a clang.

Violeta hurried down the hall toward him. Speaking in Romanian, she asked, "Can I help you?" As she skidded to a stop in front of Adrian, her eyes widened. "Oh. It's you." She immediately removed her panties. "Your father said I was to extend you the same courtesy as I do to the rest of the male members of the family."

"That won't be necessary, Violeta. I don't know what my father told you, but you can stay dressed when I'm around. In fact, I'd rather you did."

"Oh!" Her face reddened, she snatched her panties off the floor and fled back in the direction from whence she came.

Adrian tossed the suitcases inside and sighed, "I'll just have to leave them a note."

He strode to the entry table and noticed the vase of long-ago wilted flowers flanked by old tarnished candleholders, disfigured by black wax that had dripped down over their once silver beauty. "How droll."

With a deep sigh of defeat, he grabbed a pen and paper from the drawer and strode to the door of the crypt. The wooden trapdoor in the floor would have been hidden but for the large iron ring that acted as a handle. He heaved it open and the old familiar smell of mildew assaulted his sinuses. He sneezed before he stepped into space and floated downward, making a soft landing on the dirt floor. Realizing he had forgotten to bring a flashlight, he hoped they hadn't moved anything. He remembered where his parents' crypts were and without waiting for his eyes to adjust, strode in their direction.

"Ouch!" Sharp pain ricocheted through his big toe. *Damn.* In the pale light from above, he realized they had added a few more coffins. *Great. They must be having guests.*

Adrian sharpened his vision, picked out his mother's casket and scribbled a quick note in Romanian that read, "I'll be home with my darling Maura when you get up. Make sure Papa behaves himself. You know what I mean. Adrian."

* * * * *

Maura hugged her purse and loitered next to the hotel's front door. At least if she could hear people talking inside, they could probably hear her scream should the occasion arise. What was taking Adrian so long?

At last he appeared and sauntered over to her.

"I'm sorry I was delayed, *cherie*. My parents were out. I had to leave them a note and explain that we'd be waiting for them."

"Oh, no biggie. I was perfectly fine," she lied.

Adrian cleared his throat, looked down and kicked at the dirt.

Crap, he probably guessed that wasn't exactly honest. Lying was so much easier sometimes.

"Something's bothering me, though, *cherie*. I think I may need to prepare you to meet my family, but I don't know how."

"Uh-oh. That sounds ominous. Well, you said they were out. Maybe we can get settled in and then you can tell me about them?" *Is meeting them really that damned important? I've never heard of a vampire mama's boy.*

Adrian grinned and chuckled. "It's important to me and I'm not a mama's boy. But they are a little—unusual and I don't want you to be shocked."

Maura folded her arms and tapped her foot. "Can you stop reading my mind, please?"

"If you'll stop thinking so loud, I will."

She threw her hands in the air and looked at the sky. "You've got to teach me how to control that and soon. I don't want to accidentally insult your parents."

"Don't worry. They can't read your mind. Only I can and only when you get highly emotional and focused on something."

"Thank God. Wait a minute, I don't get 'highly emotional'."

"Yes you do." He stepped forward and rested his hands on her waist. "I don't mind, though. I'd expect that of an Irish redhead."

Maura rolled her eyes. "Well, I don't get in a snit often and if you'll give me a few lessons you won't be able to tell at all. So why can you read me if others can't?"

"I assume it's something to do with our...um...potential relationship."

Maura leaned back and studied his face. "Potential? I thought it was pretty actual, actually."

"Oh, it is. Don't misunderstand. I'm not sure what it means since it's never happened to me before, but my parents have had that ability from the start and they've been happily married for centuries." Maura cocked her head to the side and smiled. "Sounds like it's a good thing, then."

Adrian raised his eyebrows and sent her his intense stare. "Do you consider it good?"

"Of course I do. For God's sake, I came all this way and spent quite a wad of money to meet my 'beloved'."

"But regardless of that, they're different from you and me. Remember that." Adrian swept her into his arms and kissed her with passionate abandon despite standing in the middle of town. Maura had to admit she adored him. At first he was kind and a perfect gentleman, then he was constantly in her way and annoying, but now she simply loved him, unabashedly.

She sucked on his bottom lip as he pulled away and he smiled.

"How are you feeling?"

"Incredible. You're the best kisser."

Adrian chuckled and smoothed her hair. "Well, thank you, but I meant to say, how is your stomach?"

"Oh, I'm fine now."

"Really?"

"Really and truly."

"Good. Hold on."

He picked her up in his arms and the landscape blurred. Oddly, the only thing that went through her mind was how thankful she was for his vampiric strength that could lift a hundred and thirty pounds like a feather.

* * * * *

As soon as he knew she had her balance, Adrian set Maura on her feet. She stood in front of his once majestic home, gaping.

"Oh—My—God. Um… It's… Um…"

"I know." Adrian kicked at the brown grass. "It used not look like this, believe me. Apparently my parents thought they'd toss in a little atmosphere for the tourists."

Maura didn't answer. She merely strolled to the right until she could see around a corner, leaned toward it and peeked, as if waiting for trolls to pop out. Turning back to him, she wore the most worried expression he had seen thus far. "Is it haunted?"

"Not yet."

"Are you positive?"

Adrian found it amusing that Maura seemed more afraid of ghosts than vampires. At least that was one fear he could put to rest easily.

"I'm quite sure of it. Nobody dies here."

"Oh." Maura slapped herself on the forehead. "Duh. Of course not. You're all immortal, right?"

"I think so. I'm the youngest and I'm almost six hundred years old."

Maura raised her eyebrows. "You look damn good for almost six hundred. Can I try your brand of face cream?"

He almost made a wisecrack about the horrible mud mask she wore back in her New York apartment, but caught himself in time. She'd probably flip out if she knew he had been on her fire escape, spying on her.

Maura crossed her arms. "So you didn't um…how do I put it politely? No one dined at home?"

"Never. Well, not to the point of anybody dying. They keep servants that allow non-lethal feedings." *Among other things.*

She nodded. "So, what year were you born?"

"We're not exactly sure. I was turned shortly before I left Romania, sometime in the mid 1400s." Internally, he cringed. *Come on, Adrian. The more you can prepare her for, the better.* Taking a deep breath, he said, "I knew Vlad Tepes."

Maura's eyes popped and she gasped. "No friggin' way!"

He would have been able to feel her palpable excitement even if he wasn't a vampire closely tied to her.

"Was he really assassinated, or is he holed up somewhere? Was it true what Enric said about him? Did you witness any of his atrocities? Holy shit! Why didn't you say something when we visited his castle? Is that why you were so worried about me?"

Adrian shook his head. "No, he's gone, but I haven't been back for quite a while and I don't know who may have moved in since. There are rumors of his rising again and again."

"Are they really rumors?"

"Why don't we go inside? I have more to tell you."

Maura's face fell and she stared at the scarred front doors.

"It's all right. Only the servants are awake and they won't bother with you. None of them speak English."

"Oh! Of course, it's still daylight. So the vampires are asleep? We won't wake them up?"

Adrian smiled and shook his head. "No, darling. They're 'dead to the world' as the American expression goes."

He sauntered toward the entrance of his decrepit ancestral home, but Maura didn't budge. He sensed her vibrating adrenaline and turned around.

"What is it now?"

"I'm sorry, Adrian. I'm just…it's just that I'm a little bit…um…"

"Afraid?"

She nodded.

"Good. I was beginning to think you had no common sense at all."

"Excuse me?" She jammed her hands on her hips and leaned forward, but her feet were still glued to the ground.

Adrian chuckled and walked back over to her. "I was joking."

"Did you know that insult humor is the lowest form of comedy?"

"No, I didn't. Where did you learn that?"

"I just made it up, but it should be common knowledge."

Adrian smiled and tucked a stray hair behind her delicate ear. "I'll keep that in mind. Now I promise you, nothing will happen to you here. I'll be with you at all times."

"Are you sure? If not, I don't want you to forget those famous last words. I'll have to come back and haunt you. I'll be your castle's first ghost."

"I won't leave your side, *cherie*."

Maura crossed her arms, still not moving. "What if your mom wants me to help her in the kitchen?"

Adrian tried to picture it and almost laughed. "She doesn't cook."

"What if your dad wants to have a private chat with you?"

"I'll refuse. Come on, Maura." Adrian wasn't always a patient man and he wasn't getting any more patient under this inquisition. The sun was getting lower in the sky and he might not have enough time to prepare her for his parents and whatever guests they might be having. Why the hell did they invite houseguests, anyway? Was he supposed to introduce Maura to the whole dysfunctional extended family at once?

At last Maura walked up beside him and grasped his hand. "Okay. I'll come, but we need to agree on some kind of signal if I get wiggy, all right?"

Her original words and expressions always amused the hell out of him. Sometimes literally. All the little uniquenesses that were Maura could change any of his moods in seconds. Most often for the better, but sometimes…

"Fine, if you get 'wiggy' why don't you play with your hair or something?"

"What if I do that by accident?"

Adrian sighed and looked at the sky. "It's not getting any lighter out here, Maura."

"Okay, okay. I'll ask for a pencil. That way I'll be armed."

He couldn't believe she thought she could stake a vampire with a pencil, but he couldn't come up with anything better on the fly.

"Fine. Do you have a pencil I can keep in my pocket?"

Maura opened her purse and fished around. "I think so." She pulled out a yellow number two pencil and handed it to him, eraser first. "Be careful. Don't put this anywhere near your heart, okay?"

It was all he could do not to laugh out loud. "Don't worry. I'll place it in my right jacket pocket. Pointy-end facing away from all vital organs."

"The one on the outside of the jacket, right?"

"I appreciate your concern for me, darling, but I've been taking care of myself for nearly six hundred years."

She folded her arms again and looked as if she was readying for battle.

"Right." He dropped the pencil into his right-front jacket pocket and then extended his elbow. "Shall we?"

Taking his arm, she allowed him to lead her to the doors.

Upon ringing the bell and the doors remaining shut, he wondered if he had been locked out for some reason. Possible whys and wherefores ran through his mind until one of the doors opened to reveal the maid.

He spoke in rusty Romanian, but managed to say, "Hello. This is my friend, Maura. We'll be staying the night."

The maid stepped aside and Adrian noticed his lover appraising the maid's skimpy uniform as they walked by.

"Can you get us some tea?" Adrian asked, just to test his theory about her being non-bilingual.

The maid stared at him mutely until he spoke in Romanian. She shook her head to his question so he asked if the chef was about. She nodded and retreated toward the kitchen, leaving the two of them alone.

Maura stared after her, probably wondering why her short flouncy skirt bobbed up above the lower curve of her panties when she walked.

Adrian looked at his feet. "I'm sorry, she's...um..."

Maura looked up at him with a deadpan expression. "She sure is."

At least she was wearing panties. That much was a relief. How the hell was he going to explain his parents' sex games to her? Hopefully he wouldn't have to. Now if he could just predict what other behaviors they may have adopted over the last five centuries or so, he'd try to prepare her. Maybe it wasn't too late to forget the whole thing. They could just go back to the hotel and... No. His parents would wonder what happened and come looking for him and more importantly, he needed to know that Maura could cope with whatever happened between them in the future. She had to be tested.

"Maura, I know it looks bad, but let me show you around. Some of the nonpublic areas must look better than this. They had to put the good stuff somewhere."

Maura glanced around the large entrance hall and noticed threadbare area rugs, furniture looking as if it had been dragged up the rocky hill and portraits of some pretty frightening characters.

"If you say so."

Adrian placed a hand on the small of her back and guided her to the wide corridor on their left. As much as she wanted Adrian to be the one, if he was she hoped he didn't make frequent trips home.

On the right was a receiving parlor and she peeked inside as they strolled by. The sofa and love seat were badly frayed and the rug was worn almost all the way through in places. Dust covered the antique end tables.

"I hope you don't think this is the way we really live. My parents roughed the place up for the sake of the tour. They think it provides the kind of atmosphere the tourists are expecting."

Maura's nerve endings prickled as she eyed the portraits along the wall. Some were paintings of vampires baring their fangs. One was even in the act of biting his victim, fangs and blood evident. The terror on the innocent woman's face contrasted wildly with the evil delight in the eyes of the killer.

As if reading her mind, he slipped his hand farther over to stroke her arm. "No, they're not ancestral paintings. I don't know where they got them. Pretty gruesome if you ask me."

"More atmosphere?"

"Undoubtedly." He stopped and kissed her.

Maura melted into his arms and warm lips. Whether or not it was because she needed his comforting contact, her nipples ached and she wanted him.

Adrian? Testing…testing…Maura to Adrian.

I'm listening.

Will we be able to have sex in your parent's house while we're staying here? I mean, will they let us sleep in the same room?

That shouldn't be a problem. Are you craving something I should know about? He stepped back just enough to reach up and tweak her nipples.

Maura jumped and then giggled. She felt her juices flow like a faucet had been turned on. *Yeah. I'd love to get naked with you right now and screw your brains out, but I imagine it wouldn't make a good first impression if they woke up to hear me screaming my head off.*

Adrian licked his lips. *I don't imagine they would mind as long as it added to the atmosphere. Quick, let's duck in here.*

The first room they came to was the library and Adrian yanked her inside. Cobwebs covered several of the shelves and the maid appeared to be adding dust to the table and chairs in front of the fire. She was bending over from the waist and more of her panties were exposed as she "dusted".

Adrian strolled into the room and spoke to the girl in Romanian. She answered him in quick clipped sentences. When she shrugged at his last question he retuned to Maura.

"Apparently this room is on the tour too. She said that most of the downstairs including the dungeon is open for tourists."

An electric energy traversed up Maura's spine, making the hair on the back of her neck stand on end. "Dungeon?"

"Don't worry. You never have to see it if you don't want to. Who knows what foolish things they may have added there to entertain the tourists."

So is there someplace we can go for a quickie?

"Let's head upstairs. They don't sleep there. It should be nice and private." He clamped his hand around her wrist and began running toward the wide staircase in the foyer.

Before they reached the steps a trapdoor in the floor burst open and a pale, thin woman with long black hair shot through it. To Maura's complete shock the dark-haired, light-skinned woman floated to the floor daintily.

"Good evening, Mother." He glanced down through the trapdoor and said, "Where's Father?"

"He got up a little earlier." The woman cocked her head and cupped a hand behind her ear. "Ah... He's doing the gardener. He'll be back shortly. He has to spank Violeta for leaving the door unlocked earlier."

Adrian stood ramrod straight and quickly turned to Maura. "He's doing the gardening. Yes, he's quite the gardener."

Just then a large man, also with dark hair and eyes, strode in from the back, bowed in front of her...and sniffed. "Welcome to my home." His eyes rounded and he began to inhale deeply when Adrian's mother kicked his leg.

Adrian? Why is he looking at me like a dog eyeing a steak? Adrian?

The older man coughed, then cleared his throat and spoke in slightly accented English. "It is good to see you again, my son. Please introduce me to your friend and our guest."

"Maura, this is my mother Angelika and father Petrov. Although, he's changed his name to Vlad for the sake of the tour."

She sensed some kind of animosity in Adrian's tone. Not knowing what it could be about and since he wasn't answering her telepathically, she let it go for the moment.

"Enchanted." Vlad took her hand and placed a kiss on her knuckles. Then, she could have sworn he licked them.

Angelika cocked her head. "We have lovely guest coffins for you in the crypt, dear."

"Uh, that's all right, Mother. We'll take my old bedroom."

His father elbowed him. "No need to explain, m'boy. I'd want her in my bed all day long too."

Angelika turned to Adrian. "As you wish, dear. It's exactly as you left it."

Chapter Twelve

&

Adrian had carried their suitcases to their upstairs bedroom, relieved to see the interior in all of its hoped-for glory and opulence. Gold-accented furnishings went beautifully with the well-kept intricate handmade pieces foretelling the style of King Louis XIV. Everything in this room had been carefully maintained. *Okay, it looks like the maid is good for more than sex and snacking on.*

Maura gazed all around the room, wide-eyed.

"Adrian, this is exquisite. Absolutely beautiful!"

He smiled and nodded, noting especially the oversized canopy bed with rich red velvet drapes that could be drawn for that cozy, even more private feeling. Hopefully, his parents' "show" wouldn't last very long since he couldn't wait to get Maura into that bed and use his sexual talent to impress the hell out of her. If she could stand whatever horrors he imagined were coming, he might consider initiating their first "love bite" afterward.

"Well, I think we'd better get back downstairs before the tour arrives. Honestly, Maura, I have no idea what to expect, but you've been wonderful so far. I hope you won't be too shocked by whatever may happen next."

She smiled and bumped him playfully with her hip. "Oh c'mon, how bad can it be?"

Adrian's throat tightened. It could be bad. Knowing his parents it could be very bad. They weren't exactly normal, even for vampires. They were open about what they were, even flaunting it. Most vampires thrived on secrecy. And it wasn't just his parents. His brothers were the same way.

Little mattered to any of them but doing what they wanted, when they wanted to do it, saying any insulting or foolish thing that popped into their heads. They had enjoyed bragging about their vampiric talents and getting away with murder since no mortal was foolish enough to challenge them. One of the reasons he left home for the last time and stayed away was because he couldn't stand their arrogance or stupid antics anymore.

"Promise me you'll use that pencil request if they make you uncomfortable, all right?"

Maura snorted and appeared to still doubt their ability to horrify her. "Your parents are pussycats, Adrian. I really like them. They made me feel very welcome."

"You seemed a little 'wigged-out' when they said they had a guest coffin for you. That's the right American expression for how you felt, is it not?"

"Well, it's the thought that counts. And now that I know we'll be here in this gorgeous bedroom…" Her eyes picked up where her words trailed off. She raised her eyebrows twice in rapid succession, smiling all the while.

"*Oui, ma cherie*. I cannot wait either."

He pulled her into a hard embrace and crushed his lips to hers. She opened her mouth and met his tongue with the same intensity. It was going to be a wonderful night—or not.

Moments later, as they descended the stairs, Adrian's father grinned and called out to them. "Maura, Adrian, feel free to join in the fun when the tour group arrives."

"Not this time, Father. Because we were on the tour, it might be traumatic for them to see me participate as a vampire and they seemed like nice people."

"Ha! You still think of mortals as nice people, do you? By the way, call me Vlad."

Maura? They don't know you're mortal yet and I'd like to keep it that way, for now.

Sounds like a damn good idea, she telegraphed back.

Adrian took Maura's hand and led her to the side of the entry doors. "I think we'll just wait over by the sideboard and join the group when they get here...uh, Vlad."

The doorbell rang. "Places, everyone," Angelika cried. She ran up the stairs and waited regally on the wide landing above.

Vlad ran down the hall and disappeared into the library. *Oh no.* Adrian hoped the maid wasn't in there but guessed she probably was.

The double doors opened seemingly of their own accord as they had for Adrian the evening he arrived. Enric stepped inside first. He was slowly followed by the cautious-looking tour group.

Angelika floated gracefully down the dusty steps, then stopped at the bottom and said, "Good evening. Welcome, mortals. I am Angelika and I will be showing you around our vampire mansion. We will meet my husband Vlad in a few minutes."

As the big double doors began to shut, Adrian saw a group of older women who looked like they wanted to flee before they closed completely. When they spotted Adrian and Maura, a couple of them audibly sighed with relief. They probably figured that if he and Maura hadn't been killed after spending the afternoon there, perhaps they'd be safe too.

"Meanwhile, it would be my pleasure to escort you through our gallery." Angelika gestured gracefully to the long corridor. "Follow me."

"This vay," Enric said. He wore a big grin and winked at Angelika. Adrian, comforted by his reaction figured that the tour guide must have seen this show a dozen times and yet still willingly brought his groups through. It couldn't be too raunchy or dangerous, could it?

Angelika paused in front of the first portrait—a gruesome likeness of the stereotypical vampire actor. He had a sharp widow's peak, black hair so slicked back it lay flat against his head, a beak nose and exposed fangs.

Adrian shuddered to think what type of foolishness she'd make up about the painting. With an expansive sweep of her hand, she announced, "My Uncle Demetri. He was such a handsome vampire that many artists wanted to paint him. His likeness may seem familiar to some of you."

"Yes, he does," one of the older women whispered. "He looks just like the actor who always played a vampire in the nineteen-thirties black-and-white movies. Oh, what was his name?"

"Bela Lugosi," her friend supplied.

"Ah, yes. That's the one."

The painting was in all probability of Bela Lugosi himself, since my mother didn't have an Uncle Demetri.

Maura turned toward him with raised eyebrows. *You mean the painting's a fake?*

Phony as a rubber chicken.

She started to giggle but covered it with a cough.

The murmuring guests strolled past the receiving parlor and down the corridor following Angelika. She stopped in front of the next painting—a disgusting rendition of a vampire feeding on a terrified young woman. Their costumes suggested a time long ago in history.

She smiled wistfully at the painting as she pointed it out. "And this is my brother, Christofor. The painting commemorates his first kill. Some vampires like to have that special turning point captured in art and hung on the wall, sort of like a businessman might frame the first dollar he ever made."

Oh, come on. Who's going to believe that?

Apparently the audience did. Different members exclaimed "how grizzly", "horrible", "revolting" and the like.

When one of the young men had recovered enough to ask a question, he timidly raised his hand. "Um, you said he's your brother?"

Angelika nodded, smiling.

"It looks like that was hundreds of years ago. How old are you?"

Her expression dimmed. "A lady never reveals her age. Now let's continue."

Jordan grabbed Maura by the arm and pulled her aside. "Are you really going to spend the night here?"

"Sure."

"Are you mad?"

Maura lowered her voice. "It's all fake, Jordan. Don't worry. You should see the upstairs. It's completely different. Really beautiful."

Adrian's acute hearing allowed him to follow the tour group while listening to the girls' conversation.

"Angelika and Vlad are really nice. And, by the way, his name isn't even Vlad. It's all for the tour."

Adrian snickered. *Nice, huh? How nice is it to scare the pants off people?*

"Come on, people like to be scared sometimes…uh, Jordan."

Adrian realized Maura was responding to him, out loud and thought he'd better stop projecting his thoughts to her for now. She wasn't used to telepathy yet and following one conversation at a time was probably all she could handle.

"I guess you're right about that." Jordan shrugged.

Angelika was almost to the library. To Adrian's relief, Maura seemed content to be occupied elsewhere. Hopefully, she'd stay back. He still didn't know what his unpredictable father had planned. There was only one more foolish portrait to go. It showed another "uncle and aunt" lying in side-by-side coffins with contented expressions on their faces. When she called it their wedding portrait, Adrian almost laughed out loud.

Angelika beckoned the group to follow and turned into the library.

A handsomely dressed Vlad sat in one of the leather chairs, reading.

"Ah, this is where you are, darling! Everyone, this is my husband, Vlad."

Vlad stood up, straight and proud. He strolled to Angelika and slipped his hand around her waist.

"Welcome to our home. I hope you will enjoy a glimpse into the lives of real vampires."

Vlad kissed Angelika lovingly.

"Six hundred and forty years of marriage and we couldn't be happier. Isn't that right, darling?"

She gazed into his eyes wistfully and stroked his cheek. "Absolutely not."

Vlad beamed. "You see?" He held his wife's hand. "I have asked the maid to bring some refreshments for us, so please make yourselves comfortable, browse the bookshelves, I'm sure she'll be here any minute. Meanwhile, I'll visit with my beautiful Angelika." He took her in his arms and made out with her right in front of a delighted audience. Some of the women could be heard sighing.

Ah, so far so good.

Only moments later, the maid rolled a metal cart into the room laden with pastries.

The guests swarmed around the cart oohing and aahing. Some of the guys looked like they were ready to ooh and aah over the maid.

"Thank you for bringing our snacks, Violeta," Angelika said.

At that, Violeta walked over to Vlad and cocked her head, offering him her neck.

"Yes, thank you for our snacks, Violeta." Vlad opened his mouth wide to show his fangs and sank them into the maid's ivory skin. A small spurt of blood trickled down her neck as he fed.

The crowd gasped. Angelika simply stood and watched.

Enric laughed. "I'll never figure out how they do that."

Vlad pulled away from the maid and offered her the handkerchief from his pocket. She dabbed the blood from her neck in front of the shocked visitors and then left the room.

"Yum, that was delicious. As soon as you've had your fill of the pastries, we'll take you through our dungeon."

Angelika left her husband's side and waited at the doorway.

The dungeon, huh? Adrian had memories of the dungeon back when the villagers weren't so willing. The heavy chains and manacles were probably still embedded in the wall.

Maura?

She answered him telepathically from hall. *Hi, Adrian. I'm sorry. We got engrossed in conversation. What did we miss?*

Oh, nothing really. Why don't you take Jordan up to our bedroom and finish your conversation. I'll let you know when the tour is over.

Hell, no! We don't want to miss the whole thing.

Well, they're about to go into the dungeon. I don't think you two should see that.

Are you kidding? We wouldn't miss it!

Maura's stomach growled as she dragged Jordan down the hall. Hopefully some of those goodies she had seen the maid wheel into the library were left. Rounding the corner, Maura spotted the cart still containing some pastries and didn't want to miss out.

Just as she was about to make a beeline for the plate of lemon squares, the group began filing out.

"Excuse me," she said repeatedly after bumping into people who were too zombie-like to get out of her way. Why did they all look like they had seen more than dust and cobwebs?

Maybe she and Jordan could dash in there quickly and grab a few treats without missing the dungeon tour. Adrian stood beside his father at the front of the room and looked uncomfortable. Something about the two of them together seemed odd. Not that they didn't look like father and son. They did, but she sensed something fundamentally different in their natures. Vlad was grinning and stood with his chest puffed out, like he was pleased as punch. Adrian's shoulders slumped and he was shaking his head. Maybe she could distract him?

Hey, lover. Grab me a couple of those lemon squares, will you? I don't think we should tour the dungeon on empty stomachs. She even managed to chuckle telepathically. She heard Adrian sigh, but he swiped the whole plate and began making his way toward her. His eyes betrayed resignation, but she didn't think it was with her.

When he reached her she asked, "Is everything all right, Adrian?"

"What is it you would say with sarcasm — peachy keen?"

"Maybe my mother would have said that." Maura grabbed a gooey pastry and stuffed it into her mouth. "Yum." The lemony flavor, tempered with just the right amount of sugar, retained a little of its tartness and fresh scent, yet wasn't overwhelmed with sweetness.

Adrian smiled and kissed the top of her head as he handed the plate to Jordan. Maura snagged another pastry as it went by.

"I didn't realize I was so famished."

Adrian slapped his forehead. "You must be starving. Let me take you to the hotel for dinner."

"Now?"

"Of course. You haven't had anything since breakfast and you, well…"

"Ralphed it on the side of the road?"

"Right." He murmured into her ear, "And perhaps we could find a room there and…"

Maura felt her nipples tighten as she leaned in to kiss him. He yanked her into his arms and delivered a long, strong, passionate kiss. He was just beginning to tell her via telepathy how he wanted to caress her breasts, suckle her and fuck her all night long when they were rudely interrupted.

"Adrian, my son. You must savor your lovely mistress later. I have a big surprise for you downstairs and I wouldn't want you to get distracted." Vlad waggled his eyebrows at Maura. "Although I can't blame you for wanting to make love to such a pretty, redheaded, voluptuous woman."

The word "lecher" popped into Maura's brain and she immediately chastised herself for the thought. *Your mistress? Is that what he thinks I am?*

Adrian grabbed her hand and kissed her knuckles. "To tell you the truth, Father, I'd rather spend as much time as I can with my beloved."

Maura sighed and melted.

"Nonsense, you have eternity to enjoy each other. How often do you get to come home and see—" Vlad stopped what he was saying and wagged a finger. "I almost gave away the surprise."

"Father, just tell me what it is."

"I will not." He wedged himself between the young lovers and put an arm around each of them guiding them out of the library. "Your mother would never forgive me. She's been planning this surprise since you told us you were coming here with someone special."

Maura heard Adrian curse under his breath even though he may have been trying to do it quietly.

Angelika led the group now and Enric announced the various rooms as they passed. "This is the dining room. As you can see, the family doesn't use it much. Their dinners are alvays ready in pretty little packages." He laughed out loud. It appeared the group got the joke but their chuckles were more subdued.

When they arrived at the kitchen, Angelika said, "Excuse me for just a minute. I haven't had dinner yet and I need to see the chef for a bite to eat. You can wait right here."

As soon as she disappeared into the kitchen, the group crowded around the doorway. After a few seconds, Maura noticed them wincing. Enric grinned and shook his head in amazement. "Someday I'm going to figure out how they do that. They must have a bag of pig's blood behind their fangs or something. I know they vouldn't feed on humans."

Vlad faced the audience and winked, "Can't give away the family secrets, my friend."

Jordan folded her arms. "How do you know? How long have you been giving these tours, Enric?"

"Long enough to know ve are all perfectly safe. Don't you vorry. I vould never take you into any real danger."

Roland muttered, "Seems pretty real to me."

Vlad strolled up to Enric and clapped him on the back. "You're absolutely right, Enric. Your group is in no danger from my wife and I, but I can't guarantee what will happen to them in the dungeon." He said it so joyfully! She was amazed that the group dutifully followed Vlad toward a heavy wooden door with at least three rusty-looking iron locks.

As Maura and Adrian passed the kitchen, she hung back. Peeking inside, she spotted a handsome young man dressed in a white chef's uniform, complete with the tall, poufy hat. He had been lying down, but rose and hopped off the long metal prep counter. Angelika was dabbing her mouth daintily with a cloth napkin, blood spots evident on the napkin and on the chef's neck.

Are they actually feeding on the maid and the chef? What the hell is going on, Adrian?

He sighed. *I might as well tell you, Maura. The servants are willing, but they're food. My parents need blood to survive and the servants are poor villagers who have nowhere else to go.*

They kill them?

No. Absolutely not. They feed on them a little bit at a time. They'd never kill them. They need them to live.

What do the servants get out of it?

A place to live and a lot of money. The work isn't hard, so they probably consider it a decent job. They are even treated like part of the family.

Adrian stood behind Maura and kissed her neck. "Don't worry, darling. I won't leave your side. I already promised I wouldn't let anything happen to you."

"How many servants do they have?" she whispered

"Only three that I know of at the moment. They have a gardener too."

"They have a gardener? Someone should be fired."

Adrian chuckled. "Yes. My reaction was the same as yours."

"So you're saying this is a good thing for everyone involved. It helps the local economy or something?"

"Or something."

Unexpectedly, Adrian reached over and squeezed her breast.

"Hmm... Let's skip the dungeon, Maura. There are much pleasanter things awaiting us elsewhere."

What? Forget it.

"Maura, please...I'm getting edgy about what kind of hell awaits us down there. Besides I can't wait another minute to make love to you."

She laid her head to rest on his shoulder. *I know, lover. But as your father said, we have lots of time for that. Maybe not eternity but…*

Adrian inhaled sharply and blew out a long breath, as if trying to hold his temper.

"Oh, stop it. You're being silly!"

A massive iron key ring clanked in Vlad's hands as he unlocked the dungeon door.

Chapter Thirteen

ॐ

Adrian heaved a giant audible sigh. He wasn't going to spoil Maura's fun and he did want to test her to see if she could handle whatever might come up, right? The dungeon door squeaked an ominous greeting as Vlad heaved it open.

Adrian waited to be the last one in line before descending into the dank and moldy darkness. He had to bend over to fit through the door and his posture remained slumped on the way down the rickety stairs. The quiet murmurings of nervous excitement among the guests spiked his own anxiety.

Echoing growls from below stopped the parade in its tracks. Maura turned and grabbed on to Adrian's jacket, frantically searching his pocket for her pencil "stake".

Grateful for his vampiric eyesight, he was able to pierce the blackness and see what the crowd was reacting to. *Oh bloody hell, it was only a dog. Wait a minute. It's not just any dog!*

"Strudel" Adrian cried. He pushed his way through the crowd and ran to his boyhood best friend.

"I told you I had a surprise for you, son." When Adrian rose, holding the adorable black Yorkshire terriera souvenir of his father's trip to Scotland, he enjoyed a thorough, tongue-lapping face bath. Vlad clapped him on the back.

"But how…?"

"We turned him as soon as you left home. Of course, he ran away for a few decades, probably trying to follow you. But he came back, just as we knew you'd eventually come back too. You had to go find yourself or something. No hard feelings son, see? We're just delighted you're home, even if it took over five hundred years."

More than a few tourists gasped. Roland was the one brave enough to speak up. "Five hundred years, Adrian? Does that mean you're a..."

"Vampire? Yes, my friend."

Roland's eyes widened. "We just thought you were related to someone who worked here, or maybe it really was your family's castle but there were actors that play vampires. I never imagined the real thing even existed!"

"I'm afraid so."

Vlad bristled. "'Afraid so?' Aren't you adjusted to the wonders of this privilege yet? I thought that's what you set off to do."

"I'm sorry to disappoint you, Father. I set off to find a cure. And I have."

Adrian set Strudel down. He trotted over to his bowl of pig's blood and began lapping it up happily.

Vlad turned to see the stunned tourists, forced his frown into a jovial expression and laughed. "Yes, well, you can tell me all about that later. Not that I doubt you or anything."

Adrian rolled his eyes.

Enric clapped his hands twice. "What incredible luck, people! We have a real vampire on the tour with us! Perhaps you can be persuaded to add your own unique insights as we travel along, Adrian?"

"I'm sorry. I won't be continuing on from here. I've decided to stay with my family for a long overdue visit."

"After a five-hundred-year absence I can certainly understand that you vould. And Maura? Is she staying vid you?"

Maura stepped forward and took Adrian's hand. "Yes, I am."

That small comforting gesture helped Adrian relax. Well, that and no prisoners chained to the walls or in the iron maiden. Whew.

Enric clapped his hands. "People. May I have your attention? As you can see, now that our eyes have adjusted to the darkness, there are two cells on the left-hand side. The first one is empty. You're welcome to go inside to see how it would feel to be imprisoned down here. The second cell holds the gift shop. As soon as our host lights some candles, you can go in and purchase your souvenirs."

Gift shop?

Curious, Adrian turned to Maura. "I have to see this."

"So do I."

They walked hand in hand past the first cell that contained only straw, to the second where Vlad was lighting several tapers in brass stands that looked like they belonged in church. With the candles flickering in the darkness, causing shadows to bounce around the rock walls, the cell looked almost beautiful.

Then Adrian focused on the contents and groaned. A glass case held a multitude of plastic fangs. A basket contained several wine bottles labeled "Blood" in Romanian, German and English. Miniature balls and chains made into cheap key rings hung from a metal stand along with trays of postcards.

"Let's get out of here, Maura."

"Can't I look at the postcards?"

Adrian snagged one, handed it to her and said, "Here. I have to go back upstairs before I 'hurl' as you would say."

Strudel wagged his scruffy tail as they passed by him. Maura thought he was the cutest little dog she had ever seen.

"Don't you want to bring your doggie upstairs?"

"Not now. I have something else in mind for us."

She followed Adrian up and out of the dungeon. He grabbed her hand and ran down the long corridor past the kitchen, dining room, library and bogus paintings.

"I'll bet I know where you're taking me. Race you!"

Adrian turned enough to flash his winning smile and then took off—literally. He actually flew up the stairs and disappeared.

"Cheater!" she called out.

By the time she made it to their room, Adrian lay naked on the bed, sporting his huge erection. "Did you yell something at me back there?"

Maura began stripping as quickly as possible. "I called you a cheater."

"I'd never cheat on you, Maura." Warmth filled her to the marrow. When she pared down to her burgundy corset, Adrian's eyes bulged.

"Whoa. You are gorgeous. Let me look for a while."

She couldn't help being somewhat self-conscious about her body. She guessed all women were to some extent. Her thighs were a little thicker than she'd like. Her tummy a little more rounded than she'd like. But of course, she'd like to look like a *Playboy* bunny, so perhaps she wasn't being very realistic.

Adrian's hungry gaze traveled over every inch of her and then he spun his finger meaning he wanted her to turn around.

Oh Lord. Can a woman suck in her butt?

She turned around in a circle and began to unlace her bodice.

"No. Let me."

He patted the mattress and she lay next to him. With his teeth, he pulled the lacings to free her breasts.

Her body already knew his touch, the feel of his mouth on her nipples, his seductive scent. She shivered with barely controlled anticipation as he awoke every succulent desire inside her.

He peeled back the edges of burgundy and lace imprisoning her body. The cool air whispered across her breasts and her eyes closed on a sigh. He ran his hand down the side of her throat in a caress so tender it was lighter than a breeze.

"Adrian..." she whispered, sounding hoarse, almost breathless.

"Yes, my love?" He nuzzled her ear and planted nibbling kisses downward to the pulse point over her carotid artery. Her heart answered, beating wildly.

"I—" Totally lost in desire, she postponed whatever it was she had wanted to say. It must not have been important. Certainly not as important as the texture and heat of his tongue.

Now with no barrier to the downward slide of his hand, she tingled with the smooth pressure on each of her breasts in turn. He molded and shaped them as if they were clay...or putty. She was most definitely putty in his hands.

He slid his big hand beneath her back and lifted her enough to slip the finely boned corset out from under. As he draped it over the end table, he rolled close enough to bump his prominent arousal up against her hip.

She reached for it and enclosed his hard shaft in her hand. He leaned back and groaned in what sounded like excruciating pleasure. Maura scrambled to his side where she covered his cock with her mouth. A rush of air escaped his lungs and his erection jerked with life.

She hadn't been shy about giving blowjobs in the past and thought she was pretty good at it. This time she wanted to be perfect.

"I'm going to make love to your cock. Lie still and let me do whatever I want."

Adrian opened his eyes and leveled his hooded stare at her, betraying a mixture of intense heat and wonder. Maura smiled wickedly and licked the underside, from scrotum to head. He reared back and almost growled. His hard, beautiful cock took over the job of staring her in the face as he lay back with eyes closed.

She caressed his pelvis while she licked him languorously. Soon, she scooted a little farther down and lapped at his balls like two scoops of ice cream.

Adrian writhed and reached for her.

She paused just long enough to whisper, "Not yet. Do I have to tie you up?"

"You could try." He chuckled.

Cupping his balls, she continued to play with them. She kissed each one and then concentrated on the spot at the base where they met his shaft. He sucked in a breath.

Maura took his steel-hard cock in her hand and softly caressed it with her cheek, then slid his arousal across her slightly opened lips, just tasting it and then she caressed it with the other cheek.

"Maura, stop."

"No. I haven't even sucked you yet."

Starting at the base of his shaft she covered his cock with hot, wet kisses. Lapping at every inch, she moistened him making him even harder. At last, she slid her mouth over the tip and swirled tight circles around it, spreading his pre-cum. With the tip of her tongue, she played with the hole and Adrian moaned.

Sucking the tip, she slid her mouth down his slick shaft, dragging it back up slowly with even more suction. With her hand now free, she stroked his ass, eventually concentrating on the crack. When she inserted her finger in his hole, he gasped.

"Gods, Maura!"

She had intended to keep sucking him, while fucking his hole with her finger, but he began to shudder.

"That's it," he cried. Grabbing her beneath her armpits he lifted her face to his. "I'm so fucking hard, I'm ready to come."

"Why didn't you?"

"I want to make you feel as good as you've made me feel tonight. Maura, I'm going to fuck you now." He flipped her onto her back and tested her wetness. She spread her legs and reached for him.

Adrian climbed over her extended leg and positioned himself. "I promise you can finish what you started later on and I won't skip foreplay next time, my darling, but I simply must…"

With one thrust, he entered her. She grasped him around his back and he sighed with relief. Maura could swear she felt him pulsating inside her. They held one another as he began pumping.

Maura felt his cock fill her to the core as she closed her eyes and moaned in bliss. "Oh, God, it feels so good."

"Open your eyes, *cherie*."

She willed them to open at least halfway and found her gaze locked in his intense stare.

"Look down. Watch me fucking you." He raised his body enough so she could look down, past her erect nipples to the spot where their bodies met. Never had she felt the intense connection she felt as he undulated in and out of her — mating with her. Every stroke was an internal caress. Her heart almost burst in joy.

Intense sensations flooded her, reaching every nerve ending. She reared back and moaned. Adrian slipped one hand under her back and braced himself on that elbow. He reached for her clit and she gasped when his fingers found it. He kept up his steady rhythm, thrusting, pulling and rubbing until white heat filled her core, igniting climax. She forced her mouth against Adrian's muscular arm and screamed as she shattered in ecstasy. At the same time, Adrian jerked and bucked with his own orgasm. He roared and rode his pleasure to the last aftershock.

With one arm still beneath her, he completely enveloped Maura in his loving embrace.

"I love you, Adrian."

"And I you. You're mine, *cherie*. Forever." And then he sank his fangs into her neck.

* * * * *

"Did you…? I mean, am I…?"

"I know what you're trying to ask and I don't blame you for thinking it. No, darling. You're not a vampire. I didn't turn you, but you turned me inside out last night. I had hoped to make love to you repeatedly all night long, but after I drank from you, you fell into a deep, exhausted sleep. I hadn't intended to give you my love bite, but the passion we shared forced my canines to grow. I'm afraid I did what came naturally."

"It wasn't painful after the initial jab. Once you were sucking it felt kinda neat. Like my veins were fluttering. She stretched and yawned. "I feel like I slept for a week. What time is it?"

"The sun is up. I was hoping you'd awaken soon. I can feel the need for some of my special beverage."

"The Blood of the Warrior?"

"Yes. I'm afraid I need it."

"Why didn't you just get up and drink some?"

Adrian swept a stray red lock behind her ear. "I was watching you sleep."

Maura sighed. "You are just about the sexiest, most romantic vampire I've ever met."

Adrian raised his eyebrows. "Just about?"

She chuckled and stroked his biceps. "Okay, you're numero uno, but don't go getting a big head."

Adrian glanced down at his hard-on. "Too late."

Maura batted him away playfully. "Go have your breakfast. Play with your dog. I'll be here when you get back.

176

Thanks to you, I feel punch drunk—like I could nap for another eight or ten hours."

Adrian raised her hand to his lips and planted a long, gentle kiss on her palm. "Sleep then, darling. I'll be back to check on you soon. I imagine my parents are in their coffins by now, but you never know. They said something about more guests arriving while we're here. I'm curious to know whom they invited."

Maura ran her fingers through her tousled hair. "Oh, fabulous. I must look dreadful this morning."

"You look beautiful. I'll be back soon." Adrian leaned over, gave her a peck on the lips and rose from the bed.

He wasn't kidding about his hard-on. She figured it was just morning wood and a trip to the john would ease it without her help. Besides, she was still a bit woozy. Is this how it would feel any time he fed from her? No wonder he was reluctant.

Adrian stepped into his black jeans and after wrestling his thick, erect member into them and zipping them up, he grabbed a bottle of wine from his suitcase. As he was leaving, she watched him from the back. His butt fit the curve of his pants perfectly. His back muscles rippled with easy strength, the kind she knew any time she was cradled in his arms.

Just before he opened the door, he turned to her and said, "Last night was very special."

A broad smile stretched her lips. "It was for me too."

His answering smile glowed in his eyes and he gently closed the door as he left.

Maura sighed, deeply content and happy.

"Way to go, Susan!"

She jerked her head to the left. *Oh, hell. Why are you here, Devil?*

177

"I just wanted to congratulate you. You may have gone all the way to friggin' Romania to find your vamp from New York, but you had to do it your way and you did it."

Yes, I found him and we're falling deeply in love. She sighed again.

"If you had listened to me I could have saved you loads of money in airfare, hotels and that useless tour."

Money isn't the issue here. You can't put a price on love. Besides, it's a tax write-off.

A familiar flutter of wings fanned her right shoulder. Maura rolled her eyes to the right. *Naturally you had to show up too, Angel. What do you want?*

She crossed her arms, a stern expression on her face. "You won't be able to write off anything if you don't enter something in that little journal of yours."

Oh, crap. I forgot about the journal.

"That doesn't surprise me. You've been busy!" The devil laughed with delight as his red belly jiggled.

Well, so much for sleeping in today. I've got to get up and think of something job-related to record in the journal.

"Don't fib, now. You could get caught."

"Yeah, sure. Just talk about how you've been fucking your brains out with a vampire ever since you arrived. That'll go over well. You might get an exemption next year for being in the crazy-house."

Oh, leave it alone, both of you. I'll figure it out. Now leave. I have to get out of this bed and I don't want you watching.

"Ha! Like we're not watching whenever we feel like it."

"Devil! Don't taunt her."

"Who's taunting?"

Maura closed her eyes, slapped her hands over them and waited. When she didn't hear any more from her watchdogs, she opened her eyes. They were gone.

Hey, it worked! I'll have to remember that for next time. She
was sure there would be a next time too. She was surprised the
angel didn't give her a hard time about last night...or the night
before...or the night before that.

Maura smiled as she rose, still feeling the remainder of
deep fulfillment between her thighs. She pattered to her
suitcase, pulled on her robe and proceeded to fish out her
journal.

* * * * *

Adrian had come downstairs to an unexpected
inquisition. Angelika had been pacing back and forth at the
bottom of the stairs, waiting for him. Now seated in the
receiving parlor with his parents, he waited for Violeta to
bring him a wineglass from the kitchen.

Vlad cocked his head. "Are you sure you wouldn't rather
snack on Violeta this morning, Adrian? I imagine you and
your mortal worked up quite an appetite last night."

"Mortal? You knew?"

"Of course we knew. You think we can't smell the
difference between our own kind and a mere mortal? What's
the matter with you? Have you forgotten everything about
your heritage?"

Adrian adjusted in his chair, trying to get comfortable. It
was a losing battle since his discomfort seemed to be what his
father wanted.

Angelika rose from her seat on the couch. "I'll return with
the rest of our guests."

"Who else is coming?"

"We've called your brothers."

Adrian groaned. All he remembered about his brothers
was the torture they enjoyed inflicting on each other and
mostly on him. He was the only one who didn't want to be

turned. In fact, he wasn't entirely sure his parents didn't turn him anyway just so he'd be able to defend himself.

"How did you call them? I don't see any telephone poles up here."

Vlad crossed his arms. "We sent a message via carrier pigeon. Unlike some sons, our older ones left forwarding addresses."

Bracing himself for the worst, he faced the door with dread and waited for the parade of strange siblings from his youth.

Damian entered first, a psychotic look in his eyes and evil grin on his face. Nope. Hadn't changed a bit.

Boris, still huge, lumbered in behind him. He shot a look of contempt at Adrian, although, with a lazy eye, it was easy to avoid his glare. He flopped onto a thin wooden chair, which collapsed beneath him. Damian laughed like a hyena as his brother lay on the pile of kindling.

Perhaps, if he was lucky, Vilhelm, the oldest and cruelest of the brothers wouldn't come. But his luck wasn't with him at all today and Vilhelm walked in as all hell was about to break loose. Boris was up and ready to smash his fist into Damian's face. Damian stepped out of the way of his brother's blow with his vampiric speed and Boris punched the air.

"Boys!" Vlad transported himself between them in milliseconds.

Angelika entered slowly and gracefully. "Don't tell me they've started in on each other, already."

Adrian looked from his father to his mother. "So it would appear. Whose good idea was this anyway?"

"Hey, get a load of the runt." Damian laughed. "It looks like he managed to grow some balls after all this time."

"Behave, all of you!" Angelika stepped away from the door. "We have one more guest and I don't want you behaving badly in front of her."

Her? Who could that be? Don't tell me they dragged Maura into this.

Sashaying around the corner, he caught a glimpse of black spike heels and fishnet stockings first. Then a sparkling red gown. And…bloody hell! Vampirella encased in it like a hundred and seventy pounds of sausage in a one-hundred-twenty-pound sack. Her voluptuous bosom was forced up so far it spilled over. The waist nipped in and generous hips stretched the bottom before a high slit eased the pressure of her thighs.

She tossed her bleached-blonde head and some of her locks swished over her shoulder. In her breathy alto voice, she said, "Hello, lover. Why haven't you come to see me, lately?"

"By the gods, Mother. Why did you invite her? Our relationship ended hundreds of years ago."

"Perhaps it shouldn't have?" Angelika sat on the sofa next to Vlad and placed her hands on her knees. "Did you know she's kept in touch with us all these years? She's been more of a daughter than you've been a son."

Adrian jumped up and began to storm out. Boris blocked the door, picked Adrian up by the collar and threw him back into the overstuffed chair he had been sitting in.

"What is this? Some kind of intervention?"

Vlad inhaled deeply. "Call it whatever you like, son. The truth is Vampirella has never gotten over you and we think you two should give it another try."

He heard Vampirella sniff and turned just enough to see her dabbing at dry, invisible tears with a lace handkerchief.

"Bloody hell, people! She's just acting, can't you see that? You've no right to tell me with whom I should associate."

Boris nodded. "Yup, he grew a pair of balls all right. That doesn't mean we can't bust them, Adrian."

Vilhelm sneered. "Don't be fooled by him. I say he still has the fangs of a chicken."

Damian let out another chilling laugh. "I curse his veins."

Adrian contracted his hands into fists. "You all have hearts of dust."

His brothers began to advance on him. A split second before they pounced, Vlad flew to Adrian's aid and wedged his body between them. Hard punches landed everywhere. Adrian merely shielded himself as he did when he was boy. He wasn't going to fight back until someone split his lip.

"That's it," Adrian roared. Like a whirling dervish, he landed blow after blow, hearing an "oomph" here and an "oww" there. He picked up one body that turned out to be Damian and tossed him like a sack of potatoes against the wall. Next, he heaved Vilhelm over his head and he went skidding out the door. At last he thought he had Boris within his reach and delivered a brutal sucker punch to the chest. An unmistakable cracking sound followed as ribs broke. As soon as his bull-red vision cleared, he realized to his horror that the figure doubled over and crumpling before him was his father. As Vlad hit the floor, Angelika screamed.

Chapter Fourteen

‮ဢ‬

Maura noticed disturbing noises from the floor below. When she heard a thud and a scream, she dressed quickly, ran a brush through her hair and dashed downstairs. She didn't see anyone immediately so she ran down the corridor and skidded to a stop in front of the receiving parlor.

The oddest collection of people she had ever seen bent over a fallen body. But where was Adrian?

A woman resembling Mae West turned toward her and looked her over from top to bottom.

"Is this the mortal trollop who ruined my eternity and stole my Adrian?"

The rest of the assembly twisted their heads and glared at Maura, obvious hostility in their eyes and on their faces.

"What happened? Where's Adrian?" Maura demanded.

Angelika straightened her posture. "He was the only one able to handle the sunlight, so he downed half a bottle of that foolish wine of his and took off to find a vampire-friendly doctor. Vlad's been hurt."

A monstrously large man with a lazy eye added, "He thought he was punching me, but my father got between us. Now if he moves, his ribs could puncture his heart and he could die."

Another man who bore the family resemblance, but wore what looked like a permanent sneer narrowed his eyes and advanced menacingly toward her. "It's all your fault. We wouldn't have fought if he hadn't said he was going to waste himself on a worthless mortal. Now our dear father is mortally wounded in an immortal kind of way."

Vlad spoke up from the floor between gasps. "I'm not dead yet, Vilhelm. Now remember your mother's promise. Don't make a liar out of her."

The third brother, with psychotic-looking eyes, turned sharply toward Angelika. "Why did you have to promise the family wouldn't touch her? I want to snap her head from her body and ram it up her—"

"Stop it," Angelika ordered.

The Mae West-y woman sashayed over and dangled her left hand with long, black fingernails in front of Maura's face. "I'm not family...yet." Her finger descended and landed sharply on her, scratching a path down her arm before Maura could move away.

"Ow. What's wrong with you? How could any of this be my fault? I was upstairs writing in my journal."

The psycho brother laughed like a madman. "A journal? Stupid mortals. They record everything even though it'll be long forgotten in the blink of an eye."

The one Vlad had called Vilhelm stalked toward the door. "Perhaps we can't touch her, but we can certainly touch that diary. She may have recorded what she did to bewitch our brother."

Maura gasped. "You leave that journal right where it is!" *Holy crap. I wrote about what a fantastic lover he is—and about how he bit me!*

He cocked his head to the side. "What foolish bravery." Then he left the room in the direction of the stairs.

"So what's the trollop's name?" The bleached-blonde creature didn't seem to be speaking to anyone in particular, so Maura answered.

"I'm not a trollop and my name is Maura. Who are you?"

"I'm Vampirella and Adrian's betrothed to me."

Maura jammed her hands on her hips and leaned toward the misguided sexpot. "Says who?"

184

"She's feisty. Could be fun. When I get better."

Angelika bristled. "Forget it, Vlad. You won't be fucking Adrian's current mistress."

Fucking? Me? What the hell?

The bigger brother smiled at her. At least, she thought so. Hard to say which eye he was looking out of. "I wouldn't mind fucking her before he gets back."

"Oh no you don't!" Suddenly Maura realized what Vlad's initial drooling stare had been about. Apparently he not only fed from the mortals, but he screwed them too — and Angelika knew about it. Ick! Swingers. The two remaining brothers both looked her over like they were about to drool.

Vampirella spoke up. "Perhaps we should lock her in the dungeon for her own safety?"

"But Strudel hasn't been fed yet," Vlad said.

Maura rolled her eyes. "Oh. Perfect."

Vampirella grabbed Maura by the wrist and dragged her kicking and screaming out of the parlor and down the hall to the dungeon door. "Don't worry. I'll get the maid to bring a bowl of blood for him," she called over her shoulder. Mumbling under her breath she added, "If I remember."

Angelika called after them. "The keys are in the kitchen. Bring them to me as soon as everything's taken care of."

Vampirella had no problem gripping Maura's arm with one hand and working the locks with the other. One push and Maura went ladder surfing. She landed with a thump on her bottom, then Vampirella broke the ladder in two. Other than stinging from a few splinters, she seemed to be unhurt.

Maura heard Strudel growling, but she couldn't see a thing.

"Nice puppy. Nice doggie." She hoped she could find the cell and close the iron door before Strudel made breakfast out of her.

Adrian, help! Where are you?

Oddly enough, Strudel stopped growling and began to whimper. Was he reacting to Maura's mental cry for help from his beloved owner? Because she was connected to Adrian was she also connected to his dog?

Without further hesitation, Maura stood up and dashed toward the cell.

Wait a minute. There's wine in the gift shop!

Hoping she'd be spared for another two or three seconds, she pivoted toward the gift shop and ran for the only escape she could think of. Oblivion.

Strudel had apparently stopped feeling sorry for Maura or himself and bolted after her, barking and nipping at her heels.

* * * * *

Vampirella paced across the broken stone floor and dusty rugs in front of the oak entry. She had to come up with some kind of plan to lure Adrian away from this inferior mortal that he seemed to prefer over her. Of all the abominable insults!

She flopped onto an old stuffed chair and coughed when a cloud of dust rose and covered her face. While she was squinting and waving the dust away, Vilhelm tromped down the stairs with Maura's journal.

Wearing an evil grin when he spotted Vampirella, he stopped and leaned on the bottom of the banister. "You're not going to believe this."

"Be careful, Vilhelm. If you tell me something to hate this woman more than I already do, I'll drag her up from the dungeon in pieces and let you have your way with whatever's left of her."

Vilhelm raised his eyebrows. "Sounds like fun, but first, you should know that she's apparently on a shopping trip."

"More like a stealing trip from my vantage point."

Vilhelm shrugged. "I don't know, Vampirella. This appears to be nothing more than a catalogue of purchases, time spent shopping, traveling and plans for future purchases and where she intends to look for them."

"Let me see that." Vampirella stood and brushed the dust from her sparkling red gown, then marched over to Vilhelm and ripped the journal out of his hand. She glanced at the first few pages and turned to the last one Maura had written. "Well, if Adrian manages to get her away from here alive, at least I'll have her itinerary." She slammed the book shut.

Vilhelm reached for it. "Let me put it back where I found it so she won't know you're coming for her."

"Then when she and Adrian relax, thinking they're safe, I'll look for a moment when the bitch is alone."

"And pounce!"

They both grinned. While she was handing the book back to Vilhelm, a couple of folded pages fell out of the back and fluttered to the floor.

"What's this?" Vampirella unfolded the papers and gasped at the title.

"What is it?" Vilhelm grabbed the pages from her limp hand and read the caption.

"Mortal/Immortal Relationships. A Code of Honor!" He reared back and let out a booming evil laugh that echoed all over the entry chamber.

* * * * *

Adrian returned with the only doctor he could find and the man wasn't exactly willing or cooperative. But Maura! If anything happened to her, he wouldn't be able to forgive himself. He couldn't help thinking about how he had left her vulnerable. Angelika had promised no one would touch her. Was that good enough? He didn't trust his brothers not to terrorize her somehow. He should have put a lock on the door to her room so she couldn't even invite them in.

187

Adrian set the doctor down in front of the doors and steadied him until he could stand without staggering.

"What did you do to me? How did we get here?"

"No time to explain." Pulling on the doors, he was frustrated when they didn't open. There was no time to wait for Violeta to mosey down the hall, so he simply ripped the door off its hinges.

The doctor's eyes bugged open and he froze.

"Come on," Adrian demanded.

"I—I..."

Adrian picked up the short, gray-haired man and carried him to the parlor.

The onlookers stood back enough for the doctor to approach Vlad, still lying on the cold, hard floor.

"This is my father. You will attend to him immediately."

Adrian spun on his heel and dashed for the stairs. He met Vilhelm on the landing halfway up. "Why aren't you with Father? You'd better not have done anything to Maura."

"I didn't touch her. Mother promised the family wouldn't and we didn't."

Then Adrian saw the evil gleam he remembered so well glitter in his brother's eyes.

"Vampirella didn't make any such promise, though."

Adrian gasped. "She wouldn't dare. She knows I'd never forgive her."

Vilhelm shrugged and continued down the stairs.

Adrian used his vampiric speed to reach the room he and Maura had shared the night before. A vision of the best sex he had experienced in his nearly six hundred years on earth popped into his mind as he yanked open the door.

She was gone.

"Bloody hell!"

Adrenaline pumped through his body. Rushing to the parlor faster than he had flown before, he braced himself in the doorway and shouted, "Where is she? What have you done with her?"

Angelika looked up and hesitated.

A lump rose to Adrian's throat. "Mother?"

"She's fine, dear. Your brothers were starting to intimidate her, so Vampirella took her to the dungeon for her own protection."

Vampirella smiled like the passive-aggressive fiend she was, waved to him from the corner and pointed to her cleavage. "Here are the keys, lover. Come and get them."

"I'm not your lover." He ignored the keys popping out of her bodice and dashed down the hall.

Vampirella called after him, "Oh, you might want to feed Strudel while you're down there. I was going to, but with all the excitement I got distracted and forgot."

Adrian's anxiety turned to full-blown panic. How could she have trapped his beloved in the dungeon with a vampire dog that hadn't been fed?

He ripped the locks off the dungeon door, yanked it open and jumped to the bottom of the stairs in one fluid motion.

Maura's voice! He heard her making some weird noises. The sound was coming from the back of the dungeon. She wasn't screaming. Thank the gods!

He strode toward her voice and stopped suddenly. Is she singing? And is that Strudel, howling?

Adrian appeared at the entrance to the gift shop. Maura sat against the wall, legs splayed on the floor, waving a bottle of wine. Strudel lay at her side while she patted him.

Apparently she hadn't spotted Adrian yet, because she continued singing in a loud, slurred voice over the howling dog.

Twenty-eight bottles of wine on the floor.

Twenty-eight bottles of wine —
If one of those bottles should happen to pour,
Twenty-seven bottles of wine on the floor...

She tipped the bottle and a large splash of wine landed in front of Strudel. He stopped howling and eagerly lapped it up.

She giggled and scratched the scuff on the back of his neck. "Good doggie. Goooood doggie."

Adrian leaned against the open iron door and crossed his arms, smiling.

When she finally looked up at him, she raised the wine bottle in his direction and shouted, "Daddy's home!"

Adrian managed to keep his chuckle silent and stated, "You're drunk."

Maura giggled and poured another puddle of wine in front of Strudel. "Yup. An' your little dog too."

Adrian shook his head and scooped Maura up into his arms. "Let's get you out of here."

Maura suddenly remembered that she was mad at him and wriggled until he almost dropped her. "Oh, no you don't, stupid-head. You broke your promise." She weaved and staggered. "How could you leave me alone here?" Reaching toward him she waved her hand in front of his face. "I missed. Stand still so I can slap you."

Strudel started to whimper.

"Come on, Maura. You can yell at me all you want after I get you out of here."

"Oh, okay..."

Adrian held her in his arms, about to fly her out of the dungeon.

She shook him loose again. "Wait a minute. What about your doggie? You aren't going to leave Strudel twice, are you?"

190

Adrian leaned back and looked at her as if she had lost her mind.

"He misses you. He missed you so much for so long! And a dungeon is no place to keep a dog. Let's take him with us."

Adrian chuckled and pulled her head to rest on his shoulder. He took in a deep breath and stroked her hair. "You have the biggest heart of anyone I know. But Strudel's a vampire now. He can't go out in the sun and he has to feed on blood."

"So? There's blood in the kitchen we can take with us and we'll cover his cage during the day."

"What cage?"

"The one we'll buy him. C'mon... Look at that widdle face." Maura blew a kiss toward Strudel.

Panting, with his red tongue hanging out, he appeared to be grinning.

Adrian rolled his eyes. "I must be as crazy as you are."

"Then we can take him?"

"Yes."

While Maura clapped her hands, Adrian picked up Strudel and flew him to the opening above. "Stay," he commanded. Strudel sat obediently and waited, wagging his tail.

Maura was next. She willingly held Adrian around his neck as he scooped her into his arms and took to the air, then set her down gently in the hallway.

"We should get Strudel some breakfast. He must be starving."

Adrian put an arm around her waist to help her walk to the kitchen. "The blood needs to warm up. I'll pour some into a bowl and we'll pack. Then we can go shopping for a cage and come back for him."

"Promise we'll come back for him?"

"I'll come back. You'll be safer somewhere else." Adrian pulled a bottle of red liquid from the refrigerator and found a bowl. "I'll want to check on my father anyway."

Maura watched him set the bowl in front of his dog and pat him with a contented smile on his face. "You have a good heart too, Adrian. Are you sure it isn't beating?"

His expression saddened, but he hid it quickly.

"Let's get our things together, Maura. I want to get you outside in the sun as soon as possible. You'll be safe there."

With the vampiric speed she was growing to hate, Adrian transported the two of them down the hall, past all of the lower rooms and up the stairs to their bedroom in a dizzying blur.

"Jeez, Adrian. If I didn't feel sick before, I do now."

"I'm sorry, *cherie*. It was necessary."

"Why? Do you really think your family would harm me? I know Vampirella wouldn't hesitate, but your parents?"

He didn't answer—just set her on the bed and as soon as she had her bearings, she stood and made her way to her suitcase. "I haven't had time to wash up, fix my hair, put on makeup…"

"You can do that later when we're comfortably settled elsewhere. Right now we should get our things and get out of here."

His voice was clipped and worry lines etched his forehead. Was he worried about being unable to protect her if his family ganged up on the two of them? Adrian never seemed like the type to run from anyone or anything. Well, okay, he had run during the Crusades, but who wouldn't? She pictured hordes on horseback with machetes bearing down on anyone who got in their way. Yup, sometimes running is the right thing to do.

She tossed the few things she had unpacked onto the bed. Next, she gathered her brush and makeup, tossed them into her purse, then grabbed her journal from the desk and zipped it back into the front pocket of her suitcase. When she looked up, Adrian was already standing by the door with his suitcases, his hand on the doorknob.

"Ready?" he asked.

"Sure, but where are we going and can we take a few minutes to get there this time?"

Adrian nodded, then looked at her sadly. "I'm sorry things tuned out this way."

"Don't get me wrong, you're not off the hook yet. You have a bit of explaining to do as soon as we can find a minute to relax."

He opened the door and said, "Come. We'll talk soon."

* * * * *

The hotel in the village seemed like the most logical place to go since she wasn't looking forward to being transported again. After a quick dash down the stairs and out the front door into the sunshine, Adrian let out a sigh of relief. "We're safe. For now."

Maura insisted on walking down the steep rocky hill even if she wove or staggered. He tucked his suitcase of wine under one arm and carried his clothes and hers in the other hand. She carried her shopping trip treasures and balanced her purse on her shoulder.

She took her time in order to keep her footing, but teetered nervously every so often on her way. Suddenly she heard the voice she had been half expecting since she and Strudel shared a few bottles of wine. How many? She had lost count.

"Well, Susan. What are you going to do now?"

Oh, frig. I knew you'd show up.

"Really? How did you know?"

Because I'm plastered.

"Yes, I know." The devil waved his hand in front of his nose as if the stink of wine was too much for him.

Oh give me a break. I can smell the whiskey on your breath too, you know.

"Whiskey? I smell like whiskey? Funny. I've had vodka, gin, brandy, rum, sherry and some Jell-O shots. No whiskey that I can remember." He shrugged. "But then, my memory is crap."

Tell me about it. You can't even remember my real name.

"Sure I can. Your name's Susan."

It's Maura.

"Oh, Maura, dear…"

She recognized the light soprano voice coming from her right side.

It was just a matter of time. What do you want, Angel?

"Nothing. I'm just keeping an eye on him." She pointed to the devil with her thumb.

So far he hasn't even tried to get me into trouble. He's only told me that he's had more to drink today than I can hold in a weekend and that my name is Susan.

"That doesn't surprise me. So what did you come here for, Devil?"

"You know? I really can't remember." He shrugged and disappeared.

"Good! My work is done." With that the angel disappeared too.

Maura rolled her eyes, grateful they had reached the bottom of the hill without her tripping over a rock or her own two feet and rolling to the bottom.

Chapter Fifteen

🔊

Adrian wondered what was wrong. She kept snapping her head from side to side and scowling.

"I think I'm beginning to sober up."

"What makes you say so?"

"Because I suddenly realize what an idiot I am."

He didn't know what to say. She had probably decided they couldn't make a relationship between them work or wondered why she had wanted to date a vampire in the first place. He wasn't quite ready to hear the word goodbye, but he wouldn't blame her for dumping him while she could still catch the bus out of town.

"Let's wait until we can sit down and get you some breakfast before we talk. All right?"

"There are some things we shouldn't discuss in front of the other hotel guests, Adrian. Maybe we can just sit outside for a while. Besides, the sun feels good — and safe."

He hung his head. She probably didn't want to break up with him in front of everyone and didn't even want to be seen with him after that. Perhaps he'd just get that covered cage for Strudel and fly himself and his dog back to New York after this fiasco.

Maura walked to a picnic table in partial shade and sat on the sunny side. Adrian set their suitcases down and sat across from her.

She leveled her gaze at him and without preliminaries launched right into it. "So what's this business about being betrothed?"

"That's a bunch of bull, Maura. Vampirella and I were never betrothed. My parents like her and maybe they said something about it after I left, but it means nothing. They don't tell me what to do or who to be with."

She looked down at the table and nodded. "Have you ever been married or betrothed to anyone?"

"No." He wondered why she was bothering to pursue this line of questioning if she was just going to dump his ass and get on with life.

"Do you see us ever becoming exclusive? I'm not talking about anything legal. I know that's not terribly practical for immortals."

Puzzled, he reached across the table for her hand. "Are you saying you want to pursue this relationship after what just happened to you?"

"Well, duh. I love you, Adrian. Like I said, I'm mad at you for leaving me when you said you wouldn't, but I don't want to throw the baby out with the bathwater."

Shock waves ripped through his body. "Baby? Whose baby?"

She took one look at his face and burst out laughing. "There's no infant in the oven, Adrian. It's just an expression."

She took his other hand and tenderly rubbed them. "You didn't know I was going to wake up and come downstairs looking for you. You didn't believe your family would try to hurt me. Why you trusted Vampirella if you knew she still loved you I don't understand, but...well, maybe I can. I've had boyfriends that wanted to be friends afterward. I've even believed and trusted one or two of them."

"Exactly. I thought she knew I'd only remain cordial if she treated you decently. I never thought she'd put you in the dungeon with a vampire dog that might be hungry. How did you befriend Strudel, anyway?"

"Easy. We had something in common."

196

Sometimes this woman confused the hell out of him. "Really? What could that be?"

"We both love you—and we were both waiting for you. It just seemed less lonely to wait together."

His spirit warmed and lifted. "You have something else in common too."

"What's that?"

"You both like red wine."

Maura giggled and the light that shone in her eyes told him she was back to her happy self. It was reassuring and frightening at the same time.

"Maura?"

"Yes?"

When he hesitated, she cocked her head to the side and squinted at him, as if trying to figure out what he wanted to say. He wasn't sure what he was about to say either. There was a question he wanted to ask, but he didn't have it completely thought out yet.

"I guess it's nothing."

She shrugged. "Whatever. Not to change the subject, but where can we find a cage for Strudel today?"

"You still want to drag a photosensitive dog that drinks blood around with us?"

"Hell, no. That would be cruel. I want to carry him around with us."

Adrian laughed and rose from the table. He jogged around it and when he reached the other side she stepped over the bench to meet him. He grabbed her in a tight embrace and kissed her for all he was worth. By the time he was able to ease up a little, she relaxed into his arms and opened her mouth for their tongues to meet.

Interrupted by voices from the direction of the hotel, their lips parted.

"Look, it's the lovebirds again." Jordan and Roland strolled toward them.

Contentment seeped into his marrow as Maura left her arms around his waist and nestled her head against his chest. Her body felt so warm and right resting there.

"You caught us," he called out.

When the other couple reached them, Jordan asked, "So are you really leaving the tour and staying with Adrian's family?" Jordan looked up the hill at the creepy-looking castle with trepidation.

"Not exactly. We're leaving the tour, but I've mapped out a new itinerary for some serious shopping and sightseeing. I haven't even asked Adrian about it yet, though." She chuckled and looked up at him. "I suppose I should do that, huh?"

"We can go wherever you like, *cherie*."

"I'm happy I met up with you again, Maura. I wanted to give you my address in London. We should keep in touch. Hey, if you're still in Europe after the tour, look me up and we can go shopping together!"

Maura let go of Adrian and reached for her purse. "I'd really like that. Let me give you my address in New York too. I can show you some fun places to shop right in SoHo where my store is." Both women extracted address books and swapped contact information.

* * * * *

Maura finally felt safe enough to let Adrian leave her shopping in the town of Codlea while he took the dog carrier they bought and went back for Strudel.

They picked out the largest, most comfortable cage they could find for their pet. Maura floated around the streets of Codlea in a loving haze, realizing that she and Adrian were becoming a couple. She had found her beloved and he seemed as committed to establishing a life together as she was.

A storefront window across the street caught her eye. The clothing in the window was exactly what she had been looking for and a large sign boasted "Made in Romania".

Perfect! Maura waited for a car to pass, then dashed across the street and paused a moment to admire the styles in the window close-up. One mannequin wore a long, black velvet coat with a wide, turned-up collar. It possessed that unmistakable vampire flavor that had attracted her attention first. Gorgeous! Next to it, another pale mannequin modeled an off-the-shoulder, three-quarter-length black dress trimmed with subtle red satin. A long dress of black and silver brocade sporting a thigh-high slit made the pale, thin mannequin appear even paler and thinner.

Surrounding the three costumes were all the accessories she could have hoped for. Spike-heeled, patent-leather boots and open-toe shoes. Belts of silver metal. Rings and jewelry of every description from ornate to antique to downright creepy.

Maura almost climaxed right on the street. Thinking she had hit the mother lode, she bounded inside. All around, she saw racks of beautiful clothes, but no employees and no real Goth styles. They must be in the back.

"Hello?"

When no one answered, she called out again a little louder. "Hellooo…"

She strolled through the shop, admiring what was on display and slowly made her way toward the back. When she reached the dressing rooms, they were dark. "Hmmm…that's strange."

A door opened and a large buxom woman with platinum blonde hair wearing a too tight black sequined gown with a thigh-high slit backed out holding some shoes.

"May I help you?"

That dripping-with-poisoned-honey voice. Where had she heard it before? As soon as the woman turned toward her, she realized why it was familiar. *Vampirella!*

Maura trembled, but quickly pulled herself together, straightened to her full five-foot-five frame and glared at her. "Fancy meeting you here, Vampirella."

"Oh, it's not such a coincidence. You're here to shop for gothic fashions for your clothing store back in New York."

"How did you know that?"

"I have my ways." Vampirella slinked all around her, looking smug. "I hope you like my wardrobe. I put in the window just for you." She patted her hair like she was trying to push the teased section higher. If it hadn't been dry as cotton candy and hairsprayed into rock, the move may have looked sexy.

"How did you travel through the sun to get here?"

"There were a couple of glasses worth of wine in the bottle Adrian left behind. I'm sure he meant for me to have them—at least subconsciously. I must say I'm impressed that it works so well."

Vampirella glanced around the dressing room area. "Actually, since I won't have to worry about sunlight anymore, I'm thinking I might buy this shop when he and I are together again, now that the owner can't stay here anymore."

Maura gritted her teeth. How dare she think she could break them up? Yet the woman had her at a disadvantage, so the comment had to be ignored. She'd pursue the other subject instead. "Why can't the owner work here anymore?"

"Ask her yourself." She opened the fitting room door and stood aside to reveal a barefoot woman with deep red gashes in her neck, bound and gagged. "I meant to kill her, but she'd just eaten some nasty garlic. Peeuww...I hate that stuff, so I made her give me the shop and I fired her." Turning the shoes over in her hand, Vampirella said, "I like her shoes, though. Oh, look. They're even my size."

Maura tried to cover her horror. "I'll have to eat lots of garlic sandwiches from now on."

An evil smile stole across the sinister vamp's face. "Just the reaction I was hoping for. Adrian hates garlic too. Maybe that will convince you that he belongs with me, not you. Now because I don't want to upset Adrian too much when he gets here, I'll put you in the other dressing room. If you cooperate, you won't have to be tied up like the previous owner." Her eyes narrowed and glittered. "Just remember what I can do to you."

Maura's stomach churned. Vampirella grabbed her arm and roughly shoved her into the other dressing room. She did her best to put up a minor struggle even though she was pretty sure she had no choice in the matter.

Vampirella laughed as she did something to the handle. Maura suspected she had fixed it so it wouldn't open, but she tried to turn it anyway. The handle didn't budge. That door wasn't opening any time soon.

* * * * *

Adrian breathed a sigh of relief, satisfied that his father would be all right. How Maura had managed to forgive them was beyond his wildest imagination. Well, she did say she had a pretty eccentric family herself. He wondered if he'd meet them someday and if so, what they'd think of her dating a vampire. At least he had vampiric strength in case anyone tried to throw him into a dungeon.

Strudel yipped and wagged his tail when Adrian found him in the kitchen. He had slurped up the last of the pig's blood in his bowl and looked as content as...well, as a dog with all his needs met. With a wide smile and his tongue hanging out, he wagged his tail furiously while Adrian scratched him behind his ears.

"I'm glad Maura convinced me to come back for you, boy."

He also had to admit he was glad his family had turned his boyhood best friend and kept him undead all these years. A weird string of events, but welcome ones.

"Strudel, do you want to come with Maura and me? I have to tell you it won't be easy. We'll have to carry you around in a covered cage during the day and—"

Strudel jumped up and down, wagged his tail furiously and yipped his agreement. Adrian chuckled and picked up the delighted dog.

"We'll play Frisbee in the park after the sun goes down, but Maura and I will be sleeping during the night while you're awake. It may be a little lonely for you."

No lonelier than it is here. No one plays Frisbee with me. Whatever that is.

A shocked Adrian set Strudel back on the floor and stared at him. *Boy? Was that you? Did you just speak to me telepathically?*

Yes, it's me. Your Strudel. Don't worry, Master. I won't be any trouble. I'll stand guard over you during the night. Just please take me with you. Nobody loves me like you and your funny red-haired woman do.

Hands on his hips, Adrian studied his dog. *I'll be damned. Who knew we'd be able to communicate like this. That's got to be a first.*

I called to you and called to you for centuries, but you were too far away. I couldn't howl out loud or I'd get yelled at and locked in the dungeon. Maybe all that practice helped me develop telepathy. I have to really concentrate hard to do it, though. I'd have talked to you before, but I couldn't. I was too drunk to stand on all four paws.

Adrian shook his head. "You and my lady will get along just fine. She's a bit of a lush, I'm afraid."

Yeah, but she's fun. I really like that about her.

"She likes you too. I guess there's nothing like two or three bottles of wine and singing at the top of your lungs to facilitate a bond."

Heh, heh. Yeah, she didn't even complain about my being off-key.

"Well, let's get you into your covered cage so I can take you out in the sun with me. Don't worry. It isn't like one of those cramped bird cages."

Strudel jumped up and down and licked Adrian's hand as he bent down to pat him.

* * * * *

Meanwhile, Maura sat in the corner of her dressing room and tried to call Adrian telepathically without success. She wanted to warn him, so he'd know what he was walking into. Why it hadn't worked concerned her. Maybe it was the distance. He could still be at the castle.

An unsettling thought struck her suddenly and she shivered. What if his father was in serious condition and Adrian didn't dare leave him? Or what if they had managed to talk their son out of dating a mortal?

Just the thought made her heart ache. If so, would he come and break it off with her in person? Or would he be one of those cowardly types who just stopped calling or coming by? And yet, it was possible he'd think she left him since she wasn't able to meet him at the café they had designated for their rendezvous after. Would he, could he, find her with Vampirella lying in wait?

As she fumed and obsessed over all that could go wrong, she heard the tinkling of the little bell out front, signaling someone entering the shop.

"Well, well. It's about time you got here, lover."

"I'm not your lover anymore. How many times do I have to make that abundantly clear?"

Adrian! Adrian, I'm here in the back. In one of the dressing rooms. She's tied up the owner and locked me in!

"Oh, come on now, darlink. You know you want me."

"I want no such thing. What I need is for you to promise you won't harm Maura. That's an order."

"Ha! An order? What makes you think the little harlot is still alive?"

Silence…this was her chance. *Adrian! I'm here. I'm alive.*

"Vampirella, if you harmed one hair on her head —"

Vampirella snorted in disgust. "How can you care about an ignorant little mortal? She has no idea how to make you happy. I on the other hand —"

"Could make me utterly wretched, depressed and miserable forever."

Vampirella screamed at him. "How dare you? You'd rather have a short fling with a woman who already looks ten years older than you? She's just going to get older too! She'll get a fat double chin and her breasts will sag. Is that what you want?"

"Yes. I want Maura."

"I refuse to believe that. Look at all you could have if you just say you want me."

"I'm looking. I still want Maura — through all stages of her life."

A loud cry of frustration followed and Maura heard sounds of a scuffle. *Adrian, don't aggravate her. Just leave her and come and get me. We can zoom out of here in one of your whirlwind runs up into the mountains.*

Wait… Was that Strudel growling? *Strudel? Is that you? Can you hear me, boy? What's happening out there?*

Maura, this bitch is bad news. I'm afraid she'll tear you to pieces if she can get to you. She made a run for it, but Adrian caught her by the heel. She went down and now she's trying to scratch and bite. If I weren't in this damn cage —

How can you see? I thought you were covered?

I'm able to peek out the bottom. The cover caught on a shoe and the hem is raised.

Vampirella screamed.

What's going on now?

Holy gods, Maura, I wish you could see Adrian fighting for you. I knew he had it in him, but he keeps a tight lid on his power and energy.

What's he doing? Trying to kill her?

Don't worry about what he's doing. I'm glad to see he's unleashed his anger on her. The bitch needs to know she can't push him around.

Is he in any danger?

Well, he's out of practice, but I think he can take her.

Suddenly Adrian let out a high-pitched howl.

Ouch. That was a low blow.

Maura felt a lump of panic rise to her throat and her pulse began to pound. *What? What just happened?*

Well, put it this way. You can be grateful to him afterward, but you won't be able to show it with nooky tonight.

Oh, crap. Adrian? Adrian? Just get me out of this room and you'll see what one pissed-off Irishwoman can do. I'm ready to kick some vampire ass!

At last all was quiet. Seconds later, she heard someone gasping for breath. Maura's anger quickly skyrocketed into anxiety and her body trembled.

"Adrian? Is that you?" she called out loud.

Still no answer, but the heavy breathing seemed to go on for an eternity.

"Adrian?" she yelled, voice quivering.

"It's me, *cherie*, Where are you?"

"In the last dressing room."

"All right. Relax. I'm working on this handle. Another moment, please."

Relief washed over her. The door sprang open and Maura leapt into his arms.

"Ouch." He recoiled and dropped her onto her feet.

She jumped backward and saw the damage Vampirella had wrought. "Holy crap, Adrian!"

His full lower lip was split and bleeding. Sweat beaded his brow and dripped down his forehead to his temples. He seemed to be adjusting his jaw. Bruises had already formed and his clothes…torn to shreds.

"I'm so sorry about all of this, Adrian."

"No, darling. It is I who should be sorry. None of this should have happened. But I will take you somewhere far from here. Somewhere safe. Come, *mon coeur*." He held out his hand to her and she reached for it gingerly.

"It is all right, *cherie*. I never hit a woman except in self-defense."

"That amount of racket was self-defense?"

"Yes. Could I help it if she fell when she lunged and knocked down every display with her head?"

"Hey, I'm not blaming you. I'm glad she's a klutz. I'll bet the skintight dress didn't help her any."

Maura wondered what Vampirella looked like. She didn't much care how many bruises the uber-bitch had. She just wanted to know that Adrian had knocked her out cold.

As they rounded the corner, Maura spotted her lying motionless on the floor. Black dress split where it was too tight anyway, blonde hair smashed flat against her head and legs facing the opposite way as her arms and torso, twisted at an odd angle. Maura paused looking over the vampiress's contorted body.

"Is she dead?"

"No. We must hurry, *cherie*. Vampires heal quickly."

"I so want to kick her while she's down."

"Not now. Take Strudel's cage. I'll carry the rest."

Maura lifted the heavy cage with an oomph, but didn't complain about the weight. They'd be somewhere else in a few seconds anyway. She peeked under the cover and said, "Thanks for the play-by-play."

Yes, I can't wait to go to the park so we can play.

Maura just smiled and dropped the cover, making sure it was covering the cage all around.

Chapter Sixteen

🔊

Adrian had taken Maura to the metro train in Bucharest. From there they'd buy tickets on an overnight international train. He had to get her as far away and as safe as possible, then try to talk her into going back home without him. He knew it wouldn't be easy, but it was for her own safety, so she had to listen.

"Do you have your passport with you?"

"Where are you taking me?"

"I'm taking you out of the country, to my vineyard in France. You'll be safe there, *cherie*."

"Cool. I could use a bottle of wine right about now."

Adrian smiled, shook his head and pulled her close. If she left him, he'd miss her so much, he'd be depressed for a decade. If she didn't leave him, she'd wind up dead and he'd be devastated.

He couldn't think about that now. He simply had to enjoy every moment he had with her. It had been a long time since visiting his winery and he looked forward to seeing the *grande maison* again. The French countryside always settled him and clarified his perspective.

After buying their tickets, a long silence stretched out between them. Even Strudel was quiet or perhaps asleep.

When they were ready to board, Maura glanced around in panic. "Where's your other suitcase, Adrian? I don't see it anywhere."

"I'm afraid I left it back in Codlea. I couldn't carry you with Strudel and four cases all at once. Not for lack of strength, but I didn't have enough hands and arms. I can replace the clothes once we get to my home in France."

"So, you think the case you brought is the one with your wine?"

Adrian nodded. He hoped she wasn't going to ask for a sip. He had no idea how it would affect mortals and he didn't want to experiment on his beloved.

"I think you'd better double-check, sweetie. That one looks like the case with your clothing to me."

Adrian jerked his gaze back to his lone suitcase. Prickles traveled up his spine. The two cases looked almost identical, but she was right. This wasn't the one he meant to take.

"Damn!" He opened it anyway, hoping they were both wrong and this was the one that held his owner's reserve, but clothes spilled out. "Bloody hell."

"Is it too late to go back?"

"I'm afraid so." Adrian blew out a long breath and raked his fingers through his long, tangled hair. "Come. Don't worry about it. It will be dark soon, anyway. If I must, I can share some of Strudel's pig's blood."

"Euww. Dog food?" Maura picked up her suitcases and let Adrian take his and Strudel's cage. He was tempted to kick the suitcase with his clothes under the train, but he did have a few favorite items in there. His black Armani cashmere sweater, black Italian leather pants, black silk shirts…no, it wouldn't be worth it. His anger at himself would return a second or two after that, anyway.

What's the worst that could happen? Adrian felt as if he'd take a blow to the stomach when the worst-case scenario hit him. Vampirella could drink it, rejuvenate, be impervious to daylight, skip the time it took to hunt and feed and then come after them at his winery, knowing he'd have to go there to replenish his stock. Bloody hell.

* * * * *

The trip to Budapest, Hungary, passed uneventfully. Once settled into their private compartment on the intercontinental train bound for France, Maura finally relaxed. Adrian seemed distracted and nervous, though.

"What's the matter, sweetheart?"

He shook his head but continued to fidget. "Nothing. I'm just not very comfortable."

"Well, who would be after taking a stiletto to the groin?"

He smiled for the first time since leaving Romania. "It's not that. At least I don't think so. Maybe we should check and see?"

A wicked aspect in his dark eyes told her he wanted to test his ability to recover quickly. She glanced over at the window built into the door and noticed a curtain that could be drawn over it. Bracing herself for balance as the train chugged and bounced along, she made her way over and pulled the shade.

Next, she turned off the overhead light to suit the romantic mood coming on. "Do you think this is private enough to examine your, um…private parts?"

"I'll make sure it is." He slid Strudel's cage over to block the door should anyone wish to enter. Hearing his dog yip, he raised the cover. "Sorry, friend. I have to keep you covered up just a little longer. The lady needs her privacy and I need the lady."

Strudel wagged his tail and nodded in understanding and agreement.

Good. She had wondered how that would work. Probably living with Vlad and Angelika so long had taught him a few things about men and women. Or vampires and multiple men and women. Again, ick.

Adrian expertly unfolded one of the benches, making it into a bed, then turned to her, his intense eyes sparkling with lust.

"Come to me, *cherie*." He extended his arms and she gladly stepped between them. His balance must have been superior to hers, because she stopped feeling the sway of the train. He held her so tight, she wondered what he was thinking. To ask now would only interrupt forward progress and Maura could feel her own body's reaction begging her to go with the flow. The moisture between her thighs, her deepened breaths and clenching womb all signified her readiness whenever she thought of having sex with her vampire lover.

He scooped her up and carried her to the bed. Their eye contact remained fixed as he laid her on the textured vinyl surface. Kneeling beside her, he began unbuttoning her blouse. She pulled the hem of his shirt free of his pants and waited until he had reached the bottom of her buttons. His eyes darkened while she returned the slow torture of revealing his hard chest, button by button.

"Lift your beautiful bottom for me, *cherie*."

"I don't know how beautiful it is, but I'll hoist the one I've got."

Adrian waited until she had braced her feet against the firm mattress and raised her lower half a few inches. He yanked off her pants, the elastic waist slipped easily over her hips. Thank goodness she had a couple of these unfashionable, yet utterly practical and quickly removable styles in her wardrobe. Before she had a chance to lower her body, he cradled her butt in one hand and stroked it. "You have a remarkable *derriere*. I love every inch of it."

Maura thought there were a few too many inches to love, but thankfully it sounded as if Adrian didn't agree.

As he peeled off his shirt and dropped it onto the floor, she caught her breath. His body really was breathtaking. Well-defined muscles in his arms and his six-pack abdomen contracted when he moved. His color was a bit paler than she remembered, but perhaps it would improve once he fed.

"Adrian, if you need a little snack afterward, the café at Maura's neck is available."

"Sounds like a restaurant on a land mass that juts out into the sea."

She chuckled. "Think of it any way you like, but remember they don't serve full-course meals. Only appetizers."

He stroked her mons and said, "I have my appetizer right here, but thank you for the generous offer."

She shivered with his touch—not that it was cold, but cooler than usual and he was caressing one of her most sensitive parts.

"Adrian, let me undress you the rest of the way."

He smiled and sat mostly still while she fumbled with his belt and pants. Of course it was hard to concentrate with him rubbing her muff like that.

When at last she had pushed his pants down, she could see that his cock was dark red and fully erect. *Ah, so that's where the blood went.*

Adrian removed his black trousers and discarded them as carelessly as he had his shirt. He lifted Maura's back and slipped her shirt off, then removed her bra. As soon as they were both naked, he settled down beside her and kissed her tenderly. She sighed as he slid downward and took her breast into his mouth. She loved the sensations that rippled through her body as he took his time, sucking each of her nipples progressively deeper and harder. While thoroughly suckling at her breast, he returned to tease the apex of her thighs. She wriggled and moaned with his relentless attention to her naked body. He knew exactly how to drive her crazy with desire.

She reached for his cock, closed her hand around it and stroked up and down. He breathed deep as she increased the tempo.

"You have an instant effect on me, *mon coeur.*"

She thought she heard him growl. Or was it Strudel?

Maura grabbed the blanket that lay beside her and tossed it over the two of them. He tried to help spread the coverlet, but quickly lost interest in being modest and returned to feasting on her breast. No, the growling was definitely from Adrian. It became muffled as he slid down under the blanket to tongue her… Wowza!

She trembled and moaned with joy as he went right to work on her clit. Automatically arching her back only served to push her sensitive nub farther into his mouth. Maura felt the beginnings of her earthquake much sooner than anticipated. She bucked, quivered and gasped. A shattering 7.5 on the Richter scale hit her personal epicenter and rippled all through her body. She barely muffled her screams of ecstasy by pressing her hand over her mouth. Adrian hung in there as she came again and again and extracted every last aftershock he could give her.

Warm bliss spread, while the blanket heated up as if it were electric, set on high. When she felt capable of forming sentences again, she said, "Damn, I was smart to fall in love with a vampire!"

Adrian crawled back up to her eye level, the saddest look in his eyes. His expression gave her pause.

"What's wrong?"

He shook his head. "Nothing." He tossed the blanket off and kissed her shoulder.

"Oh yeah? Don't tell me it's nothing when your face says it's something. Now spill it!"

Adrian looked downward at his hard-on. "Spill it? On command?"

Maura did her best not to laugh, but she lost the battle. Mirth bubbled up and her irritation vanished in a loud guffaw.

"Your hearty laugh…joy dancing in your eyes…how did I live without that?"

Inevitably, her laughter made him smile and chuckle at what she knew was an intentional misunderstanding.

She cleared her throat a couple of times and composed herself. "Tell you what, I'll help."

Maura slid down next to his cock, took the base in her hand and licked the firm shaft. Adrian rolled and landed on his back, saying, "Ohhh."

Once she had wet his entire length, she lowered her mouth over the tip, swirled her tongue around it and sucked. She went down on him, letting her tongue drag over the sensitive underside.

"Does that hurt?"

"*Non.*"

Because he didn't wince or complain of pain, she really turned on the suction and pulled up slowly.

"Did that hurt?"

"Oh, glorious torture." He smiled and winked. "I'm fine."

There was no way she'd let him forget their lovemaking. She intended to make enough mind-blowing memories to sustain him through whatever eternity he had after she was gone.

Soon he began to shake and moan, evidence of his orgasm building. "Stop, *cherie.* I'm getting close."

She looked up into his eyes, grinned around his cock and sank down on it again, faster and firmer. Hanging on to the base with a death grip as tight as a cock-ring, she argued and insisted on pleasuring him without saying a word.

Ripples signaled his impending climax. "Maura!" It was too late. He groaned and shot cum into her mouth.

Maura drank every drop. As soon as he had regrouped, he pulled her up over his chest and cradled her head in the hollow of his neck. "*Je t'aime,*" he whispered, hoping she didn't hear the quaver in his voice.

* * * * *

Maura awoke expecting to find Adrian next to her. After three eager and impassioned couplings during the night, she thought even a vampire would be exhausted. Instead, the sunlight that spilled into the compartment covered his half of the pillow. As soon as her eyes adjusted, she found him huddling next to Strudel's cage near the door.

"Are you okay, sweetie?"

"I will be. I just had to share breakfast with Strudel. You're right about dog food. Disgusting."

"Sorry about that. You can come to me for snack time if you ever need to." She sat up and looked out the window. "Where are we?"

He stood and pointed toward his pants. "Getting close to our stop. I was about to wake you." She tossed him his clothes and he hopped into his pants. He hesitated when he went to pick up the shirt. It still lay in a pool of sunlight hitting the floor.

"You're sensitive to the sun again?" It was said as a question, even though she knew the answer.

"I'm afraid so. Would you mind handing me my shirt?"

She grabbed it off the floor and tossed it to him, then stood to retrieve the suitcases from the rack. "Don't you want fresh clothes?"

"After I wash up. Would you be so kind as to go first? If the sun is coming in the bathroom window, I'll need you to close the curtains before I can go in."

"Wow. This photosensitivity is a total pain in the ass."

He raised his eyebrows and was about to speak when she cut him off. "No, I meant for you. Only for you. Not me. I don't mind doing whatever I can to help."

He seemed to relax. "Good, because it may be tricky getting me off the train. Last night I was able to borrow someone's satellite phone and call my driver. He'll pick us up in the funeral limo. It has tinted windows in front and curtains in the back."

Lovely. "How long does this usually last? I mean after you get some Warrior Wine into your system?"

"The benefits of my special product take effect almost immediately." Adrian sighed and sat on the end of the bench closest to the door. "It's only a thirty-minute drive to the house. I'm sorry I won't be able to give you the scenic tour."

"The tour can wait. How's Strudel this morning?"

Adrian smiled and glanced at the cage. "Asleep. He's on the opposite schedule. I don't really know what to do about that. I spent some time patting and playing with him quietly last night while you were sleeping. He understood your need for sleep and was determined to be quiet."

Maura stretched and popped a crick in her back. "Ah. That's better. You two must have done a great job because I slept like a baby even on this hard, plastic slab, or maybe you just wore me out last night." She winked. "Either way, I feel very relaxed and well rested this morning."

Adrian's sad smile returned.

"What's going on with you lately?"

"Huh? Oh... I'm just sorry to be a bother. Do you think you could check out the bathroom soon?"

"Of course." Maura scrambled to her feet, found her clothes from the evening before and wriggled into them. While the train chugged along, she made her way to the restroom with the towel and washcloth provided. The track must have been straighter since she wasn't weaving and being pitched from side to side as she had been the night before.

A quick peek out the window before she drew the curtain confirmed the lack of mountainous terrain, therefore a straight path through some beautiful countryside. It had to be France. While she washed up, she obsessed about how to get Adrian off the train through the bright morning light without watching him fry.

She had seen enough episodes of *Buffy the Vampire Slayer* to remember Spike covered in a blanket or his long, black leather coat running from one shadow to the next. Sometimes after only brief sun exposure, smoke would pour off him anyway. She shuddered, picturing the same thing or worse happening to Adrian.

What would happen if they tried to take one of the train's blankets? Would they be arrested and stuck in a nice, dark jail cell? What if they suspected he was a vampire? Did the French countryside have its own Buffette the Vampire Slayer? Maura smiled. Well, at least that sounded unlikely.

Maybe the conductor would snatch back the blanket back and her beloved would burst into flame. *Bloody hell.* A lump rose to her throat as she realized she was even picking up his expressions now.

The train slowed down. She finished her business with lightning speed in order to get back to their compartment and let Adrian take his turn. They had to figure this out as soon as possible. When she yanked open the bathroom door, Adrian was waiting just outside.

"You'd better hurry and get dressed. I'll be there in a moment."

She glanced around to be sure they were alone and asked, "How the hell are we going to get you off the train?"

"I'll tell you as soon as I get back."

* * * * *

Safely seated in his limo, Adrian blew out a sigh of relief. Not only was he safe from the sun, but Maura hadn't asked too many questions when he told her he could control the conductor's and passengers' minds as he slipped past everyone under a "borrowed" blanket. The only question he really hoped she wouldn't ask was "Have you ever used it on me?" If she did, he still wasn't quite sure what he would say.

Maybe it was a good time to introduce another topic of conversation and distract her before the possibility occurred to her.

"*Cherie*, I have been hiding something from you."

"I knew it!"

Her face looked almost jubilant, confirming her right to worry...for a moment. As he watched her expression fall, he quickly launched into what he hoped would be an observation she probably hadn't missed anyway. That way she could be right again.

"We must be on the lookout for Vampirella. If she discovered my wine and used it herself, not only will she have the ability to travel in sunlight without stopping for meals, but she'll also know exactly where we're headed."

Maura nodded solemnly. "I thought of that too. I didn't know if she knew where your winery was or not. I guess she does, huh?"

"She does."

Maura didn't ask anything more. That was unusual for her. She simply fidgeted and looked out the window.

"Now you are the one holding something back, Maura."

"I shouldn't ask. I don't really want to know the answer."

"Oh?" Adrian suspected she wanted to ask about his relationship with Vampirella and there was little he could say to reassure her. Yes, they had been intimate...and it had been an on-again, off-again thing for a couple of centuries. Even when he knew what they shared wasn't love, he took solace in her willing body. Yes, she had felt the sting of rejection and probably wanted him back simply for spite alone. Unfortunately, he knew her well enough to realize she could and would do anything to get revenge.

"Do you prefer really buxom women? I mean, I'm having a hard time understanding the appeal. Vampirella doesn't seem to have much in the personality department, but she sure does have the physical attributes men seem to value highly."

Adrian leaned back and studied her face. Was she really worried that her body didn't measure up? *Unbelievable*.

He gripped her chin, forcing her to look in his eyes. "I have no complaints with you or your body. You are my beloved. She is my nothing. You must remember that. She will try to convince you otherwise. Never, ever believe what she says."

Maura nodded slowly. Or maybe he had too forceful a grip on her chin. He let go and she rubbed the spot below her sensuous bottom lip.

"Okay. I get it. Is that what you wanted to tell me? That she might try to chase us down and tell me lies to get you back? No shit. I didn't just fall off the grape truck, you know." She patted Strudel's covered cage as if it were the dog inside.

He stared at her in wonder. Women could confuse him at the best of times, but this one had a way of surprising and confounding him regularly.

"So about that mind control…"

Fuck.

Chapter Seventeen

𝕤𝕠

After Adrian fessed up, Maura thought over the implications of what he'd done while they rode to his vineyard. So he'd used it on her once to show her what making love with a vampire could be. Okay, maybe twice. So what? And that was only if you considered astral projection the same as mind control. She had definitely enjoyed the sensations he'd created remotely. Hot damn, who could object to that?

Maura sighed inwardly as she relived the experience. She was simply grateful it was her beloved, her Adrian and not some sort of stray succubus or something. Not that she really knew what the hell she was talking about. The only stray demon she knew anything about was her drunken devil and he was a what, not a who. What did he mean by that, anyway?

It occurred to her that she was having quite the conversation with herself as they rode in silence and her "friends" hadn't shown up recently to interject their two cents, "recently" being the operative —

"Oh, Susan. Tsk, tsk." A light pressure touched her shoulder. "Do you really think we'd leave you all alone to struggle with this when you need us?"

Speak of the devil. Crap!

"It's good to see you too."

Crap and a half. Crap and three-quarters. Crap squared. She refused to look to her left or right.

"Has anyone ever told you how completely ungrateful you can be?"

Only you.

"Well, you're lucky we don't do this for the thanks we get."

Oh no. You said "we". That means—

"That's right, Maura, dear. I'm here too."

Damn. The flutter of wings sounded in her right ear like a train rushing through a tunnel.

"Someday, you'll thank us."

I think not.

Adrian reached around her back and squeezed her arm.

"We're coming up to my estate, *mon coeur*. Out of your window you will see my driveway."

High, thick hedges parted to reveal an impressively long, stone-lined drive that split manicured lawns all the way from the entrance to a drive-through under a columned, covered entrance. Whew. "Covered" meant he could step out of his car and walk right in. How embarrassing would it be for the lord of the manor to rush in under a blanket?

A soprano voice said, "Why are you more concerned for him than you are for yourself? Have you forgotten there's a disgruntled female vampire on your tail?"

Maura quickly jerked herself back to reality and searched the area for an unwelcome foe. She could see no sequined gowns sparkling in the sun. No bleached blonde hair lurking in the bushes and the only person who appeared when they pulled up to the front door was an elderly gentleman in a gray suit.

He stepped up to the car door and opened it. "*Bienvenue*, Adrian…and your lovely guest."

"Maura, this is the estate's manager, Bertrand, and may I present to you, Maura Keegan."

"You certainly may." He smiled at Maura but not in a lecherous way. He simply made her feel welcome. "Will you be requiring a guestroom?"

Adrian shook his head and looked sad. "We'll be staying only a few hours. If you could ask the cook to prepare a hearty lunch for Maura and then pack another suitcase of my owner's reserve. I'll be showing her the cellar, then packing an overnight bag. We'll be on our way soon after that."

"What about Strudel?"

She wondered how Adrian would explain the presence of a vampire dog. It was bad enough that the staff knew they were working for a vampire man, but a dog they couldn't communicate with that drank only blood? How would he explain that?

"Ah, yes. My dog. He prefers his meat fresh from the butcher shop. In fact, he likes it so fresh that you may as well procure live animals from a farmer and have the cook slaughter and feed him on the spot."

"Strudel likes pig's blood," Maura said.

Adrian shot her a look.

Maybe she shouldn't come right out and give instructions to his staff, but their little dog deserved to have the diet he was used to and seemed to like. She wouldn't mention the red wine, however.

"Yes, Miss Maura. I understand. I'll take care of it immediately. Would you like some in bottles, ready to go?"

Adrian raised his eyebrows and cleared his throat, apparently surprised that his manager knew what Strudel was. "No, Bertrand. I think it's best if Strudel stays behind. I'll come back for him as quickly as possible."

Oops. Maybe they didn't know what their boss was! Maura puzzled it out. Of course they did. How could they not?

"Yes, Bertrand. Thank you. That would be most convenient."

As soon as Bertrand departed, Adrian stared at her. "What were you thinking?"

"That they know what you are and if they can accept that, they can certainly deal with your adorable little dog. How could they work for you and not know, Adrian? Do you think humans are stupid?"

"Now that's a loaded question, because that's exactly what I used to think centuries ago when I bought *le maison*. *Mon dieu*. Are you psychic or —?"

She looked up at him with her most innocent expression. "Or what?"

He didn't answer. He simply stared at her. Perhaps wondering how she knew they knew.

"You've never worked for someone else, have you, Adrian?"

He looked up, probably scanning his lengthy background. Eventually, he said, "No. Even in war, I procured positions of independence. Advance scout, usually. I'd go ahead of the rest, knowing I could drink my fill of the stragglers and deserters already at death's door and then report on the enemy's location, all in record time."

"I should find that disgusting, but I don't. If that's how you avoided snacking on your staff all these years, I'm sure they appreciated it."

"I guess you are right, *mon coeur*."

"When you work for a boss, you pay attention to his or her habits, fine points and innuendos, so you can either please them, or at least stay out of trouble. Eventually, you know what he's going to do or say before he does. I wouldn't be surprised if your driver told Bertrand to have your owner's reserve ready upon your arrival."

As she spoke the words, Bertrand returned from the kitchen with a suitcase. He looked surprised to see Adrian and Maura still standing there and placed it beside the front door, his meaty cheeks turning a little pinker.

"The cook has been told of your dog's needs, sir. Will you be requiring anything else?"

223

Adrian stood dumbfounded. At last, he bowed to his manager and said, "No, Bertrand, but thank you." It was said with unmistakable respect and gratitude.

Bertrand seemed pleased as he smiled and bowed to Adrian. "You are most welcome, sir. We're happy to see you on your visits and glad to assist you with whatever you need."

Maura couldn't help being touched by the affection and loyalty of Adrian's right-hand man. As they made their way to the cellar, she felt a certain pride. Odd since she didn't do anything but hook up with a good man—an undead one, but everybody's got their little quirks, right?

Adrian placed his hand on the small of her back and escorted her to the door of his wine cellar. Before they reached the bottom of the stairs, Maura's gaze met rows of stacked barrels. The cool cellar held a surprisingly fresh woody scent. Not at all like the musty cellars or dungeons she had been in before. Just the fact that she could add the word "dungeons" to her list of subterranean habitats boggled her mind.

"*Cherie*, forgive me." Adrian took her hand and led her to the left side of the enormous room. The entire end wall displayed racks and racks of identical bottles. "Ordinarily, I would be proud to show you the entire process, but we have no time. I'm afraid I'm beginning your tour at the end."

"Don't worry, sweetheart. I understand why we're here. Is all of this your owner's reserve?"

He tucked one hand in his pocket, wrapped the other one around her waist and strolled down the long row. "*Non, mon coeur*. I wish that were the case, but only the last rack at the end of this row is mine. Some four hundred bottles when it's full."

She hated to ask, but couldn't shut her eyes to the harsh realities they would have to face. "What happens when that's gone?"

"It takes several months to produce a single bottle. The barrels on this end are Blood of the Warrior in various stages

224

of fermenting, but I have other orders to fill. As such, I must be conservative with my own stock, otherwise I'd eventually have to go on a diet."

A rustling sound came from behind the furthest barrels and an imposing figure stepped out from behind them. The bleached-blonde hair and black sequined gown gave her away. Holding one of his special bottles like a gavel, Vampirella said, "That may be sooner than you think, lover." And she charged.

Adrian swept Maura behind him and spread his arms to shield her.

The black-clad bitch brought the bottle down hard, smashing it to pieces on Adrian's skull as if pronouncing sentence. A death sentence for both of them.

Maura screamed. Before she could think about how to make her feet move or where to run, Vampirella lunged at her. She evaded her by leaning back in a *Matrix*-like move and Vampirella dove right over her, skidding to a stop on the floor. The only glitch was that Maura didn't have that elastic recoil in order to right herself after a move like that and fell splat on her back.

As Vampirella picked herself up, her blonde beehive hung over her forehead and her fangs descended. The expression "seeing red" finally made sense. A red light glowed from where her pupils should have been. She advanced on Maura as if nothing could stop her.

Feeling totally helpless, Maura was sure this was it. *Goodbye, weird world. It was interesting while it lasted…*

Adrian rose. Barely noticing his swift movement, her position suddenly shifted. She had been picked up like a flower vase and set aside, out of harm's way.

Adrian's fangs projected out of his open mouth and a hissing sound like some sort of supernatural steam filled the air. Vampirella, still baring her fangs, grabbed two precious bottles and threw them at him. Then she tried to charge past him to get to Maura, but hugged the wine rack. Perhaps she was hoping his fear of wasting that precious lifeblood would protect her, but it didn't. He swept her aside and she went hurtling into the wine racks. The racks tipped. Some of the bottles fell and landed on top of her while others smashed on the floor.

She grabbed at the bottles blindly, throwing them at Adrian as he advanced on her. He reached out and seized her wrists only to have her drenched arms slowly slip out of his grasp as she struggled against him. She launched herself at him and cried, "Darlink…" but he merely stepped aside letting her crash to the floor and lie across wet broken glass.

Vampirella's black gown, now soaked with wine, stuck to her legs as she pushed herself up. Her expression was one of fierce rage as she lunged past him, going for Maura's throat. She grabbed her neck with one hand.

Never had Maura experienced terror like this. The pressure around her throat so severe and crushing she thought she'd breathed her last.

Adrian broke Vampirella's chokehold and swept her aside, hard. She landed with a thud against the barrels, rocking the whole pyramid.

Maura watched, horrified, as her beloved apparently lost his mind and grabbed bottle after bottle, hurling them at Vampirella's head. She held her hands up in front of her eyes and cowered against the barrels.

Maura couldn't just stand by, frozen in horror and let this happen. "Wait, Adrian. Stop!" She grabbed his arm and held on for dear life. "You're wasting the last of it! The Blood of the Warrior is almost gone."

Her voice seemed to reach him even through the depths of sheer fury. He slowly turned to her, panting. Maura ran her hand over his cheek and whispered. "She's not worth it, Adrian. Let her go."

Vampirella scrambled to her feet and rushed toward the stairs.

He slumped against the nearly empty wine rack and slid to the floor. One more bottle fell to the floor and shattered, as if to punctuate the end of battle—the end of his nearly normal life. He may have won, but at what cost?

Maura kneeled beside him. "Are...are you all right?"

He hung his head. Dark, wet hair that had fallen loose during the frenzy obscured his face. His deep breaths seemed to quiver, but he didn't answer.

She stepped a little closer and touched his arm. When he didn't move or stop her, she rubbed his back, softly. "What do we do now, Adrian?"

"We send you home."

* * * * *

"I'm not going to argue any more with you, *cherie*. You are in danger." Adrian sat on his throne-like chair, sipping a glass of wine from one of the last half dozen bottles of his owner's reserve. He had showered and dressed in black leather pants and a black shirt with open French cuffs, minus the cufflinks.

"You can't make me go home. I'm not a child or your servant to order around." Maura sipped her glass of regular red cabernet and crossed her legs at the knee. "Besides, I've done hardly any shopping and found no place to order further inventory. If I want this trip to be partially paid for, I'll need to do that."

"You came to find your vampire lover. Now that you have found him, you must lose him. There are six bottles of wine left, so in six or so days, he'll turn into a monster."

"Yeah, just my luck. The luck of the Irish."

He turned to her, his expression deadpan.

"I was being sarcastic. The Irish are not a lucky people, you know. That saying originally referred to bad luck. Lord knows how it got screwed up. Now it's just ironically cruel."

"No one knows that better than I do, Maura. I came over during the potato famine. When most of the people had either dropped dead or emigrated, I followed what was left of them to the United States. I had heard there was some unrest between the North and South and fortunately for me, the bloodiest war in US history was just about to break out."

"The Civil War?"

He nodded.

"Didn't you have your owner's reserve back then? I thought you had it since the Joan of Arc days."

Adrian shifted uncomfortably in his chair. "I ran out once before, *ma cherie*. Remember when I told you not to ask about where I obtained my sample?"

She sat in the nearby wingback chair. "Yes. Do you finally trust me enough to tell me?" Maura set her glass of wine down and leaned forward.

"I had a bloody arrow, first. It was given to me as a gift when I made it known how much I admired her. To obtain the essential ingredient a second time, I had to get it from the black market. It took more decades than I care to remember to locate such a precious commodity. I did what I had to do to survive until after the War."

Hope filled her heart as she came up with a brilliant idea. "You found more on the black market. Then we just need to locate more. Have you tried ebay?"

Adrian gaped at her until one side of his mouth raised. His expression softened, as if he were looking at an amusing child.

"I'm serious! Or we could move to the Middle East."

He let out a groan and shook his head. "Wars are not the same these days. We fight with bombs now. We'd be in danger of getting killed by a bomb ourselves. And there's no guarantee I wouldn't hurt you if I got hungry—beloved or not."

"You wouldn't!"

He swirled the wine to coat his glass. "I would." Casually, he stuck his nose over the rim and inhaled deeply. Closing his eyes, he leaned back and sighed. "I will miss this, but never doubt that I will miss you much more." He leveled his gaze at her, staring intently. "If I caused your death—"

"Stop it! I'm not leaving you until the last possible moment. There's still hope until there's absolutely no wine left."

"I admire your persistent optimism, but I'm afraid it's already too late." A stern, almost frightening glare penetrated her. "Do you really want to prolong my misery?"

What the hell? Maura crossed her arms and held his glare. "I think I should make you as miserable as possible while I can, you broody bastard. I didn't realize I was such a pain in the ass."

"That's not what I meant and you know it."

"Well, shit! You have a few days left to drink wine, take strolls in the sunshine and make love. What's wrong with you? Don't you want to enjoy what little time we have left together and possibly come up an alternative plan?"

Adrian threw his hands in the air, stood abruptly and strode to the door. "Remember this. Vampirella is as stubborn as you are. I doubt she'll leave us alone, but I will think about it, *cherie*." Then he walked out, leaving her to think too.

A slight pressure tapped her left shoulder. "Are you willing to listen to a little advice now?"

She rolled her eyes and glanced at the devil standing there with an uncharacteristic expression on his face. For once, he wasn't arrogant, mocking or sarcastic. He appeared to be concerned.

Sure, why not. What is it you want to tell me?

"If you'll forgive the cliché, 'Hell hath no fury like a woman scorned.' And I should know."

Not to minimize that, but I'm feeling a little furious myself right now.

"Adrian's trying to protect you, dipshit! Look at what he just sacrificed for you."

Maura's fury ramped up. Rage threatened when the angel landed on her other shoulder and tried to soothe her.

"Maura, you cannot doubt his love for you. I'm positive he wishes he could change the situation and would if he could."

Then why won't he even try? Why is he sending me away if it's all the time we have?

The devil elbowed her cheek.

"Oww…"

"Did it ever occur to you that he might have the same hope you do? But you may be getting in the way of his finding it? All he's trying to do is keep you alive. And as long as you're alive, there's hope for the two of you to be together again."

Maura could have slapped herself upside the head. No. It had never occurred to her. *Why didn't he say that, then?*

"So he wouldn't get your hopes up just to dash them if he fails."

Okay, if that's the case, what am I supposed to do?

"Why don't you do the rest of your shopping in London? They seem to have more of what you were looking for anyway."

The angel patted her hair. "Maybe you can visit that nice friend from the tour, what was her name?"

The devil answered without hesitation. "Jordan."

Oh, sure. You remember her name, but not mine. Thanks a lot.

"Pay no attention to him when he's goading you. He did have a point before he ticked you off, Maura dear."

She won't be back just yet, but I could stay at a bed-and-breakfast or something. Then I can call her when she gets back.

"There, now doesn't that sound better? Go shopping, buy lots of shoes and when she gets back you can take her out to lunch and have a nice visit."

Maura nodded and her two advisors fell silent. Her thoughts turned to her friends back in New York for the first time in days. She hadn't called Quilla to check on the shop. Would Barb be sympathetic or would she give her a big "I told you so?" Maybe Haley would understand. Perhaps she could rally the troops and all of them would take her out, get her rip-roaring drunk, then home safely where they'd leave her all tucked in so she wouldn't roll out of bed and onto the floor.

Sadly, that would only help until the next morning. She'd probably feel worse than before and life would go on, with or without Adrian. Her heart ached. It was that second eventuality she couldn't imagine dealing with.

"What do you say, Susan? One final fuck and then say goodbye with a little dignity?"

Maura groaned.

The angel flew over to her left shoulder and shook her finger at the devil's red belly. "What do you know about dignity, anyway? You're not helping. Please stop it."

The devil gaped. "Oh, now little miss goody two-slippers is getting nasty. I'm really scared." He stood on Maura's shoulder and folded his arms. "I know what I'm talking about. I may not say it the way you'd like me to, Angel, but Susan understands. 'Thank you and goodbye sex' can be some of the sweetest of all expressions of love."

Maura downed the rest of her wine and burst into tears.

* * * * *

Adrian lay in his bed that night, deep in thought. Pictures of his recent life rolled through his mind like a movie, always starring Maura. They had spent a jovial evening playing with Strudel out on the lawn. She had laughed just as freely as she had cried that afternoon when she didn't know he was watching.

Now she was in the adjoining bathroom getting ready to make love to him for the last time. He could only guess at the thoughts and emotions running through her now, knowing this was their last night together. His own sadness was hard enough to deal with.

He had tried to explain the difficulties that would lie ahead and make her understand that if she were hurt or worse... Well, how many regrets could one man carry? He had frightened himself in the wine cellar. Blind rage hadn't overtaken him since before discovering the Blood of the Warrior and he had no wish for her to see him at his worst again.

There were years in which killing hadn't meant much more to him than walking into a fast-food restaurant and ordering up a meal. Then, after his utter revulsion of Vlad the Impaler's peacetime behavior, he had vowed to stick to the smorgasbord that existed after battles and there were always battles being fought. Won or lost, they'd be fought again.

During that time, he had heard the most amazing story. He was told of a young woman who showed extraordinary leadership and bravery in battle. She was the equal of any warrior. But by the cruelest twist of fate, she was labeled a heretic by the church and executed. So much for giving your all for God and country. Then, rumors of miracles performed by the nineteen-year-old French martyr from the deep sleep of death spread like wildfire. Being undead, it moved him in a way that nothing else ever had.

He met the son of one of her jailors a few years later. She had been incarcerated for a year while the king and all of his advisors tried to decide what to do with her. This jailor confirmed for him the intense spiritual faith she had displayed all during that year and even at the end, at her execution. He believed that if anyone could perform miracles, it would be this incredible young woman.

People began saving whatever souvenirs they could sell after her death, knowing what a public figure she was. Most thought her a hero. She led armies into battle for her beloved homeland and drove the English out of France. If she hadn't, today's French cuisine might consist of crumpets and ale.

But she had insisted that she did it all because God spoke to her and told her to. For all of her pain, sweat and dedication to the purpose set out for her, she was labeled a heretic and burned at the stake. That particular death gave Adrian the willies more than any other. Stakes and fire. Not a vampire's first choice.

Adrian held on to her story as personal inspiration. So what if she was a young woman? If there was a god and Adrian didn't know the answer to that, he imagined that deity could talk to whomever he bloody well wanted to. Why should he have to speak to the clergy, especially ambitious, easily threatened nincompoops like those who killed her for believing she was answering his direct line?

His jailor friend had told him of something that was hushed up and now he might be the only person on earth to know about it. While in prison Joan d'Arc received the stigmata. Her hands and feet had to be bandaged to staunch the flow of blood, yet it did little good. The blood wept from the spots where Christ had been nailed to the cross many centuries before.

Something yanked Adrian out of the fourteenth century back to the present. Maura. He sensed her standing in the doorway. A radiant light shimmered from the bathroom behind her and highlighted her figure beneath the floor-length, sky-blue satin nightgown she wore. He had seen her in it from her balcony in New York, but she looked different this time. Her red hair had been brushed to a high luster and softly fell around her shoulders. It framed the face he loved. Both innocent young woman and sinful vixen in one. He wasn't about to speak and break the spell, he merely reached for her and she hurried into his arms.

"Mon coeur."

He could only manage those two words and no more would come. She didn't seem to have any either. He held her for a long time without moving. When she pulled away, her eyes were wet, but she smiled for him.

Cupping the back of her head, he pulled her toward him and kissed her lips tenderly. While caressing her back and buttocks, his inner fire flared. She responded as if his heat had ignited hers. Slanting their mouths at the same time, they deepened their kiss as if responding to some inner choreography. Tongues probed and swirled. They nipped and nuzzled each other's necks, lips and ears. Passion led the way, with no need for restraint.

Responding only to the wants and desires of their hearts and bodies, they followed the frenzy that would bring them to their inevitable mating. He dragged her negligee up and over her head. Tossing it aside may have been construed as careless, but since he was preventing it being torn off as it got in the way, he felt downright considerate.

Adrian grabbed her torso and pulled her up over his face, holding her there as he nipped and suckled each of her breasts. She braced herself against his shoulders and tossed her head back, moaning her pleasure each time he took a nipple into his mouth and suckled thoroughly. Eventually, he rolled toward the middle of the bed, gently positioning her onto her back.

Without a word, he spread her legs and crawled to the space between them. They made eye contact and smiled while he lowered his mouth to her mons. He let her view the full length of his tongue as he licked his way from the bottom of each ridge to the top. She bent her knees and rose up onto her elbows to watch. That didn't last long. As soon as he began to flick her clit with his tongue, she automatically closed her eyes and moaned. Soon after, she vibrated and sounded like she was hyperventilating. Her center yielded easily as he inserted two fingers into her hot, wet chasm while her undulating and moaning only encouraged him to stroke harder and faster. The volume and frequency of her cries followed in sync with his swift lapping and finger-fucking.

If he thought about how he'd miss her, he wouldn't be able to stand it. All he could do was block out the sadness and give her something to remember. The staff had been warned to ignore any noise coming from their room. Fortunately, Bertrand accepted the instructions graciously and without question, avoiding the necessity of having to explain that his love could raise a racket when she orgasmed.

In minutes Maura screamed and shook with spasms. As soon as he thought she was about to relax, he mounted and joined with her. She sighed when he buried himself within her slick channel. He grabbed her around the waist and rolled so she was on top. Pulling her up enough to sink back down on his entire length, she moaned and then took control. She fell forward, braced her hands on his shoulders and raised her ass in the air. With a sensuous swirling motion, she impaled herself until her pussy ground into his pelvis. He reared back, closed his eyes and groaned in ecstasy. She slipped into an easy rhythm of raising and lowering her core on his heated staff.

He lifted his head and captured in his mouth the breast that rocked back and forth over him. As he suckled her nipple, his finger found the sensitive bundle at her apex and stroked. Soon she built up to another peak, shrieked and bucked with more spasms. It happened again...and again. Her fluid gushed. He flipped their positions again and may have been able to make her come until morning if she didn't pass out, but he began to shake and slip into bliss too. Paroxysms of rapture overwhelmed him and took him to a place he had never been before. It must have been some kind of ultimate high where he felt as if he'd escaped the confines of his human shell. Yet he existed outside his body for only a moment. A fleeting instant in which he came within a whisper of reclaiming his soul.

When eventually his shaking stopped and his body calmed, he pushed himself up and observed her to be sure she was all right. Her head was turned to the side, her eyes scrunched shut and she was wearing an unfamiliar frown. Hearing a tiny whimper, he was beside her in a flash, cradling her.

"Are you all right, my darling?"

She rolled into his arms and bawled like a baby.

Chapter Eighteen

❧

Maura felt like a fool. She had wanted to give him a night of passion he would never forget, instead she wound up blubbering all over him and couldn't stop. Even noticing her black mascara darkening his chest didn't slow her down. To his credit, he was incredibly gentle and sensitive, for a killer. He held her, stroked her back and murmured softly in her ear. She didn't understand what he was saying since he was speaking French, Romanian or some combination of romance languages, but the translation was clear. He loved her. He was heartbroken too and wished their love didn't have to end.

He held her until at last her tears were spent. She let her limp hands slip to the bed and when she could, she pushed herself up to a sitting position. The constriction in her throat prevented any semblance of conversation, so she simply reached for the tissue box on Adrian's nightstand and blew her nose. With another one, she wiped at the mascara under her eyes and finally managed a few words. "Sorry…I must look awful."

"I want to remember you just like this."

"Why? So you won't regret your decision to send me home?"

He shook his head sadly. "No. I'll always regret my folly and what has to happen because of it. But know this. I couldn't bear cutting your life short. Few people are as alive as you are."

"Talk about cutting things short, we've had only days together. Days! It took me thirty-eight years to find you and took you six hundred years, give or take a decade, to find me. How is that fair?"

Adrian took her hand and intertwined their fingers. "I knew I would have to mourn your loss someday, yet I never dreamed it would happen so soon, or like this...because of my own anger. I wish I could make it up to you somehow."

"You were protecting me from Vampzilla. If she wasn't so thick in the head, believing she could somehow force you to take her back, it never would have happened. I wish there had been something else handy to throw at her, but I guess—"

"If I had been thinking straight, I'd have broken open a barrel and staked her. Hell, I should have killed her back in the dress shop, but I didn't out of respect for our families. Something like that is apt to start a feud."

"And that would be bad?"

He sighed. "I need to think." Adrian got out of bed and paced in circles around the room, as if racking his brains. It was all Maura could do to shut up as she watched him scrunching his forehead, then sighing and shaking his head. Wandering among his things, he would occasionally pause and finger a fine piece. A vase on the mantel. A small gold box on his dresser. He appeared to be filled with regret, self-recrimination and anger. She imagined he couldn't see the vineyard for the tangle of vines.

There were so many questions. Once he had reverted, would he even care about being among humans again? Where would he go in order to avoid hurting people he loved who tried to help him? Or innocent people with full lives ahead of them who happened to be in the wrong place at the wrong time? Clearly he couldn't stay here in his villa or go back to New York.

Maura pulled the sheet over her and tried to think of a way to begin a dispassionate discussion. "I hate to interrupt, sweetheart, but I need to know something—in case there's some kind of breakthrough in the future. How do I find you? Where will you go from here?"

He turned toward her and sighed. "I don't know. Africa seems like a possible option where famines are leading to massive deaths. Perhaps I can relieve the suffering and pain of starvation while keeping myself alive until I find another cure—another miracle." He dropped his head in his hands. "Does anyone deserve three? Especially someone who didn't deserve the first one?"

"We have to try. Both of us can think over the weekend and come up with any and all possibilities. We can meet in London and share ideas."

He sat next to her and looked into her eyes with his intense gaze. "How can I go to London without a shred of hope to offer? My fermenting wine in the barrels won't be ready for months. Meanwhile, I'd have to shortchange all my buyers' shipments to fill my own needs. My rich and powerful vampire clients wouldn't take being cheated well. Not well at all."

Maura pushed Adrian onto his back and poked him in the chest. "Look, you made a decision. Some decisions work out well and others don't. But it's no use wishing you had made a different one. If you really want to make it up to me, you'll spend a couple of days getting your head together and then join me in London. This can't be our last night. It can't end like this."

"I have to agree that parting after creating such a miserable memory isn't the way I want it, either. I don't mean the sex. That was the most...the best..."

Maura looked up at him in awe and whispered, "It was? Really?"

Adrian raked his hands through his hair. "Regardless, I think we need some time to regroup and get used to the idea of some time apart. I think you may be right. If I can find the time and peace to think rationally, I may be able to figure out a way we can be together someday in the future."

"Oh, thank God. You're finally being reasonable. So, where should I meet you in London?"

"Don't worry. I'll find you."

* * * * *

Maura stood in the dusk on the doorstep of Jordan's flat across the Thames River in Putney. She rang the bell and hoped to find her friend at home, happy to see her. She could barely wait for someone to talk to. Someone who wouldn't think she was completely nuts if she talked about vampires.

Maura had shopped 'til she dropped in London for the past two days, logged everything in her journal, but couldn't write about what had happened with her immortal lover. Why hadn't he met her yet? He was supposed to meet her today. That meant daytime, didn't it? He had a few more bottles of wine so he could still move about in daylight, couldn't he?

How she had lost her handwritten notes from the Code was beyond her comprehension. She had hidden the pages in the back of the journal for safekeeping and they were no longer there. Perhaps with all the rushed exits she and Adrian had made recently they had slipped out somewhere along the way. A horrible feeling in her gut said they may have disappeared, because she no longer needed them.

The front door opened a crack. "Maura!" Jordan threw open the door to her modest townhouse and hugged her.

The warmth of touch from another human being sank deep into her soul. She hadn't realized until that moment how badly she needed the contact.

"Jordan, I'm so glad you're home. I hope you don't mind my rotten company. I'm just going to apologize in advance."

"You sound like you're in quite a state! Come in and tell me over a cup of tea what's gone wrong."

Maura followed her inside, grateful to have a quiet, private place to talk with her friend.

"Jordan, it's Adrian and me."

"Oh dear. Better switch that drink to wine, then. Or what do you Yanks use to soften the sting of a relationship gone bad?"

"Chocolate ice cream right out of the carton with a giant spoon. But it's not that. We're still very much in love. There are just some major complications."

Jordan offered her an understanding smile and hug and then led her into the dining room. "Sit. I don't have any ice cream, but I can be a fair hostess with some blueberry scones. I'll even heat them."

Maura shook her head. "No, I don't need food. I need a friend."

Jordan sat on the opposite side of the table and placed her hand over Maura's. "You have one. I won't repeat a word, but I think we'll at least need a cup of tea."

"Thank you. Tea sounds wonderful as long as it's not that watered-down herbal crap."

Jordan chuckled. "No, we don't believe in watering down our tea or our alcohol. I'll have a nice strong cuppa for you in just a minute. Shall I put a shot of brandy in it?"

"Better not. It'll just make me more depressed and you'll have a sloppy drunk on your hands."

"I'll be right back, luv." Jordan rushed off to the adjoining kitchen and Maura glanced around, taking in the homey surroundings. Lace curtains in the window framed and softened the streetlight from the sidewalk outside. A built-in china hutch in the corner, painted white like the rest of the room, held colorful bone china cups and saucers. Unmatched chairs surrounded the dark cherry dining table at which she was sitting. Matching upholstered seats tied them together and looked perfect in the charming English home.

In moments, Jordan returned taking two bone china teacups from the corner cupboard. She stopped in mid-stride and stared at Maura.

"You're smiling."

Maura nodded. "Your home is lovely. So unexpectedly peaceful."

"Yes, that's the way I like it. You may not think it goes with the Goth-looking girl in front of you, but it was my Auntie's home. When she left it to me, I kept it much the way it was. I really like its charm and many wonderful memories were made here."

"You're an interesting dichotomy."

Just then the teapot began to whistle and Jordan rushed back to the kitchen with the teacups. "We can let it steep as long as you like," she called over her shoulder.

Maura's thoughts returned to Adrian as they did every few seconds, regardless of any other distractions surrounding her at the moment. She didn't want to give Jordan the impression that they were breaking up even though, essentially, it had to happen.

When Jordan's doorbell rang, Maura sat up straight, all her senses heightened. *Adrian? Is that you?* When she received no answer, she cursed under breath. Maybe it was just a delivery or something, hopefully not more guests. She needed her friend all to herself right now.

She heard Jordan open the door and say, "Vilhelm, what a nice surprise!"

Vilhelm? Not Adrian's mean older brother. It couldn't be.

"Hello, Jordan. This is my friend, Ella. May we come in?"

"Of course. It's nice to meet you, Ella. What a lovely dress."

No! Don't invite them in. Maura's blood ran cold as she pushed herself up onto trembling legs and peered into the kitchen. There stood Adrian's sociopathic brother and Vampirella, in a long sparkling blue gown, three sizes too small, as usual—and they were inside the house.

"I have a guest already, but I can introduce you and offer you a cup of tea—"

"Actually," Vilhelm said, "we don't have to stay long. We just wanted to know if you could tell us where to find a mutual friend of ours."

When Maura could force her legs to cooperate a little better, she darted around, looking for a quick exit. Knowing how vampires could outrun her, she doubted she'd get very far, but she had to try. Moving as quickly and quietly as she could, she made her way toward the back door. Just as she put her hand on the doorknob, she glanced outside and spotted an imposing figure in the garden. *Crap! It's Adrian's giant brother, Boris!*

Jordan called out to her, revealing her presence as the other guest. *Shit. Shit. Shit.*

"Maura?" Jordan had obviously taken them to the dining room to discover she was missing. "She's probably in the loo."

"I think I know where she is," said the saccharine voice of Vampirella. "Take a look back there."

Oh no, she can probably smell me.

Jordan entered the parlor at the back of the house while Maura pretended she was innocently admiring the houseplants. She prayed she'd be safe as long as Jordan was there and even more, she prayed Jordan would be safe if she didn't panic.

"There you are," Jordan said. She walked over to her and put an arm around her waist. "Some friends of yours, Vilhelm and Ella, are here asking about you. How fortunate that you just happened to be visiting."

Maura clasped her arm and with a tremble in her voice, whispered to her. "It's too late now, but you just invited vampires into your house."

"What? But Vilhelm and I met on the tour and became friends. He said he was on a waiting list. When you and Adrian left, he was able to take the spot you vacated. Nothing was said about his being a vampire, although...he's sexy as hell."

Vilhelm entered the room, his posture straight and confident. "Jordan was kind enough to invite me to drop in if I ever came to London. So I did and I've brought a friend. She just wants to talk to you, Maura. She wants to know where Adrian is."

"If I knew, I certainly wouldn't tell you."

Jordan looked to Maura, then to Vilhelm and Vampirella and then back to Maura. "Make yourselves comfortable." Her voice barely whispered, "Can I get anyone a cup of tea?"

* * * * *

Adrian scoured the tourist attractions first, sure he'd find her roaming the city since she'd never been there before. No one could shop for two days straight, right? He had called to her telepathically and grew more and more concerned as sunset descended over the city and she hadn't answered him.

Realizing that a woman who owned a shop might be a shopaholic herself, he thought that maybe he'd misjudged her. Just because he'd go crazy shopping that much didn't mean she would. If she could shop nonstop for days, he'd have to go to the shopping district and try to find that Goth shop she was so keen to visit. At least he might find people who had seen her. She probably struck up a conversation, knowing Maura. Perhaps they'd even know where she was going next.

Adrian didn't want to ride the tube and didn't feel like wasting time, so he found a spot in an alley where he could begin his whirlwind of a run and hope there would be another empty place on the other side where he could reappear. Probably, since deliveries didn't happen at this time of day, he could find a place behind one of the shops.

Under his arm, he secured his briefcase holding the last precious bottles of wine...the ones Bertrand had brought up from the basement before the disaster. Disappearing in a swirl of dead leaves and cigarette butts, he materialized behind some quiet shops on the edge of the larger shopping area.

Now to find the right place. Adrian hated to ask for directions. Absolutely hated it. It made him feel stupid, so he opted to browse the front windows as quickly as possible while calling out to her. He breezed around the nearest corner taking long, quick strides.

Maura! Where are you? Every nationality seemed to be represented on the streets of London. Some browsed slowly, making him impatient to get around them, without knocking someone down. He hadn't realized what a modern New Yorker he had become.

No gothic-looking shops and no answer to his telepathic communication quickly led to frustration and alarm. Throwing in the towel, he stopped a young woman who seemed to be dressed in what he'd call classic European casual. What Americans would call business casual clothing.

"Excuse me. Do you know of any gothic clothing stores in the area?"

She looked at him as if he were a shit statue, turned up her nose and walked on without answering.

What the hell? He thought that only happened in New York. Now he knew why he never asked for directions.

Continuing on what felt like a fruitless search, he wondered if Maura could have left London. Maybe she had come to her senses and gone home. Deep in his gut he doubted that...not that she had no sense, but he knew she wouldn't give up on him.

Maura? I'm here. Tell me where to find you!

The faintest sound echoed in the distance. He thought he heard his name. Adrian stopped suddenly and listened. A shopper, apparently not paying attention, plowed right into him, knocking him off the sidewalk.

"Oh, terribly sorry," the girl said.

When he righted himself, he noticed she was dressed in some sort of "punk" style. "No problem." He was torn as to whether or not he should ask this young woman about the Goth shop or stand there and listen for another cry. Bloody hell. He'd do both if it would help him find Maura.

"Perhaps you can help me find a shop I'm looking for?"

"After almost pushing you into a bus? Of course."

"I don't know the name of it, but it's supposed to be around here somewhere. They sell gothic clothing."

The girl raised her eyebrows and took a long look at him. He was, of course, wearing all black. Boots, leather pants, a long, unbuttoned trench coat and black dress shirt beneath. His hair was slicked back and held with a black rubber band.

"Oh, I think I know the place you're looking for. It's not around here though. You'll find it in Paddington."

"Paddington." Adrian had heard of Paddington bears. The New York toy stores were full of them one year. He could picture those cute, cuddly teddy bears wearing yellow raincoats and hats in store windows, but didn't have the faintest idea where Paddington was.

"How do I get there?"

"The tube goes to it. There's a station there." She pointed to the familiar metro sign less than a block away.

"Thank you."

So he had to ride the subway after all. If he heard her call again on the way to Paddington station, he'd just have to get off as quickly as he could and hope she'd keep it up so he could follow her voice. *One more try. Maura? Mauraaaa!*

No sound greeted his inner consciousness and the only noise his ears picked up were the sounds of the city. Traffic. People. The occasional blare of a horn.

Adrian hoofed it down the stairs to the subway. A quick glance at the map showed the way to Paddington station.

There didn't appear to be many stops on the map between where he was now and his destination. *Thank the Gods.*

He boarded the right car and waited to be whisked away to Paddington, where he'd hopefully find a clue as to Maura's whereabouts. Perhaps while there he'd pick up one of those cute bears for her. She could hug it in his stead until he could return to her. If he could return.

An uneasy feeling came over him as the train pulled away. No matter how he tried, he couldn't shake it. Perhaps he was heading in the wrong direction? Too late now. He'd just have to keep going and hope for the best.

As the train pulled into Paddington station, he barely heard it, but he could have sworn she called his name again. This time the timbre was different—more urgent.

He charged up the stairs, expecting to see shops with fuzzy, adorable teddy bears in the windows, but instead he found himself in the red-light district. Dark streets, abandoned-looking brick buildings. Women dressed like hookers. Maura definitely didn't belong in this environment. Bloody hell. Maybe she came here and something terrible happened to her!

No, he had heard her. She was alive somewhere and calling for him. *Damn it, Maura, where are you?*

Adrian, if you're…London…river!

At last he heard her a little more clearly. Not every word, but enough. The river, it had to be the Thames.

He spotted the closest person and ran over to her. The woman, wearing a very short animal print dress and fishnets, leaned against a streetlamp.

"Excuse me."

She turned and smiled, eyeing him as if he were her next john. "You want a date, luv?"

"No, ma'am. I'm just looking for directions. Where can I find the nearest bridge across the river?"

She crossed her arms. "It'll cost you."

"How much?"

"Twenty pounds."

"That's ridiculous. I'll bet you get twenty pounds per hour and all I want is a minute."

She frowned and checked her watch. "All right. Five pounds per minute. Pay first."

Aggravated but desperate, Adrian reached into his coat's inner pocket, pulled out a five-pound note and handed it to her. "Now talk fast."

She shrugged, turned and pointed southeast. "Chelsea Bridge. You might want to take the tube, it's quite a distance."

"No time," he said and whooshed off with his vampiric speed. He couldn't care less if she saw him effectively disappear.

Adrian ran in the direction indicated until he reached the river. At the edge, darkness covered his reemergence. He spotted the closest bridge and walked at a fast clip toward it while calling to her.

Maura. I'm by the river near a bridge. Shall I cross?

He received a faint reply. He was no nearer, but he thought he heard her say, *Yes.*

Give me some clue as to where you are.

Neighborhood… South End.

He began to walk south. *Keep talking, darling. Let me follow your voice.*

He heard her sing in a tremulous voice. What the heck was she singing anyway?

Devil with the blue dress, blue dress, blue —

Shit. He lost her. He must be going in the wrong direction again. Possibly he was south of the South End. Adrian turned north and jogged a few paces until he picked up her voice again and it began to get louder.

Devil with the blue dress on.

I hear you. I'm coming. Are you telling me that Vampirella is there?

Bingo! And that's not all. A moment later, she began a new song. *Let's do the Mash. It's called the Monster Mash. The Monster Mash. It was a townhouse smash —*

Bloody hell. Sounds like everyone showed up. Keep singing. I'm getting closer!

Adrian broke into a flat run.

By the time Maura resorted to a chorus of *do ahhhh, do ahhhh,* her voice was fading.

He realized he must have passed her and turned around. When her voice came in strong again he was in a neighborhood of townhouses, so he charged up the nearest side street. Her voice continued to come to him stronger until he spotted a figure standing in the shadows outside one of the flats.

Maura, is someone standing guard at the front door?

Probably. Boris is at the back. I can't see the front door from here, but you have more brothers, right?

For the moment.

Chapter Nineteen

🕭

Vampirella strolled back and forth across the carpet in front of Maura as if trying to intimidate her. Little did she know her silence wasn't bothering her a bit. All the better to concentrate and use her telepathy with Adrian.

When Maura said she couldn't give Vampirella any more answers, she had begun this furious pacing and didn't take her eyes of the two mortals the entire time. She had to be waiting for one of them to blurt out something to get her to stop. Jordan looked like she wanted Maura to tell her something, anything, just to make her go away.

Adrian, be careful, okay?

Of course I will, darling. I can take any of my brothers alone, but if they get together, I'm not so sure.

Then I'll head to the back door and block it.

No, don't! He'll go right through you.

Maura sighed. There had to be something she could do to keep the brute in the backyard. She glanced around the living room and spotted a metal plant stand. If she could grab it and wedge it under the doorknob before he reacted to a scuffle or a warning from someone else, it might hold him off.

Okay, I have a plan, but you have to tell me when you're here.

There was no need to for Adrian to tell her anything. The sounds of a fracas breaking out on the street reverberated loud and clear and soon after, something crashed into the front door. Vampirella jerked her head and ran toward the sound.

Maura bolted off the sofa and grabbed the plant stand. She knew the amaryllis was going to fall onto the carpet and spill dirt everywhere, but she'd just have to pay for the cleaning and buy Jordan another plant—if they lived longer than the plant did.

The amaryllis tumbled to the floor, Maura wedged the metal stand under the back doorknob and Boris crashed into it, in that order. She got out of the way as fast as she could, expecting another crash. Surprisingly, when silence followed, she stepped aside, glanced out the window and saw Boris ascend toward the roof in that flying leap vampires can do. A thud sounded above her head.

Meanwhile Vampirella was yelling from the kitchen. "Stop it, you two! Vilhelm, be careful! Don't you dare kill my betrothed!"

There she goes again with that damned betrothed nonsense. Adrian, if you can't kill her this time, at least straighten her out, okay?

I'm a bit busy right now, cherie.

Maura heard groans and growls coming from above. "What is that? Sounds like a wounded bear."

Jordan wandered over to the fireplace. "I think it's coming from the chimney."

"Get me the hell out of here!"

Maura burst out laughing. "I think you have a vampire stuck in your chimney."

Jordan raised her eyebrows. "Well, I'll call the chimney sweep first thing in the afternoon, then."

Maura stumbled over to her friend and hugged her. "One down. Two to go."

"Don't you want to watch what's going on out front?"

She shivered all over, again. "No. I definitely don't. I want to stay far away from all those fangs."

"Then I suggest we run." Jordan headed for the back door.

At that moment the noise stopped and Vampirella walked around the doorjamb. "I suggest you don't."

Adrian? Are you all right?

All Maura could hear was panting. One person, panting. Alarmed, she shouted. "Adrian?"

Vampirella pointed a sharp fingernail at her. "Don't move, or you'll be sorry."

"Jordan, quickly. Invite him in!"

"Adrian, come in!"

An agonizing few seconds passed before he limped into the living room behind Vampirella. "I'm alive, *cherie*. But my brothers are unconscious."

"Good! Your other brother is stuck in the chimney."

Adrian leaned over and placed his hands on his knees as laughter bubbled up from deep in his diaphragm.

Vampirella frowned at him. "You should be ashamed of yourself! Those are your brothers. Your family."

As soon as he could straighten up, Adrian's black eyes glittered and he hissed at her. "Do not presume to tell me who is or isn't my family. As far as I'm concerned, I have no family — and I have no betrothed, either. I never did."

"But darlink!"

"Don't darlink me!" he roared.

He looked over her shoulder toward the two women who were grasping each other's hands and shaking, then his voice softened.

"Jordan, do you have somewhere else you can stay for a while? Possibly a long visit?"

"I..." She squirmed uncomfortably. "I guess I'll have to move now. Won't I?"

"It would be best if you did," Adrian said. "Now that two of them have been in, you can't keep them out."

Maura put her other hand on Jordan's arm. "Don't worry, you can come home with me."

"To New York?"

"Not necessarily. I have another home."

"Thank you for the offer, but I have relatives who'll take me in."

Maura connected eyes with Adrian. *My mother moved back to Ireland. Can you take me there?*

I'll get you both to safety, then I must go.

Oh, no you don't. I met your crazy family. Now it's only fair that you meet mine.

He hung his head. Tangled hair obscured his eyes. *Shit.*

* * * * *

The place was exactly as she remembered it. Green rolling fields, stone walls and white, thatched cottages. A bicycle leaned against the side of the house on Drury Lane and Maura guessed it belonged to one of her cousins. It was too small to be an adult's bike. Oh, but it couldn't. Her cousins were all grown now, even Patrick, the youngest.

Adrian stood on the doorstep of the whitewashed cottage after Maura stepped inside the kitchen. When he didn't follow, she twisted her head to look at him and wondered why he was just standing there. As it dawned on her that he needed an invitation, she slapped her forehead and said, "Come in, Adrian," hoping her excited aunt didn't notice the hesitation.

"Yes, please come in, we won't bite," she chuckled.

Ironic phrase, isn't it, cherie?

Maura giggled nervously until her aunt grabbed and hugged her as hard as she could, just like Maura remembered her doing. Fortunately she was now taller didn't have to worry about being smothered by the full-figured woman's bosom.

"Sure 'n it's been too many years since you came to see your old auntie, Maura. What's kept you so busy?" Then she eyed Adrian and raised her eyebrows. "Oh, I see. I wouldn't bother with a broken-down old woman like me if I had a man like that at home." She burst into the rich, deep laughter Maura so loved.

"I'm sorry, Aunt Colleen. This is my...friend, Adrian. It's not his fault. I'm afraid I've been tied up running my business."

"Ah, you Americans worry too much about business and not enough about the important things, like family. Now come sit down in the parlor and introduce us all around."

Maura held her hand as they followed her aunt into the next room. Clearly she was happy to see her, even on short notice.

"Kathryn! Your daughter's here!" she yelled at the top of her lungs.

A moment later her mother burst through the back door and ran to hug her. "How did you get past me? I was outside hanging the laundry, but had my eyes peeled for you the whole time."

"I don't know, Mom. Maybe a sheet was hanging in your line of vision or something." *What can I say? My boyfriend flew me here as soon as the ferry docked?*

Maura was delighted to see her mother glowing in robust health. It was doubtful she'd ever move back to New York, having never really made the adjustment, anyway. When her husband died, it was an easy return to her roots. They shared a kiss and strong hug, which her uncle interrupted.

"Now where's my Maura?" he shouted from his easy chair. Maura guessed his rheumatism must be acting up since a cane leaned against the side of his chair. She crossed to him, leaned down and offered him a kiss on the cheek. Not enough of a gesture apparently, because he took her face in his hands and planted a hard kiss squarely on her lips.

"That's more like it! Now sit down and tell us everything."

Her aunt held one finger in the air. "Wait on the good parts until I get back with some tea, darlin'."

She was right. It had been too long. She never realized how much she missed her boisterous relatives.

Her mother cocked her head in Adrian's direction. "How about introductions first?"

"Oh, of course. How rude of me. Mother, this is Adrian. And Adrian, you can probably call her Kathryn."

"Absolutely. No one stands on ceremony here, so don't 'Mrs. Keegan' me."

"Very well, Kathryn. I'm delighted to meet you."

Liar.

He answered Maura with a telepathic chuckle as he kissed her mother's hand.

"And this is my Aunt Colleen and Uncle Michael."

He took Colleen's hand and kissed it too while she giggled.

Michael said, "Welcome to our humble home. Adrian, is it?"

Two long strides later, Adrian shook her uncle's hand. "Yes. Pleased to meet you Michael."

"What? No kiss for me?" Michael's laugh boomed and echoed around the sparsely decorated room.

Aunt Colleen elbowed Maura. "And does this handsome brute have a last name? I want to know what your new name's apt to sound like."

Maura and Adrian stared at each other, not because of any telepathic conversation going on, but because they were both tongue-tied. Heat invaded her cheeks.

Kathryn broke the silence to Maura's relief. "Don't embarrass them, Colleen. If there's news like that, they'll be sure to tell us."

Colleen simply shrugged, let out a "Humph" and returned to the kitchen.

"Sit, for heaven's sake," Uncle Michael ordered.

Glancing at the hall on her way to sit next to her mother on the sofa, Maura asked, "So where are Patrick, Sheila and Maureen?"

Her mother smiled and brushed Maura's hair away from her face in the same affectionate way she always had. "The girls are married now. Maureen lives in Dublin and Sheila in Killarney. Patrick's at work, but said he'll meet us at the pub. I called him as soon as you told me you were coming. He's getting as many of the family together as he can on short notice."

"Sorry about that, Mom. I hope I'm not an imposition."

Michael made a gruff noise. "You should never even think such a thing. There's always room for family and friends. You can sleep with your mother and Adrian can take the girls' old room."

Still standing, Adrian interjected, "Actually, I won't be staying."

"What? Just because we won't let you sleep with our niece until you marry her?"

Maura knew she was turning bright red. She could feel it. "Will everybody stop talking about marriage? We just started dating a little while ago."

Aunt Colleen hurried in with the tea tray and placed it on the ottoman in front of her husband. "You promised not to talk about anything good until I got back and I clearly heard the word 'marriage' mentioned just now."

Exasperated, Maura threw her hands in the air. "We're not getting married!"

Aunt Colleen jammed her hands on her hips. "Then why bring the lad home to meet your family?"

"I'm almost sorry I did."

"Don't worry, *cherie*. They can talk about it if they want."

"Before we do?" Maura sighed. *We've got to get out of here, somehow.*

I'm afraid we're stuck until after tea and whatever they've planned at the pub. Why don't you change the subject?

Yeah, right. Don't be surprised if it keeps coming up. You just said you didn't mind if they talked about it. To them that means you're interested and I'm just too blind to see it. They'll have us as good as engaged by the time we leave the pub.

* * * * *

"Maura, Adrian, let me introduce you to the fine lads seated at the bar," Aunt Colleen yelled over the noise in the dark pub. The patrons quieted to a murmur and she smiled her thanks. "Now closest to us here is my son, Patrick."

The young man lifted his mug as if toasting the newcomers.

"And next to him is Connor. He's your third cousin, Maura, dear."

They received the same one-mug salute.

"And then there's Michael and another Patrick, but we call him Paddy. They're Connor's brothers, so your third cousins, also. And then Sean and another Michael, but we call him Mickey. They're married to a couple of your Uncle Mike's second cousin's daughters and at the end we have Brian and another Brian." She shrugged. "We just call them both Brian and they're not related."

"Pleased to make your acquaintance," Adrian said in his polite, gentlemanly way.

Uh-oh. He'd better not be too polite or they'll eat him alive. Maura chuckled inwardly at the thought of a vampire being eaten by a pack of Irishmen.

Small groups of women sat at the two round tables in the one-room pub and Aunt Colleen strolled in their direction so she could introduce each of them, one person at a time—like either Maura or Adrian would remember any of their names or who was related to whom.

"Here we have Kate, Darcy, Megan and Maureen." The first four women offered jovial greetings with such thick accents, Maura wasn't sure what some of them had said. "Kate is married to one of the Brians and Maureen is Sean's sister."

"Oh, of course," Maura said. "I can see the resemblance."

Maureen said, "I don't see it. I'm much better-lookin'." And the women laughed.

Aunt Colleen continued on without missing a beat. "At the next table I want you to meet Caitlin, Mary Ann, Maura and Geraldine."

"Mary Ann and Maureen look like twins," Maura said. "You can't tell me they don't resemble each other."

Both women pointed to themselves and simultaneously said, "I'm the better-lookin' one."

As soon as the ladies stopped laughing, they slurred their greetings and Maura realized why she didn't quite understand all the words.

"There's more coming, later on. Now let's make Maura and her...friend feel welcome, everyone!"

Patrick got off his barstool, clasped Adrian on the shoulder and offered to buy him a beer.

Before she could see what he said or did, her aunt pulled her over to the first table of ladies and pushed her down onto a hard, wooden chair. "Maura here lives in New York City."

One of the women, possibly Darcy, quipped, "We must seem very sophisticated and intimidatin' to ya." And the table's occupants erupted with laughter. The same was happening over at the bar.

While Aunt Colleen waddled off to the bar and shouted her order over the din of the pub, Maura's mother pulled a chair over and sat beside her.

"It's so nice to have you here, honey."

The woman her aunt called Megan leaned forward and looked Maura straight in the eye. "So, how is it you and your handsome man decided to visit your poor neglected mum?"

Maureen elbowed her. "Isn't it obvious?"

"They make a lovely couple, don't they now?" Kate chimed in.

All the women nodded.

"Whoa, ladies. We're not here for any particular reason. It's just time I visited my mother, that's all."

A woman from the next table called over, "Sure 'n we believe that one. Do you have any other tall tales for us?"

The bar erupted with feminine laughter and on it went.

Maura was thrilled when Aunt Colleen returned with a pitcher and three mugs. She could check in with Adrian telepathically and see how he was doing while she was busy downing her ale.

As soon as she had a mug full, she took a long slow glug through the foam. *How are you doing over there, sweetie?*

I thought you said insult humor was the lowest form of comedy.

In my opinion, it is, but here it's been raised to an art form.

So how do you suggest I handle it?

A good offense is the best defense.

In other words…

Dish it right back. They'll love it and respect you for it.

Her mother was whispering in her ear, so she had to turn her attention away from him. Just then gales of laughter boomed from the bar and ricocheted all around the pub.

Good, he's making friends. "What did you say, Mom?"

"I said you'd better be careful of the beer. It's much stronger than you're probably used to."

"Oh. That's right. Thanks for the reminder."

Soon the pitcher was empty and Kate took it back to the bar for a refill. The door opened again and more relatives she couldn't quite remember poured into the pub. They were greeted by hearty welcomes and more introductions.

The ale kept coming, the relatives kept coming and soon Maura thought if she didn't find the bathroom, her teeth were going to float. She knew exactly what was going to happen the minute she left the room. Everyone and their cousin would be talking about her behind her back. Well, there was no way to prevent that.

"Excuse me for a minute, ladies. Nature calls."

They didn't even wait for her to leave the room. As she passed the second table she overheard wild assumptions flying around. One of the voices even belonged to her dear aunt concocting some sort of crazy story. Couldn't she just show up for a visit without everyone expecting some hidden agenda?

She knew Adrian could hear every word of it if he cared to listen. There was no way to prevent that, either. If he brought it up, she'd simply laugh it off and hope that would put him at ease. Laughing, though a welcome distraction, wasn't easing her pain.

* * * * *

After hours at the pub meeting everyone who lived anywhere near the village, they strolled the dark lane. Adrian had to chuckle to himself. Maura wasn't kidding. Aunt Colleen introduced him to the whole lot of them as Maura's "friend" wink, wink.

By the time they left, he had heard several whispered rumors about his being about to pop the question. Some said he was nervous and putting it off. Others guessed Maura was still in the dark regarding her impending status as an almost married woman since she kept on denying anything of the sort.

Because they suspected he was planning something secretly, they agreed not to spoil the surprise—unless he happened to do it in front of them and wouldn't that be grand! So now almost the entire town was following them at a respectful distance as everyone made their way home. He guessed some of them were taking quite a detour since there weren't nearly enough cottages to house all of these people.

He had seen Jordan and Maura to safety and now it was finally time he took care of his own. Maura had been a good sport. More than that. She put up with his family and a psychotic ex-girlfriend without leaving him in a wake of dust and now he had returned the favor.

"*Ma cherie*, you know I must leave soon."

She didn't answer right away. She had been quiet, staring at the road most of the walk home. "I wish you didn't have to go just yet. We haven't had a moment of privacy."

"I know. Believe me, I wish we had anticipated this and spent some time together before showing up, but you're safe now. That's the important thing. If my estimate is correct, Vampirella won't have any more of my wine after today, so keep yourself indoors after dark once I leave."

Patrick strode up beside him and clamped a hand on his shoulder. "So, we'll see you at the pub tomorrow afternoon, then."

He said it as if it were a given. Nothing had been mentioned before. He hadn't been consulted. He was about to make his excuses when Maura looked up at him with shimmering eyes.

The words lodged in his throat.

"I...I'm afraid Adrian's leaving tonight," she said softly.

"What? How's that, mate? You just got here."

"He has business to attend to."

"Sure 'n it can wait one more day."

Adrian squeezed Maura's hand. She looked up at him, her aquamarine eyes brimming with tears.

"I guess I can spend the night if your uncle's invitation is still good."

Maura's expression brightened, considerably. "Of course it is."

"Then it's all settled!" Patrick said. "That means I can sleep tonight and talk with you man-to-man at a more civilized hour." With that, he clapped him on the back and returned to the rest of the crowd.

What the hell does that mean, Maura?

"Don't panic. Irishmen don't discuss marriage, unless it's to complain about it and then they'll be talking about their own. He probably wants to know which soccer team you support."

"Fine. I can handle that, but I have to confess the topic of conversations I overheard tonight made me uncomfortable, especially since I'll be leaving before the sun comes up. Will they be inventing some wild stories about how I ran out on you?"

"Not if I pretend I'm okay, not crying my eyes out."

"Damn. You don't pretend well, *cherie.*"

"I'm going to insist on some time together tonight...*alone!*"

* * * * *

The thick carpet of grass shone bright green right through the dark of night and Maura's head had almost stopped spinning. Adrian laid her supine after sweeping her off her feet and running with her to a deserted, quiet location.

She felt slightly guilty for disappearing without telling anyone. She was sure her mother would understand, but Mom had conked out as soon as her head hit the pillow. Uncle Michael was asleep in his chair by the time they arrived home. So after Aunt Colleen roused him and took him to the bedroom, they snuck out the back door and took off.

So what? Even if they were discovered missing for a couple of hours, to be alone with Adrian on their last night would be worth it. As she thought about how neither of them knew the duration of their separation, she fought off her sadness.

"*Cherie*. I know how you feel. I'm feeling it too. We should just admit it. Trying to hold it in puts a barrier between us. There should be no barriers, especially tonight."

"How can you tell what I'm feeling? Are you reading my mind?"

"No, *cherie*. I can see it in your eyes."

He leaned over and kissed her. His kiss began tenderly, but soon the pressure on her lips increased and he flattened her to his chest until she was barely able to breathe...unless that's what taking a woman's breath away felt like. When he finally released her, he nuzzled her neck and whispered sweet nothings. At least, she didn't understand the language he was speaking, so to her it was sweet and meant nothing. She guessed it must be French. The language of love. He said "*toujours amore*" several times. She had to find out what that meant. She hoped it was something like "I love you tons". She knew she had tons of love for him since the weight of it was crushing her heart.

Without a word between them, they unbuttoned and removed one another's clothing. Lying in the soft grass, a cool breeze passed over and she shivered.

"You need a blanket, my love?"

"Don't you dare leave me to get one. Just making love will heat me up from the inside out."

Adrian chuckled. "I wasn't going to leave you, *cherie*. I was going to *be* your blanket." He placed himself on top of her gently and kissed her again. With desperate hands, she clutched him to her. She parted her lips as if to invite his tongue inside for further exploration. His kisses lingered and deepened. He caressed the inside of her mouth, her teeth and lips, thrusting and withdrawing. Adrian kissed her longer than she had ever been kissed before and heat was no longer a problem. She was burning for him.

An involuntary mewl escaped her when, at last, he lifted his lips from hers. A hunger she had known only with him begged for more, so she laved and nibbled his neck. She had felt his arousal from the time he lowered his body onto hers, but now she felt his hard cock jump. It felt even larger than before, if that were possible. Maura longed to be filled with every square inch of his luscious satiny pole. Before he mounted her, however, she wanted to make a memory to accompany him wherever he went. She wanted him to remember her lips sliding over, suckling and making love to his most sensitive, intimate part.

Maura rolled her lover onto his back and slid down beside him. He grinned as if he knew what she was up to and fully intended to cooperate with it. She intended to knock his socks off—figuratively speaking since his socks and every other stitch of clothing lay on the ground in a heap.

She positioned herself between his long legs for better access. While salivating and swirling her fingers through his black pubic hair, she looked up at him without raising her face. She hoped her attempt to look seductive and sultry was succeeding. He growled, fueling her desire to deliver a stellar blowjob.

Scooting closer, she balanced on one hand and seized his erection. Holding it in her hand by the base, it pulsated in her fist. With long licks, she lapped from the base to the tip as if his cock were a delicious ice-cream cone. He moaned his consent and lowered his back onto the grass.

Maura relished her feminine power, though she knew it wouldn't make this man her sex slave. Nor should he be. She wanted an equal, not someone she could manipulate with promises of sexual favors, as some women did, or worse, threats to withhold affection. She just wanted to make him come hard, grunting with gusto!

Maura continued her slow torture by swirling her tongue around and sucking his balls, one by one. Then, for good measure, she'd sink down on his shaft and swirl that around too. Talk about tonsil hockey!

Adrian moaned and stroked his hand over her head to encourage her. Ha! Like she needed encouragement. His positive reactions were the best motivation in the world.

After moving on to a thorough lapping of his shaft, she sucked the tip into her mouth and tongued his hole. Then, without warning, she took him as deep as she could in one fluid motion. He arched and let out a loud grunt. She loved surprising him, especially sexually. Maybe in the solitary nights ahead, she'd be able to think of all sorts of new surprises to add to her repertoire—as long as she had her trusty vibrator handy.

"Don't think about those lonely nights, Susan. Just enjoy the now!"

Oh for heaven's sake, Not you. Not now. Do you have something to say that can't wait? If not, please be brief and go away.

Of all the nights for her inconsistent companions to show up. She squeezed her eyes shut and tried to will them away.

"I just said it. Weren't you listening?"

I'm trying not to.

"Then I'll say it again. Don't think about the lonely nights ahead. That'll ruin the moment. In reality, you have no idea what lies ahead. Everything could change in an instant."

Okay. Got it. Now go.

"Has anyone told you that you can be quite rude?"

No and being rude to my id, my conscience, or whatever the hell you are doesn't count.

"Fine. Have it your way. Just remember I gave you permission to let go of the things you can't control and live in the moment, fully."

Noted. Goodbye.

Apparently she had inadvertently increased her suction while the little devil was annoying her. Adrian eased her head back until he pulled his cock from her mouth with a loud pop. "Maura, I can't take any more without coming in your mouth."

"Was I hurting you?"

Adrian chuckled and flipped her onto her back, looming over her as she got comfortable.

"You can hurt me like that any time." He suddenly became somber. "I mean, when we're together again."

She was about to say something, but he had started suckling her breasts and whatever it was seeped out of her head. The profound sensation created by his suction on her nipple spread through her abdomen and elicited an involuntary muscle contraction in her core. His enthusiastic attention to her breasts had her writhing beneath him, bringing her to the edge of bliss.

She fisted his hair and murmured his name while he transported her to another level. In that place she couldn't think about sad events that hadn't happened yet. She could only concentrate on and cherish every moment of his loving her.

When his talented mouth had finished its work at her breasts, he trailed his lips down her stomach to her mons. He laved her labia thoroughly before sliding his tongue upward to stimulate her bud. She arched and moaned in bliss. When he inserted two fingers into her opening, he stopped licking her clit and began suckling it. Maura's bundle of nerves was building to an electrifying climax. Just before her body erupted, she felt as if a rocket launched and she exploded into orgasm. She allowed herself complete lack of control, shaking and quaking, quivering and shivering, flying and crying out his name.

When she returned to earth she lay sprawled and limp as rag doll, panting. When she could speak coherently, she asked. "Will you really come back for me?"

He scooted up beside her and his eyes bore into hers. "How can you doubt it? As long as I'm undead, I'll look for a cure. The moment I have one, I'll come for you."

Cupping her chin, he bent down and kissed her. His lips were so warm.

"Adrian, how can you be undead with warm blood running through your body?"

"It's the wine, *cherie*. A bottle a day keeps the chill away."

Maura chuckled, briefly. "Do you really have to wait for those barrels to ferment? Can't you just drink the stuff like grape juice?"

Adrian stroked her cheek as he brushed her hair away from her face. "No, my love. Each barrel receives a cup of wine from the barrel before. It takes a full nine months to infuse the contents with the same power to temporarily un-curse the cursed."

"Well, can't you ask your customers to share some of theirs with you? After all, you've been supplying them for how many years?"

"Most of them have been my clients for several decades."

"Then ask them! What can it hurt to ask? All they can say is no."

"I'm afraid most of them won't be as sympathetic as you'd hope."

Maura nodded sadly.

"Darling. I can't bear to see you so sad. I hate to ask for help as much as I hate asking for directions, but I will ask, if it makes you feel better."

"Yes, it would." She sighed, then had a wicked thought and smiled seductively. "I guess if you don't want to see me sad, you'll just have to look at me from behind."

Adrian rolled off and let her up. "Are you talking about doggie-style or the other, um…?"

"Ugh, not the other—at least, not now. I was talking about the hands and knees position, using the usual door."

"That's good. Your vagina's plenty tight and I know it will be more pleasurable for you that way."

Maura moved to her hands and knees, facing away from him. "Thanks. I swear all that hoopla about the other orifice was made up by men with extra roomy partners. And I'm willing to bet they aren't as massively endowed as you."

Adrian rubbed her ass and chuckled. "You may be right, *cherie*."

She felt him close the distance between them as soon as she parted her legs. Her wet entrance had cooled in the night air until he plunged inside. The heat of passion quickly spread through her again as soon as they fell into a mutually stimulating rhythm. Being filled with him made her feel complete…not in the sense that she wasn't a whole person or that something was missing. It was more like fulfillment she couldn't achieve by herself with her imagination and trusty vibrator, or with any other man. The guide was right. She was ruined forever as far as mere mortals were concerned once sexual comparison stepped in.

Adrian had incredible staying power. He reached around and massaged her clit with his finger. Sensual shivers shot through her and radiated all over. A glorious orgasm was looming and she intended to hold on for the ride of her life.

Her moans escalated until she climaxed and they turned to screams. Electric jolts and spasms racked her body, followed by vibrations and tremors pushing her up to an out-of-body spiritual high. Still hammering into her and continuing his love massage, Adrian tugged her tighter against his body and lifted her hands off the ground. Before she knew it, her knees left the earth also and she had the sensation of flying. If she hadn't opened her eyes, she would have thought they were soaring.

Adrian had secured her with one arm thrown across her chest and was now standing while fucking her feverishly. She hadn't started down the other side of her climax when she sensed another one rolling in on her.

His arm rested underneath her breasts and they jiggled enthusiastically. Maura doubted any mortal man could perform a feat like this. As if to show off, he shifted slightly and cupped one of her breasts with this hand, squeezing it and pinching the nipple and with the other hand he continued to rub her sensitive clit.

She moaned so loud she was sure to wake the dead if they were within earshot of a cemetery. How she managed to climb above the peak she had just jumped off was beyond her comprehension. Her clit, now white-hot, was almost too sensitive to tolerate any more stimulation, yet she had no intention of asking Adrian to stop as she bounced up and down upon his strong cock. Only his arm and his cock itself kept her from falling. Her legs, still bent, rested against his thighs for balance but did little to hold her up. She bounced like a paddle ball. The feeling of total trust in him engulfed her — and then another orgasm exploded. She rocked violently against him as he jerked into her. His loud grunts and her shocked cries would have been heard over a howling hurricane.

Several spasms and aftershocks later, she felt Adrian's thighs tremble. Panting, he lifted her off his genitals and slowly set her down to kneel on the grass. Maura's whole body went boneless and she collapsed on her side, laughing.

He lay next to her, grinning into her face. That's when she realized she couldn't stop laughing — that her laughter was turning into hysteria and that she didn't care if she made a spectacle of herself. Tears leaked out the corners of her eyes and rolled down her cheeks, yet she just kept laughing.

Adrian propped himself up on his elbow and shook his head, but his smile didn't fade. Maybe he understood how cleansing tears could be. Happy tears. Sad tears. Even tears that form as soon as a bug hits your eye will make it feel better.

Maura's tears plus gasps of laughter momentarily purged her soul of whatever niggling doubts and fears remained there. Eventually, she was able to get herself under control enough to emit mere chuckles and at last, just a few soft giggles escaped between deep breaths.

Adrian leaned over and kissed her. "You're unforgettable. Make no mistake. I'll find a way to return."

"You'd better."

"I don't know what time your family wakes up, but the sky seems to be getting lighter and knowing how ridiculously overprotective they are—"

"Yeah, they're a bit old-fashioned, all right. Uncle Michael was the only one who went to bed early, so I imagine he's the only one who could face the dawn today." After thinking about that for half a second, Maura said, "Yeah, we'd better get back."

Chapter Twenty

ဆ

As soon as they opened the back door, they heard the shower. "Whew. We can sneak in without him hearing us," Maura whispered.

"I'm afraid not, lass." Uncle Michael stepped out of his bedroom, leaning on his cane.

"Damn." Maura put a sweet smile on her face and said, "Uncle Michael. Top o' the morning! I thought you were in the shower."

"Don't you be actin' innocent, Miss Keegan. You're old enough to know better. I'll have you know I've been waitin' up for you ever since I heard you two sneak out together."

"Oh."

"And I'm not in a good mood for lack of sleep. Understand?"

"Yes, sir."

"You don't have to 'sir' me, lass. I'm just your uncle, but your mother will be hearin' about it, to be sure."

Maura nodded. How could she appease the dear old man?

"That's Patrick in the shower. He has a job to go to. And what is it you do, Adrian?"

"I own a vineyard in France and a museum in New York."

"Ah, good. So, are you two to be married soon?"

Maura bit her lip and looked to Adrian, hoping he'd think of something clever to distract Uncle Michael from this line of questioning.

"No, sir."

Maura rolled her eyes. *Great. Just great. That'll really help.*

"You kept my sweet young niece out all night, but you don't intend to marry her?"

"I'm neither young nor innocent as you pointed out just a minute ago, uncle…in fact, I'm—"

Uncle Michael waved at the air in front of him and made his gruff noise.

"It's…complicated, sir." To his credit, Adrian was being respectful and patient.

Uncle Michael leaned on his cane and shuffled toward them. "Complicated, is it? I don't think it's any more complicated than askin' you to take your things and leave."

"Uncle!"

"No, Maura. He's right." Adrian laid a hand on her arm. "I still have that important business to attend to and putting off goodbyes won't make them easier."

She looked at the floor, but eventually nodded.

"I won't forget what I promised you."

She looked up at him and forced a smile. The concern on his face was impossible to miss. His forehead furrowed and he looked into her eyes with his intense gaze. He bent over and brushed her lips with the most tender of kisses.

Maura cupped the back of his head and forced his lips back to hers. She opened to him and silently begged him to deepen it. He responded as the only man who loved her would. He answered her probing tongue and kissed her as she wanted to be kissed with uninhibited passion.

Eventually Uncle Michael cleared his throat.

Adrian reluctantly pulled away from her. "I'll just get my suitcase, sir."

"It's already at the front door, lad."

Calling Adrian "lad" was a good sign and she was glad to hear her uncle say it even as ridiculous as it might be to think of her almost six hundred-year-old vampire as a lad.

He strolled to the front door with Maura trailing behind, picked up his suitcase and with his hand on the doorknob said, "*Je t'aime. A tout a l'heur, ma cherie.*"

Maura couldn't speak. The lump in her throat prevented words from coming. She hugged herself and nodded. Tears burned her eyes and she could barely see as Adrian left the cottage and her life.

Biting her lip, she trembled. Her uncle hobbled up beside her and put a hand on her shoulder.

"Maura, it's for the best...whatever it is. Life has too many complications as it is."

She couldn't stop the tears from gushing forth and her body shook with sobs. Uncle Michael wrapped an arm around her in a firm one-armed hug.

"Not to worry, lass. If it's meant to be, it will be. Come. Sit on the sofa with me. Tell me why this one's so special."

Uncle Michael sat on one end and placed his cane against the side of the couch. He extended one arm, as if inviting Maura to curl up against his chest. Feeling like a little girl and suddenly missing her father, Maura did just that.

She wound up curled into a fetal position on the couch spilling her guts. She told Uncle Michael everything. Everything!

After an hour of sniffling, talking and confessing her sins, her uncle finally spoke. Stroking her hair, as one would pat an Irish setter, he said, "So, you're in love with a vampire," as if it were the most natural thing in the world.

"Yes, uncle."

"And to be with you safely, he needs to find or make enough of his special wine...his Blood of the Warrior, is it?"

She nodded against his leg.

"And there's this old girlfriend, another vampire, who thinks she can get her hooks into him if you're out of the way?"

"Yes," she barely squeaked. "And I'm afraid. If she finds me without Adrian to stop her..." She couldn't even finish her thought, but there was no need. Uncle Michael got the picture.

"I think I know the answer to this, lass. A bit of Irish magic should do the trick."

Maura sat up at stared at him. "Magic? Do you know something about magic, Uncle Michael?"

He smiled until his round, red cheeks dimpled. "I know some things, but better than that, I know someone who knows much more about it than I do."

Getting excited, Maura grabbed his hand. "Who? What?"

"I know you heard your grandmother talk about the little people. Wee magic folk. Fairy tales some said they were. Others just thought your gran was daft, but I think you believed the tales. I remember your blue eyes, so big and round, drinking in every detail as she spoke and you asked questions, as if you knew she was telling the truth."

"Yes, I remember."

"Your gran was the daughter of a woman and a man."

Though confused, she didn't interrupt. Irish stories had to be told a certain way and sometimes they were long and drawn out.

"The woman, your great-gran, was the daughter of a woman and a leprechaun."

She opened her eyes wide and gasped at this new information. "What does that mean? How can that help Adrian, uncle?"

"I'm not able to help your vampire, darlin', but I think we can protect you from the other one."

"We?"

"The side of the family you've never met. The descendents of your great-great-grandfather. Perhaps they can persuade some of the remaining wee folk to help. All I can do is call them and ask."

Maura squeezed his hand. "Oh, please! Please do."

"Careful, lass. I may not walk well, but I can still lift a pint. T'would be a shame to lose the use of me fingers too."

"Oh!" Maura let go of his hand and giggled. "Sorry, uncle. I was just so excited."

"I understand, darlin'. First you find out we have some magic folk in the lineage and now you're going to meet them. Well, providin' they say 'yes'. They tend to keep to themselves."

"Of course. How can we persuade them?"

"You leave that to me."

* * * * *

Three nights later, Vampirella shuffled up to the doorstep of the little white cottage on Drury Lane muttering to herself.

"As if the little human could hide from me. Ha! It was ridiculously easy to find her. I'll never understand why mortals bother to keep those census, birth and death records when they're here today and gone tomorrow."

Smirking, Vampirella adjusted her tight black gown, then rapped on the door and waited. "The little tart may be here today, but she'll be gone today too."

The door opened a crack and an older woman peeked around it. "May I help you?"

"Why yes." Vampirella tried to sound sweet, innocent and English. "My name is Jordan and Maura's my mate. Can I come in?"

"Oh, I'm afraid not. We have a houseful already. I'll send her out to ye, though."

"Thank you, kindly. That would be very good of you."

The woman smiled, but if Vampirella didn't know better, she'd swear her expression was sly…like she knew something was up.

"Maura, dear. Your friend Jordan has come to see you."

All Vampirella's worries vanished when Maura stepped into view. The door was only partially open, but she stood in the doorframe, close enough to grab, looking surprised to see her.

"Vampirella, what are you doing here?"

"I've come to talk to you about Adrian. Can you walk with me?"

Maura crossed her arms and stood her ground. "How stupid do you think I am?"

"Enough." Vampirella laughed, opened her mouth exposing long fangs and lunged for her neck.

As if a force field had been erected, Vampirella bounced off something that flashed and sent a shock through her before she came close to Maura's neck. Suddenly the door opened wide to reveal the oddest collection of guests she'd ever seen. Two sets of three tiny people stood atop each other's shoulders and they all wore odd green costumes. A few regular-looking humans joined them, along with what must have been half the town in the background. Flutters of multicolored wings swarmed around her face and she tried to bat them away like flies.

An elderly gentleman with a cane said, "Ah, those would be the fairies yer tryin' to shoo. They won't be leavin', just so you know."

"Who are you people?"

A little man topping one of the three-person towers said, "We're Maura's family and we understand you've been causin' her trouble."

Before she could answer the other top little person, a woman, answered him. "Oh, yes, Shamus. It sounds like this is the vampire who wants to separate our Maura from her beloved."

Vampirella fumed, her hands closed into fists. *Who the hell are these little jerks to tell me who is the problem and who is the beloved?*

She laughed out loud, but the sound seemed to ring false. This gathering had caught her off guard.

The first little man said to the little woman beside him, "Oh yes. This is the one, Shannon. She's pea green with envy, all right. I can see it, sense it and smell it."

"Well, what shall we do about it, Shamus?"

Shamus produced a wooden stick from behind his back. It was only a stick to Vampirella, but it looked more like a walking stick next to the little man.

"I think it's time to let me shillelagh decide," said the little man and he waved it in a wide arc.

Shimmering dust fell over Vampirella and she felt strange. Very, very odd. The world around her seemed to grow and the little people became bigger. Soon, they looked like giants.

"What kind of crazy spell is this?" Vampirella demanded. She was suddenly surprised not only by the large size of the "little people" in front of her, but also by the small sound of her own voice. It seemed very high and even though she was shouting, not very loud.

She glanced all around, surprised to see herself surrounded by the fabric of her black dress looking like hills of coal.

The others were laughing at her. Laughing! How dare they!

Glancing down at her body, Vampirella saw that she had become a tiny, perfectly round green sphere. "What have you done to me?"

The little, now big, man who had been at the top of the column jumped down and landed right next to her. She tried to step away but rolled instead.

"Well now, Vampirella. It seems as though your envy turned you from pea green into…" He shrugged. "Just a pea."

The crowd behind him burst into uproarious laughter.

"You'll be sorry," she squeaked. "No one laughs at Vampirella. You hear me?"

"Barely," said the woman Shamus had called Shannon as she jumped down and landed beside him.

"Let me by," cried a big booming voice. "I can't see a thing back here."

Suddenly Maura's voice rose among the still laughing crowd. "Be careful, Uncle Michael! Watch where you put your cane. You might accidentally… Oops."

And that was the last thing Vampirella ever heard.

* * * * *

The next morning, Maura gathered both her suitcases, tossed them onto her single bed and prepared to pack. Her mother came up beside her and surprised her with a big hug.

"Good morning, Ma."

"Top o' the morning, my dear daughter."

"I wish I could stay longer, Mother, but I've got to get back to my shop. Poor Quilla has been holding down the fort too long. Besides, I have all kinds of clothes to sell and some European contacts now. I'm anxious to get back and set everything up."

"I hope you're not so anxious you won't see your special man."

"Adrian? Of course not. Don't be ridiculous. When Adrian returns, I'll make time for him in my life. Mother…I don't know if you can understand, but he is my life."

Her mother smiled as she turned her around. "Oh, I do understand. All I want is for you to be happy."

Adrian appeared in the doorway. "I'll do what I can to make sure that happens, Mrs. Keegan."

"Kathryn. I told you not to 'Mrs. Keegan' me, remember?"

"Yes, Kathryn."

"Adrian!" Maura ran into his open arms and hugged him as hard as she could. "What happened? Why are you back so soon?"

"I could leave and come back later I you —"

"Don't you dare! Just hold me and tell me what's going on. Everything. And then I'll tell you what's happened here."

"No need. Your Aunt Colleen saw me outside and couldn't wait to fill me in."

She squeezed him tight. "Isn't it wonderful? We don't have to worry about her anymore."

"Yes, that's almost as wonderful as what I have to tell you."

"Then tell! What are you waiting for? An engraved invitation?"

He reared back his head and laughed. "Let's take a walk. I want to tell you in private."

Kathryn nodded and stepped aside. "You two lovebirds are special. I can see how right you are together and I'm happy for you. Take a walk. Take off for the airport. Whatever you need to do is fine."

Maura charged her mother and hugged her. "Yes. We are. I'm so glad you know it too."

"How could I not? Your father and I shared the same looks, the same laughs. I only wish you as many, if not more, years of happiness."

"Kathryn, you may get your wish." Adrian looked at Maura with some sort of deep meaning and she couldn't wait to find out what it was.

"Then go. Be together. Be happy."

Maura took Adrian's outstretched hand and almost skipped out of the cottage and down the road with him. "What do you have to tell me, Adrian?"

"You were right. I called upon each of my clients and every one of them offered to share a few bottles with me. Most had plenty in reserve. Even those who didn't have much left over were willing to give me what extra they had."

"That's terrific! So, you have enough to get you through until the next batch is ready?"

"More than enough. But that's not all of my news."

"Really? What else could there be?"

Adrian stopped walking and spun her to face him. "How would you like to share my life? Forever."

"Be immortal? You want to turn me?"

"No, *cherie*. There's no need to turn you. One of my clients told me about another way."

Maura could hardly believe what she was hearing. A way to be with Adrian forever? Without becoming a vampire?

"Tell me. Tell me right now!"

Adrian reached into his breast pocket and produced a small vial.

"It looks like water."

"It's Florida Water, my love. From the fountain of youth."

Maura's jaw dropped. She took the vile and gazed at it. "So it's true…" she murmured.

"Yes. I went to quite a lot of trouble to get it too. I'd show you the alligator bite on my leg, but it's already healed."

"Alligators?" Her eyes popped open. "You wrestled alligators to get this for me?"

"*Oui, cherie*. Not only that, but I had to ask for directions." He gave her a soft smile. "It's yours if you want it."

Maura held the vial at eye level then suddenly shifted her stare to Adrian. "It won't make me young and stupid again, will it?"

He laughed. "Certainly not. You'll stay just the way you are. And more importantly we can stay together."

"You, me and Strudel? Always?"

"*Oui. Toujours*. Always."

"Then it's down the hatch!" Maura tipped her head back, poured the water into her mouth and swallowed it in one gulp.

"That's it?"

"*C'est tout*. That's it."

Maura cuddled up to him and he enveloped her in his arms. "*Je t'aime*, Adrian."

"*Je t'aime, cherie…pour toujours*. For always."

As they kissed, deep and slow, a familiar voice whispered in her left ear. "Way to go, Susan."

Oh, dear God. Not now. Why now?

"I thought you might finally like to know what we are?"

This better be good.

"Oh yes, Maura dear. I think you'll be relieved."

Okay. Spit it out.

"We come by when you need to weigh the pros and cons of a decision. Guess who's the 'pro' and who's the 'con'."

"Oh, don't be such an ass. We're your own good judgment, dear."

"Speak for yourself, White Fairy. I'm her own common sense."

"Common is right!"

"Sure. Whatever you say. You know friggin' everything."

281

"Hey, I always knew these two were right for each other."

"Oh really?"

Zip it! Do me a favor, both of you…

"Of course, Maura, dear."

"What is it, Susan? Just name it."

Trust me to make my own decisions and never, ever bother me again! Especially at times like this!

"Oh, my! We've been terribly rude to you, dear. Haven't we?"

Ya think? Jeez!!!

"Gotcha, Susan. You proved you can take care of yourself quite well. From now on we'll be a quiet little voice way in the back of your mind."

Thank you.

"Don't mention it."

Don't worry. I won't mention this to anyone!

Also by Ashlyn Chase

ஜ

Being Randy

Death by Delilah

Demolishing Mr. Perfect

Love Cuffs *with Dalton Diaz*

Quivering Thighs

Wonder Witch

If you are interested in other stories by Ashlyn Chase, check out her book at Cerridwen Press (www.cerridwenpress.com).

Heaving Bosoms

About the Author

ॐ

Kidnapped by gypsies as an infant, Ashlyn Chase was left on the doorstep of the Massachusetts home in which she grew up-at least that's what her older siblings told her. It seems that story telling runs in the family.

She worked as a psychiatric nurse for several years, holds a degree in behavioral sciences and has been trained as a fine artist, registered nurse, hypnotherapist, and interior designer. Writing is one career she wasn't formally educated in, yet by sheer determination she's become a multi-published, award-winning author.

Most writers whether they're aware of it or not, have a 'theme', some sort of thread that runs through all of their books, uniting the whole mishmash into an identifiable signature. Ashlyn's identified her theme as involving characters who reinvent themselves. It's no wonder since she has reinvented herself numerous times. Finally content with her life, she lives in beautiful New Hampshire with her true-life hero husband and a spoiled brat cat.

Ashlyn welcomes comments from readers. You can find her website and email address on her author bio page at www.ellorascave.com.

Tell Us What You Think

We appreciate hearing reader opinions about our books. You can email us at Comments@EllorasCave.com.

Why an electronic book?

We live in the Information Age—an exciting time in the history of human civilization, in which technology rules supreme and continues to progress in leaps and bounds every minute of every day. For a multitude of reasons, more and more avid literary fans are opting to purchase e-books instead of paper books. The question from those not yet initiated into the world of electronic reading is simply: *Why?*

1. *Price.* An electronic title at Ellora's Cave Publishing and Cerridwen Press runs anywhere from 40% to 75% less than the cover price of the exact same title in paperback format. Why? Basic mathematics and cost. It is less expensive to publish an e-book (no paper and printing, no warehousing and shipping) than it is to publish a paperback, so the savings are passed along to the consumer.

2. *Space.* Running out of room in your house for your books? That is one worry you will never have with electronic books. For a low one-time cost, you can purchase a handheld device specifically designed for e-reading. Many e-readers have large, convenient screens for viewing. Better yet, hundreds of titles can be stored within your new library—on a single microchip. There are a variety of e-readers from different manufacturers. You can also read e-books on your PC or laptop computer. (Please note that Ellora's Cave does not endorse any specific brands.

You can check our websites at www.ellorascave.com or www.cerridwenpress.com for information we make available to new consumers.)

3. *Mobility.* Because your new e-library consists of only a microchip within a small, easily transportable e-reader, your entire cache of books can be taken with you wherever you go.

4. *Personal Viewing Preferences.* Are the words you are currently reading too small? Too large? Too... ANNOYING? Paperback books cannot be modified according to personal preferences, but e-books can.

5. *Instant Gratification.* Is it the middle of the night and all the bookstores near you are closed? Are you tired of waiting days, sometimes weeks, for bookstores to ship the novels you bought? Ellora's Cave Publishing sells instantaneous downloads twenty-four hours a day, seven days a week, every day of the year. Our webstore is never closed. Our e-book delivery system is 100% automated, meaning your order is filled as soon as you pay for it.

Those are a few of the top reasons why electronic books are replacing paperbacks for many avid readers.

As always, Ellora's Cave and Cerridwen Press welcome your questions and comments. We invite you to email us at Comments@ellorascave.com or write to us directly at Ellora's Cave Publishing Inc., 1056 Home Avenue, Akron, OH 44310-3502.

COMING TO A
BOOKSTORE
NEAR YOU!

ELLORA'S
CAVE

Bestselling Authors Tour

MAKE EACH DAY MORE *EXCITING* WITH OUR

ELLORA'S
CAVEMEN
CALENDAR

✝ WWW.ELLORASCAVE.COM ✝

erridwen, the Celtic Goddess of wisdom, was the muse who brought inspiration to storytellers and those in the creative arts. Cerridwen Press encompasses the best and most innovative stories in all genres of today's fiction. Visit our site and discover the newest titles by talented authors who still get inspired - much like the ancient storytellers did, once upon a time.